# I've Got a Plan For That!

## Rowland McGabhann

# I've Got a Plan For That!

### Rowland McGabhann

**DoctorZed**
**Publishing**
www.doctorzed.com

This edition Published 2023 by DoctorZed Publishing.
www.doctorzed.com

Books may be ordered through booksellers or online:

ISBN: 978-0-6457955-1-6 (hc)
ISBN: 978-0-6457955-2-3 (sc)
ISBN: 978-0-6457955-3-0 (ebk)

Cataloguing-in-Publication entry can be found at the National Library of Australia.

Cover image South African Flag © Iloveotto | Dreamstime.com
Cover design © Scott Zarcinas

rev. date: 21/06/2023

*To David 'Spud' Murphy,
for his valuable contribution.*

## ACKNOWLEDGEMENTS

Thank you again to the team at DoctorZed Publishing for all their support in getting this book published. Onec more to Dr. Scott Zarcinas for his invaluable insight and wisdom in the art of storytelling. Thank you also to everyone who provided 'real time' advice on location in all the countries mentioned in this story.

## !

### PROLOGUE

**SCOTTVILLE, SOUTH AFRICA**
**NEAR PIETERMARITZBURG**

Aurora McCormack nudged her companion. 'There is movement.'

Sun Yee On responded. 'Right on time,' as she checked the time on her watch.

They had been watching their target for over a week now. The had rented a small disused shop from where they could observe the comings and goings of the personnel and security.

The place in question was a suspected illegal orphanage. Based on the information they had received, it could only be described as a 'puppy farm' for humans.

A call from a friend asking for help had brought them here a couple of weeks ago, which had led them to where they were watching now. Young people of all ages had been disappearing, alarmingly, and the information they had been provided with had brought them here to rescue one of the orphans who was in grave danger. The information was that she was inside.

Aurora glanced at her partner, noting her mixed-race Chinese/ Japanese features, and was reminded of when she and Sun Yee had met in Melbourne, Australia, last year. An adventure that had brought them together in unusual circumstances, to say the least.

The memory of those circumstances now brought a wave of sadness to her. As an undercover member of the police task force, she had been embroiled in an investigation that included the assassination of her father, something she was still coming to terms with.

It hadn't stopped there. There had also been a plot to explode a nuclear device and an attempted assassination on the Prime Minister of Australia. It had only been the intervention of her long-lost cousins that prevented the explosion and the attempted assassination, and which also resulted in her being thrust together with Sun Yee On.

Sun Yee was an orphan raised by the state in China and groomed from an early age to be part of the elite security squad, and later an unofficial assassin for the state.

But the bond that developed between them during that time had grown into something more potent. They then decided to partner and help people who could not receive help from conventional means, which was the reason they were now here.

While in Australia, they had met the daughter of a family entangled in a recent adventure. Again this was thanks to her cousins, the Savage brothers, Charlie, Desmond, and Vincent QC, or as they recently had been christened, 'The Umbrella Crew', because good things happen whenever they take somebody under their wings.

The daughter in question was Christina Herrero. Her parent owned one of the largest transport companies in Australia.

Christina, though, was a doctor who worked in South Africa and also donated her time to Médecins *Sans Frontières*. While working there, she was approached by a mysterious connection to help recover a young girl they believed was being held at this location she and Sun Yee were now staking out.

That is when Christina reached out to Aurora. She explained that she had minimal trust in the authorities as corruption and bribery were now rampant in the country since the change of government in 1994. The girls did not take much persuading, especially as Christina's parents, Felipe and Rosa, agreed to finance the operation.

All that said and done, Aurora and Sun Yee now found themselves here with very little information to go by. Christina had implored them to act as soon as possible as she believed the girl was in grave danger. It turned bizarre when they had asked for the girl's name and description.

'She is unlikely to respond to a name. I have been told she is probably badly traumatised and possibly drugged,' Christina had said.

When they asked to describe her, the explanation was just as vague. 'They described her as a mixed breed in the local vernacular.' Which Christina translated as similar to anything but African.

'So how will we identify her if there are many of them?' Sun had asked.

'She will have a tattoo inside her right thigh: Z652. Please, that's all I know. They refused to divulge any more. They said it would endanger her further if it were found out she was being searched for.'

They had reluctantly agreed. At least the information provided by Christina's source had provided them with this location.

Now all they could do was wait.

# 1

After observing the suspects' movements for a week, they had found a chink in their armour. When the staff changed from daytime to night shift, they rotated the security staff at the same time. But before they were allowed to return, they had to wait until the nursing staff had regained their positions, giving them twenty minutes to locate the girl and escape through the rear entrance, which would be without a guard. They intended to return the girl to their rented place and return to Durban, where Christina awaited.

The time of changeover was now. Sun Yee nodded at Aurora, and they slipped out into the darkness. They were dressed all in black, looking like a couple of ninjas, Aurora thought, they slid silently into position, ready to move.

The entrance to the central part of the building was now accessible, as the security was reserved for the wards where the orphans were housed. They planned to access the main area while the staff were changing, then enter wherever the orphans were being housed, rescue the girl and escape, all while the change occurred. They knew it was risky, but Christina had convinced them it would be too late if they did not act.

As soon as the coast was clear, they entered the unlocked door. Once inside, they went to the lower floor. The only information the source had provided about the interior was that it was where they suspected the orphans were housed.

'This must be it,' whispered Aurora as they arrived at a heavily padlocked door.

'Keep watch,' Sun said as she went to work on the lock.

In seconds she had it open. The sight that greeted them as they entered stopped them in their tracks. It was surreal. The dim lighting gave the place an eerie feeling, but the site's appearance was stranger. It had the appearance of a morgue. The place was surgically clean, and all the occupants were housed in separate plexiglass cubicles. They all appeared to be asleep, but on inspection, they could see they were hooked up to IV.

*Probably sedated*, Aurora guessed.

'What the hell is going on here?' Sun Yee asked as they stepped inside.

Aurora moved closer to look at one of the occupants. 'Look, they are all dressed in surgical gowns; how will we have time to look for a tattoo?'

Sun Yee, by this time, had begun to search. 'Look,' she said as she held up a chart attached to one of the cubicles. Aurora took it to see that it had no name, only a number.

'Let's go,' she exclaimed as they inspected the charts. It appeared that there were about twenty orphans housed here. They were able to discount any males.

Finally, it was Sun Yee that discovered who they were looking for.

The girl did not look more than fifteen; she bore a remarkable resemblance to the American actress, Zendaya.

'Found her. She is sedated. We will have to carry her,' she said as she realised she was also restrained. As she released her, she turned to Aurora. 'I don't know what we have gotten mixed up in, but this is unlike any orphanage I have ever seen. This is more like an isolation ward.'

'No time for that now, I can hear the staff returning. The security will be here any moment,' replied Aurora, as she hoisted the young girl on her shoulder with ease, suddenly thankful to have the physical build of an Olympic athlete due to her mother's Maori heritage and her father's Irish Viking background.

'Lead on. I am right behind you.'

Sun Yee dashed for the rear entrance, only to be confronted by another security gate.

'For fuck sake, this place is more like a maximum-security prison than an orphanage,' Aurora cursed.

Sun Yee went to work on the lock and had it open in seconds. They went to the rear door and opened it cautiously.

'All clear, let's go,' she said.

Just at that moment, all hell broke loose. Alarms started sounding, and they could hear shouts coming from inside.

Dashing for the safety of the darkness that the undergrowth surrounding the complex provided, they were blinded by the lights of a vehicle blocking their path just as they got there.

They froze in their tracks!

# 2

**DUBLIN, IRELAND**
*SIX WEEKS EARLIER.*

After Charlie and his brothers had completed their adventure in Australia in search of some long-lost relatives, resulting in them discovering a distant cousin of their grandmother's brother, Aurora McCormack, they had returned home to Ireland.

During their time Down Under, Desmond had discovered some long-lost relatives of his girlfriend, Maria, a member of the Heart family, with whom the Savages had become entangled with on the island of Mallorca during another of the brothers' adventures.

The Herrero family, who owned a transport company and were involved, had agreed to provide the company's Boeing 737 jet to take everybody back home to their country of origin. Their first stop was Mallorca, where Felipe and Rosa Herrero had left for 'a better life' in Australia in the 60s. But back then, they were known as Diego and Monica Suarez.

Bill Heart had married Rosa's (Monica's) sister, Meris, and owned a large *Finca*, a Spanish hobby farm. Charlie reckoned it could be better described as 'a wealthy man's country estate', which it was. Bill Heart was a retired former London mob member and now the unofficial chairman, using his home as a meeting place and an open house for everybody to party in there while visiting the island's sights and sounds.

Charlie, the older of the Savage brothers, had a casual relationship with the *Gobernadora* of the island, Christina De la Vega, something she had initiated. With her help, they were afforded the island's freedom and, as a result, were invited to all the elegant events held by the wealthy and powerful.

So, arriving in Ireland for some much-needed rest had been a welcome relief. The brothers stayed with their parents, or at least Charlie and Desmond did. Vincent Savage QC preferred the comfort of his luxury apartment in Ballsbridge and came up with some excuse about meeting a client.

'He is full of shit!' their father, Charlie Snr, snarled. 'Still thinks he is better than everyone.'

Helen, his wife, just tutted. 'No wonder he doesn't want to visit us. All you do is complain. I wish wherever he is going, he would take me!' she groaned.

Their dad was just about to get into it when Des interrupted. 'If you two start, you won't be coming with us tonight,' he warned. He and his brothers planned something special for that evening when they were to show their guests their hometown.

They had decided to avoid being outdone by Bill Heart and had pulled out all the stops to show the best that Dublin had to offer. Vincent had finally deferred to his brothers, who had decided on a traditional pub crawl.

'I have a plan for that: 18 holes,' Desmond roared, which meant 18 pubs, with a drink in each. For want of a better plan, that was what was decided.

The big night out began in the old docklands of Temple Bar, now converted into the most popular night spot in the city's centre on the banks of the River Liffey. They had booked rooms for everybody in the Hard Rock Hotel beside Temple Bar and had commenced their evening with the pub crawl.

Aurora and Sun Yee had arrived the previous day to announce their partnership's formation to help people reconnect or find missing relatives.

First, Charlie led the group to a couple of non-touristy pubs so that the non-Irish could experience real pub life in the Emerald Isle. The first stop was 'The Foggy Dew', where they shared their first honest pint of Guinness.

Des laughed when he saw the expression on some of their faces. 'It's an acquired taste. That is what you told me when you forced Vegemite down my throat in Australia,' he said, crying with laughter.

They then proceeded to 'The Auld Dub,' where a sing-song began. Charlie Snr needed no encouragement and took the stage where there was a piano—and launched into a medley of old Irish songs. He had been gifted with great musical talent and a rich baritone voice.

In no time, he had the crowd in the palm of his hands, and they would have stayed there all night if Desmond had not dragged him out.

Dinner was next at 'The Oliver St. John Gogarty', named after the famous poet of the same name. They had reserved a whole floor of the restaurant.

From there, they headed to 'The Temple Bar', owned by none other than U2, the famous rock band. The party was still in full swing late in the evening, with the Spanish women trying to teach a bunch of drunken Irish to dance the flamenco to the delight of everyone.

Finally, Aurora drew Charlie aside. 'Sun and I would like to discuss something that has come up.'

The brothers had earned the nickname 'The Umbrella Crew' because it seemed they had a strange way of protecting anybody under their influence when they got involved. For this reason, Aurora had resigned from the police and decided to use some of her cousin's unusual methods in their investigations. She convinced Sun Yee to keep Charlie in the picture.

Charlie could tell that she was concerned, and nodded. 'You get Sun Yee. I will get Des. He will not want to be left out. We will go somewhere quieter. The others can party on. I am sure we will not be missed,' he said as his dad launched into song.

That was when they explained they were off to South Africa to help their first client!

# 3

## SOUTH AFRICA

Aurora and Sun Yee took a direct flight to Johannesburg and transferred to an internal flight to Durban, where Christina Herrero worked and lived. Christina ran a clinic in Johannesburg. When they arrived, she met them, thanking them profusely for coming. They then went straight to her house.

When they were settled and had a drink in their hands, she began to relax, and then launched into her strange story, explaining what she had discovered so far.

'You must understand that helping with the staggering number of refugees and orphans on this war-torn continent is a human tragedy. Remember, Africa is one of the primary sources of child trafficking, and because of that, in trying to deal with the situation, we are often forced to deal with questionable people and organisations. So when I got this request for help from a source, I would typically be very suspicious of it. But they convinced me this girl would be killed within days if I did not intervene. When I asked for more information, I was greeted with silence. All they would tell me was that the only way to identify her would be by a tattoo on her leg.'

When Sun Yee and Aurora heard that identification would be a number tattooed on her inner thigh, horrifying visions of the Nazis in World War Two flashed into their minds.

After staking out the location the informant had provided for the last few days, they were confident that, besides the obvious fact that it could have been a better-looking place, it seemed to operate normally. 'Normally', that was, except for the fully armed civilian security staff, which they attributed to the current state of lawlessness in South Africa.

They devised a plan to retrieve the girl just after dusk. They had found an unattended easy entry point during the staff change. Christina had pumped whoever was behind this impromptu rescue for more information. All she could find out was that they would be held in a secure area.

But now things had taken a turn for the worse.

As soon as they were outside the orphanage, Sun Yee realised something was off. The response to their break-in was disproportionate to the small security staff at this place.

'Run!' she yelled.

They were sprinting for the darkness of the surrounding area when the lights brought them to a halt. They froze for what seemed to be an eternity until a familiar voice came out of the darkness.

'Will you stand around all night, or will we leave?'

'Charlie?' Aurora yelped in disbelief. She had left her cousin in Ireland weeks ago and had spoken to him numerous times there in the last few days.

'What are you doing here?' she asked.

'Trying to rescue you,' he roared.

Sun Yee broke the impasse, grabbing the girl from Aurora and putting her in the back of the Toyota Pajero where Charlie was sitting with the engine racing. She jumped in the back alongside the unconscious girl when Aurora finally decided to move, bailing into the passenger seat as Chaz gunned the car away.

'What are you doing here?' Aurora demanded again.

'Nice to see you too,' he snapped back.

'Enough, you two. There will be plenty of time for that later. Right now, it sounds like everybody in Africa is after us. I don't know who this girl is, but she must be important to somebody,' Sun Yee On yelled as they accelerated, wheels spinning on the main road.

'Hang on. They are sure to be in pursuit. Is there anything to identify you back at your hideout?' he asked over the roar of the engine.

Sun Yee replied, 'No, as always, it was sanitised before we left. There is nothing there.'

'Good, now all we have to do is avoid getting captured before our ride arrives.'

Chaz swung the 4WD off the tarmac and into the savannah.

'Where are we going?' Aurora asked as she held on for dear life as they bounced over the rough ground.

'There,' he replied, pointing toward what appeared to be a football field, one of many that dotted this country where soccer or football, in Africa at least, was close to being a religion.

Coming to a stop at the pitch's perimeter, Charlie picked up his satellite phone and dialled.

A voice, answered. 'Ready?' a native-sounding male asked.

'Ready,' he replied.

'On our way, two minutes,' as he disconnected the call.

Within seconds, they could hear the sound of an approaching helicopter. In the distance, the commotion of the resulting search drowned any chance of them being detected.

A Bell 429 seven-seater helicopter descended in the centre of the park. Chaz immediately drove the vehicle as close as possible as the door opened, and a young African male jumped out.

'Let's get moving; this is not what you call a scheduled flight,' he shouted over the rotor.

They quickly transferred the unconscious girl to the rear, which was set up for rescue and had a bed where they could secure her. As soon as they were ready, Chaz instructed the girls to get in as he went to speak to the young guy who was standing beside the Toyota. Handing him the keys, he said something into his ear, then turned and jumped into the co-pilot seat, giving the thumbs-up to the pilot.

As they lifted off, Chaz could hear Aurora in the headphones he had just put on.

'Where is he going with your car?' she asked.

He shrugged. 'No idea. He owns it now, or I should say, he and his father. Meet Solomon Nkosi,' tapping the pilot on the shoulder, which prompted him to wave.

'When it came to the question of the price for this little trip, his son Shaka set his eye on my truck, so it solved two problems in one. I didn't have to dump the car; he got what he wanted.'

She was about to launch into more questions, so Chaz got in first.

'I know you have a hundred questions, but take care of your ward now. We are only twenty-five minutes from where we are meeting Christina. We will have plenty of time to unravel what she has got you guys mixed up in. I can tell you this: it is a lot more than some simple kidnapping.'

# 4

They touched down on Christina's property, a large, gated compound on the outskirts of Durban where she had a second home and clinic. Her primary residence and clinic were in Johannesburg, but when they learned the location of where the girl was being held, they decided to relocate their operation here.

Christina had reasoned that Durban was a bustling holiday destination to a relatively safe area, despite its diverse cultural mix. Located on the coast in the traditional homeland of the Zulu tribe, its perfect climate for sugarcane had lured a huge influx of Indian and Asian communities over a hundred years ago, who brought with them their Hindu and Muslim religions. The minority culture were English speaking Europeans, remnants of the time when the British ruled Southern Africa.

As soon as the rotor started to spool down, Christina rushed to the chopper's door, accompanied by two male attendants with a mobile bed. The still unconscious girl was transferred to the bed and quickly taken to the clinic for treatment, while Christina, the girls, and Chaz headed inside.

'I can't believe you did it. Since Charlie arrived and told me who was behind that orphanage, I have been unable to sleep,' Christina gasped. The look of confusion on the girls' faces made her pause. 'You haven't told them?' she turned to Charlie.

'Believe it or not, we had little time to sit down and chat, so no, I haven't told them anything,' he replied as they continued inside.

The girls followed closely behind him and were greeted by the sight of Charlie's brother, Desmond, and Bill Heart. Adding to their shock was the imposing figure of Sergei Stalin, someone they had become deeply involved with back in Australia.

'Somebody get them a drink before they collapse from shock,' Desmond yelled to his girlfriend, Maria Heart. The presence of Bill's daughter also elicited gasps from the girls.

'Is the whole world here? Can someone tell us what the hell is going on that you thought we needed this much help?' Aurora demanded, her cornrows bobbing up and down as she shook her head in disbelief.

'Calm down, cousin. You're getting ahead of yourself. All of these guys are here for another mission, and I decided to join when Bill told me who was running that orphanage,' Chaz said, intervening to defuse the situation, knowing his cousin's famous temper.

'Who?' she asked, her curiosity piqued.

He paused and then replied, 'The Sysue Mafia. Translated to "The Angels", they control most of the crime in this country and act as a police force for all the warring factions. When we discovered they were behind this place, we realised there was something much more than the recovery of some orphan. So, I decided to see what you had gotten involved in.'

Sun Yee stepped forward. 'That sort of explains why you're here. But why are all these guys here?'.

# 5

Christina had her staff make everyone comfortable before hurrying to attend to the young girl's condition, leaving the others to explain what was happening.

Charlie stepped in. 'You can thank the presence of these guys,' he said, indicating Des, Bill, and the menacing hulk of Sergei, 'to our illustrious father, Charlie Snr. He gave some scammer 85,000 euros, thinking he was investing in Bitcoin, almost giving access to the family trust. Only the sharp eye of Vincent, our lawyer brother who looks after all the financial matters for the family, prevented it. Since we became comfortably well-off, thanks to Desmond discovering lost Nazi treasure on a previous misadventure on the Island of Mallorca, our father started believing he was a big-time businessman. At least, that's what he told his friends to account for his newfound wealth. None of us believed him.'

Aurora and Sun Yee looked at them with confusion. 'What are you talking about?' Aurora asked.

'Let me continue. He then convinced Des that he should do something about these "Bums" that had come up in discussion, to the point where he demanded that his "Gang busting" sons should take action. This happened one night over numerous drinks, and we had no choice but to agree or suffer the pain of listening to our dad indefinitely. So when I heard Dad talking him into it and Bill was searching for a suitable hacker, I asked him to check out what he could find about the kidnapping and where you were staking out. That's how he found out who was behind that orphanage you were targeting. I decided to tag along.'

'Cyber Crime?' Sun and Aurora echoed.

'Bill had been dragged in because Des had no idea about cyber theft, and he was the obvious choice.' Bill Heart was a 'retired' member of the London Mob and now owned a restaurant in Mallorca. Unofficially, he was accepted as the 'godfather' or 'Head Chap' in London. However, this kind of crime was beyond his expertise. Why don't I let him explain,' Chaz said, handing over to Bill, who was comfortably seated in a chair.

'When Des asked me how we could catch one of these hackers, the "Chaps" laughed at me and said that stuff was all orchestrated from Africa, with so many countries—forty-five, to be precise. It was impossible to police. Most big businesses dealt with the problem by paying a ransom and trying to keep it quiet from their clients. Cyber theft is a crime that most middle-aged people fear.'

'So why come here?'

'I didn't say they had a free ride. Remember the movie, *To Catch a Thief*?' Bill asked. Des sadly believed everything he saw in the cinema. The girls shrugged. 'In the film, they use a thief to catch a thief. So that's why we're here—to hire a hacker to catch a hacker. You see, I was able to trace the likely origin of the crime to South Africa, which also happens to be where the best computer hacker is.'

'So why did so many of you come?' Aurora asked, glancing at Sergei.

Charlie answered, 'Well, you see, there's a problem. He is in prison.'

# 6

Before the conversation could continue, Christina burst back into the room.

'Come, you have to see this,' she urged, prompting them to follow her.

They quickly fell in behind her as she led them to the part of the building serving as the clinic.

The rescued girl was in a room by herself, connected to various apparatus, monitors, and an intravenous drip. She remained unconscious but appeared to be comfortable.

'What's wrong? Does she have a problem?' Aurora asked.

Christina beckoned them to follow her into a small room where they could still see the girl through a window as she received treatment.

Christina took a deep breath before speaking. 'This is not an ordinary kidnapping. It's something far more sinister. I had heard rumours about something like this, but I never thought I would encounter it.' She held up the chart that Sun Yee had taken from the girl's bed. 'The information recorded on these charts goes far beyond what is required for an orphan with no means. Every possible test and compatibility cross-reference has been conducted. There is no logical reason for this unless it involves major surgery,' she paused, 'or tissue typing.' Their confused expressions prompted her to explain further. 'The only reason these tests would have been conducted is if the patient was either going to receive an organ transplant or donate one.' She paused. 'This girl has been held captive and tested for compatibility with a wealthy recipient. We have stumbled upon a "puppy farm" for humans. People being specially prepared for selected customers.'

Chaz jumped in. 'But isn't that practice illegal?'

Surprisingly, it was Bill Heart who answered. 'Yes and no. When Chaz asked me to look into the place where the girl was rumoured to be held, I contacted a reliable Russian/Israeli contact who does a lot of business in South Africa. That's how I found out about "The Sysue Mafia". I know they are involved in trafficking, and by that, I mean people. So when Chaz mentioned that you were rescuing a kidnap victim, it seemed to fit the picture. But something like what Christina is describing would be well beyond the capabilities of those guys. If this is true, then they must have had significant assistance. So, to answer your question, from what little I know about organ trafficking, it is considered illegal in most countries. However, private transactions still occur, primarily involving the sale of kidneys since it's the one organ we can spare. Although it's illegal to receive money for it, many people "donate" a kidney for genuine reasons. But there is a thriving market for brokers to arrange sales. In almost all cases, they are willing participants, regardless of the moral issues. The few reported cases of kidney theft are just stories, not due to any sense of remorse, but rather because both parties need to be tissue-typed to determine compatibility. That's a challenging task if you're stealing it.'

Sun Ye On, an orphan herself, spoke up. 'Christina, have you ever known of such a place to exist?'

'I think we've found one in Scottsville. The information on this chart covers one year. This girl has been monitored and prepared for a special recipient. Moreover, based on what I can gather, her compatibility with the recipient is extremely rare and almost impossible to match. Whoever she was being prepared for will be desperate to have her back.'

'But how can you tell if they need her organs right away?'

'Because they have already harvested one of her kidneys within the past six months.'

This revelation prompted a gasp. 'So they already have what they wanted.'

Christina shook her head.

'I'm afraid not. According to this chart, she is scheduled for a complete heart-lung transplant in two weeks!'

# 7

They all returned to the central part of the house. Aurora spoke first.

'Whoever is looking to recover that girl cannot be allowed to. It would be murder.'

'I agree. I had no idea she was a subject for organ harvesting. I didn't even believe anything like this existed,' Christina replied as she got drinks for the shaken group.

'You'd better tell us all you know about who contacted you about this girl and where they are. Because as soon as they hear about the raid on the orphanage, they'll be looking for her. And I'm guessing, judging from what's going on here, they'll do anything to get their hands on her quickly. Do they know how to find you?' Chaz asked.

A worried look crossed her face. 'You have to understand the magnitude of the problem we face. The number of orphans due to all the conflicts and, in many cases, just simple poverty, leads to many without any documents or family background. Many governments on this continent don't have the will or the resources to look after them. The responsibility falls on aid agencies such as the Red Cross and Médecins Sans Frontières, and the many volunteer groups that operate in these depressed areas. In this case, I was approached by a shadow agency that works in the grey areas of the crisis. People approach them to locate lost ones and the like. They told me this was a missing relative and, for reasons they could, or would not reveal, said she was in danger. They provided the location where she was being held.'

'Why didn't they recover her themselves?' he asked.

'They are based in Israel. That's where a lot of the illegal transplant orders are brokered. That's probably where the recipient is,' she replied.

Chaz stepped in. 'Okay. Enough talk. Time for a plan. First thing, Des, you guys need to get on with what you're here for...'

Aurora interrupted. 'You never explained what brought you here; something about your dad being robbed online?'

Desmond replied. 'That's the easy part. He also nearly managed to let them have access to the family trust. Only by luck, Vincent was checking something and noticed some unusual activity and was able to intervene before too much damage was done. So it was decided that we do something about these crooks. This brings us to Bill and Sergei, who found it possible to trace the activity back to the country of origin, but after that, it would require the services of an expert hacker. The one they were consistently referred to was a young hacker from here in South Africa. The only problem is that he's in jail for some hacking crime.'

Sun Yee spoke. 'So what do you plan to do?'

'Get him out, especially now because of what's happening with this girl. It's even more important that we get the help of this guy. I'm sure he would be able to trace the people who are hunting her.'

'Isn't there anybody else available?' Chaz asked.

'Believe me, we've tried,' Bill replied. 'We got our friends in the police to reach out to a contact they had in the CIA, and they confirmed that this guy was their number one target, not to catch, but to recruit. But consistently, this guy's name kept coming up.'

'Okay. I agree that this guy would be invaluable. But right now, we must get this young girl to safety and figure out what we'll do to rescue the rest of the inmates there. So you guys do what you must do, and myself and the girls,' indicating Aurora, Sun Yee On, and Christina, 'We'll figure out things here,' Chaz suggested, which was greeted with agreement all around.

It was agreed that everybody would use Christina's place as their base. But until they could get their rescue victim to safety, it would be better for Des and Co. to make themselves scarce.

# 8

As soon as they departed, Chaz started to make plans. 'First thing, do you have anywhere you could go where you could take care of this girl until we figure out our next move?' he asked.

Christina thought momentarily, then replied, 'My parents bought a place on the Vaal River, a holiday home near Vanderbijlpark. When I moved here, they bought it so we would have a place to get together when they visited. And it would be perfect as it is secluded. Nobody would know about that.'

'Perfect. I will contact our friends with the helicopter to arrange for your departure while we figure out what to do about rescuing those people. You prepare yourself and whoever else you need to treat the patient,' Chaz said.

When he had received the news from the others that perhaps Aurora and Sun Yee could be heading into danger, he reached out to Bill and Sergei.

However, it was Christina's father who put him in touch with Solomon Nkosi and his son Shaka. They ran a private transport company here and, with him footing the bill, were only too happy to help. They were well accustomed to flying in this dangerous country, and from what Chaz had seen the other night, they were very skilled at it.

By the time Christina returned from planning their departure, Chaz informed her that Solomon would be ready at any time from daybreak.

'I have arranged your departure for tomorrow afternoon. The reason is that we hope with your help we can use the helicopter to aid in the release of the orphans,' Chaz explained.

'How can I help?' she asked.

'Do you have any contacts with a major news channel that would like the scoop of the century?' he replied.

She thought for a few minutes, then had a 'got ya' moment.

'Sharlene Ndlovu is one of the emerging new-age reporters prepared to ask hard questions. We became good friends when we realised we were fighting the same battles. She works for News 24. What do you want me to ask her?'

Chaz grinned, glancing at Aurora and Sun Yee. 'Ask her if she would take a helicopter ride tomorrow morning to record the potential release of a large number of "orphans" who are being kept as potential organ donors to wealthy clients that are greedy and trying to jump the queue. And tell her to have reporters and cameras at the location. If she asks for the location, tell her she will get it thirty minutes before the police receive a call. That will give her plenty of time to set up at a safe distance and watch the action live and exclusive.'

It was apparent from the reaction when she answered Chris's call that they were real friends, as she had her private number. After speaking to her for some time, they exchanged goodbyes, and she hung up.

'She is in. I will call back when we work on the final details. In the meantime, she will arrange for the ground crew to be ready to move when we provide the location,' Christina relayed.

Chaz began to outline his plan, which would be implemented precisely at eleven am. This was when the helicopter was to arrive with the camera crew and allow time for the ground people to get into position. 'That's when we go in.'

'How do we do that?' Sun Yee asked.

Chaz grinned and replied, 'We will walk in the front door!'

# 9

**DUBLIN,**
*SIX WEEKS BEFORE*.

'Do you know the trouble you have caused with your little investment? If I had not discovered the hack into our family trust in time, we could have potentially lost everything,' Vincent Savage QC ranted at his dad, who had managed to get taken in twice by the same hacker or whatever name there was for the people that fleece the unsuspecting over the internet. 'You let him get you twice!'

Charlie Snr thrust his chest out. 'I don't know what you are blaming me for. It should be the mongrel that posed as a policeman that you should be out there catching instead of trying to blame me,' he argued.

Des was sitting in on the inquisition of his dad. He grinned. What his dad was saying made much sense. During a misadventure he had inadvertently dragged his family into, he had made amends by discovering the location of a lost Nazi fortune that, after arranging with the local officials and his sticky fingers, had left them and all involved pretty well set for life. It had been decided that all business decisions be left in the hands of Vincent and Bill Heart.

Des, like his brother Chaz, could not be bothered by how the family trust was going or whether they should invest in cryptocurrency. Hence, he was sitting here with his girlfriend, Maria Heart, Bill's daughter.

They had only recently begrudgingly accepted that they were in a relationship. Something that, to everybody else, was obvious.

This had all started when some guy masquerading as a police officer convinced him that there was a possible cyber-attack on the family and that he was the nominated trustee. That was not surprising, as the guy had just invented the position. He convinced him that they needed to verify the password for the account but told him that he was not allowed to say it; instead, he was to text it to a secret government number that only the top people could see. So that's what he did.

When Vincent asked him how he had the password, he replied, 'That was easy; you are always writing it on bits of paper. I am a bit smarter. I put it on my phone in case you forget it completely. You should be thanking me,' he roared.

To which his son retorted, 'So what happened with the credit card?'

'He rang me back the next day and said that as they verified the security on the trust fund, he felt he should check out the credit card.'

'Let me guess, he asked for the number on the front and the expiry date, right?' His father nodded. 'And then he asked for the three numbers on the reverse, correct?'

Again a nod. Then added, 'I also could give him the amount of the last purchase; it was lucky I remembered it,' he cried.

'You realise he managed to get away with over eighty-five thousand Euro. But it will take months to repair the damage. Luckily, the credit card company contacted me, and I discovered his hack on the trust fund,' he said.

At that point, Chaz arrived and calmed the situation. As they relaxed with a drink, the conversation descended into the usual family abuse of each other. A practice only they were allowed to engage in.

Charlie Snr began to gain a voice. 'I don't know what's wrong with you geniuses. When you were young, if somebody did what that scumbag did, you would have hunted him to the end of the earth. Now you are too big in your boots for the little man. "The Umbrella Men",' he retorted, 'from where I'm standing, I'm getting very wet!''

This brought howls of laughter, prompting their mother, Helen, to intervene. ' You know he is right, if you were stupid enough to give a credit card to this gobshite. On top of that, leaving valuable information about where he can find it. Remember, this man is renowned for not squandering his money on food and rent.'

By this stage, they were collapsing around the place in laughter. Charlie Snr did not know whether to be grateful for his wife's support or be annoyed by the attached insult.

Des jumped in. 'You know, Mam is right. These bastards are fleecing lots of unsuspecting people like Dad. There must be a way to track them down,' he said, which began a discussion late into the night over numerous drinks.

Later that week, Bill reached out to his contacts to see what could be found. But it was Sergei, through his Russian mafia connections, that discovered that a large amount of this crime originated in Africa, with South Africa being the epicentre for a lot of the activity. When Bill reached out for somebody who could trace these guys, one name came up repeatedly; they went by the handle 'ASTRA'.

The authorities in South Africa believed they had captured the person in question, and they were currently in detention in prison in Durban. Still, strangely, no charges had been laid yet.

'Well, Chaz is already helping Aurora and Sun Yee On with something they are involved in. I say we go and have a chat with this person,' said Des, who was greeted by a howl of delight from Charlie Snr.

'They are screwed now. The Umbrella Crew are on the case,' bringing groans from the brothers, who hated that the nickname that their mother had given them was starting to stick.

# 10

**DURBAN, SA,**
*PRESENT DAY.*

Sharlene Ndlovu greeted them at the arranged meeting place. Christina rushed to greet her, and after hugs and greetings between the two firm friends, she explained she had decided to report from the ground but assured them the helicopter had already picked up the camera crew. She was in radio contact with them, awaiting her instructions.

After introductions were made and final details were hashed out, Aurora indicated to get on with it. Chaz nodded in agreement and asked Christina if she was ready to call the Police.

'Remember, just as we rehearsed. Tell them there is about to be a rescue attempt to free a young girl who has been held captive for her organs to be harvested. If they ask how you know, say that you are a nurse working there and were warned of the rescue attempt. Don't forget to add that many captives are being held there. You got afraid and ran. Before they question you more, tell them you have already called the press, then hang up,' Chaz instructed.

After she completed the call and disconnected, they all gave her silent applause. 'That was perfect. They will have to roll in force now that they know the press is involved. Now it is over to you,' Charlie said, pointing at Aurora and Sun Yee.

When they questioned how they expected to breach the facility, knowing there were armed guards inside, Sun Yee said, 'We won't get past the lobby.'

'Correct, and that is how we get inside, by getting thrown out...' He went on to explain, 'This all comes down to timing. I will appear as some friend along to provide support. This will be your show, two women frantically looking for some kidnapped relative. You don't have to make much sense; all you have to do is create enough disturbance to get us ejected as the police are arriving. That might take a bit of creativity if we are put outside before they arrive.'

Sun Yee glanced at her girlfriend. 'Not a problem,' she replied.

The girls dressed as if they were going on a talk show, which is precisely what they were hoping for. They strode across the street and walked in the front entrance. Charlie followed, dressed in casual clothes and with an expression on his face as if questioning why he was there.

Aurora poised in the centre of the lobby. The reception desk was at least two metres away. Then in her loudest voice, she shouted, 'Get me the director of this place. My sister and her cousin are held captive here, and I want her released at once.'

A young African man hurried over. 'Please keep your voice down. The director is not here; I am in charge.' That was his first mistake.

Sun Yee took up the action. 'Then you will take us directly to where our friend is held,' she demanded.

By this stage, Chaz could see the guards emerging, guns ready. But these were just thugs used to fighting, shooting, and killing and typically did not deal with unarmed, well-dressed, beautiful women. They hardly glanced at Chaz because he was acting as uncomfortable as the guy trying to get them to leave.

'You will have to leave. You are causing a disturbance. There are only orphans here,' he pleaded.

That only made them louder. Suddenly, they turned back-to-back and slid to a sitting position on the floor.

'We are staging a sit-in. We will not leave until you produce our friend and any of her friends that want to go,' Aurora decided to add, displaying their long legs, much to the delight of the guards.

This gave Chaz a chance to check where the entrance to the cellars where the kids were. As soon as he had orientated himself, he moved to the door, glancing outside for the arrival of the troops. Nothing yet, shaking his head in the direction of the girls.

By now, the guy had lost his patience and nodded to the guards to escort them out. They approached with trepidation, not knowing how to manhandle two beautiful women and, more importantly, dressed like persons of importance.

This caused them to hesitate until one of them, who decided to take charge, grabbed Sun Yee by the arm and dragged her to her feet. She put up a struggle, but it was all an act; she could have finished him and two more of the guards while he was deciding what to do.

They allowed themselves to be escorted outside to find that the police had yet to arrive. Sharlene waved from their vantage point. Already, a crowd was gathering. She put two fingers in the air.

'Two minutes,' Aurora nudged Sun Yee. 'We have to stall.'

# 11

They were figuring out how to stall when the opportunity presented itself.

They were deposited on the road before the entrance as the guards and the African man in charge began to return inside. Seizing the opportunity, Sun Yee grabbed the young manager and propelled him into the centre of the street.

'We will not release him until you release our friends,' she yelled as Aurora joined her.

In the confusion that resulted, Chaz slipped back inside and quickly went to the entrance that led to the orphans. He quickly disabled the lock by squirting superglue into the mechanisms, then hurried back to perform the same on the entrance locks as he stepped back outside to witness the standoff. The sound of approaching sirens was music to his ears.

A convoy of police vehicles roared into the street, screeching to a stop as the officers jumped out and began to cordon both ends of the road. An imposing African man in uniform stepped out of the lead vehicle.

Aurora and Sun released the manager, who made a bolt for the entrance of the orphanage, quickly followed by the guards. Before he could enter, Charlie stepped in front of the startled man.

'Before you even think about covering up what is happening here, I suggest you look at the helicopter broadcasting everything down here, and if you look over there,' pointing in the direction of Sharlene, who had descended on the man in uniform, 'that is the intrepid reporter Sharlene Ndlovu, who is here on the tip-off of an illegal 'orphanage' used for organ theft. If you think your bosses have enough clout to stop the police from investigating now that they are on national television, you might want to consider your next move. It does not matter whom they have bribed. When the Government and the police see the outcry something as evil as this will cause, I am sure they will see that taking down such a terrible thing would be a good career move. Plus, anybody that cooperates might save themselves from going to jail for a long time. And if you were considering locking yourself inside until you could get some help, think again. I have disabled all locks. Your call.'

He headed to where Aurora, Sun, Sharlene, and the officer in charge were in deep conversation, explaining what they suspected was happening inside this place.

Moses Khumalo was the commander of the central Durban police station. When word of this suspected kidnapping and the involvement of national news agencies arrived at the station, and as soon as he was informed of where this was occurring, he realised that the premises where this was taking place was allegedly connected to the Sysue Mafia. He decided to lead the raid himself.

Corruption was rife in the South African police force, as well as many other government departments, all the way to the very top, and if you wanted to survive, you turned a blind eye from time to time. But if there was any truth to this, he wanted to ensure nothing got swept under the table. If this was true, it could make him a national hero, sound currency to have in his position.

'Ladies, please allow me to speak. If, as you say, somebody is being held against their will, then let's go and investigate,' he announced to the cameras that were thrust in his face.

He pushed through the group of protesting reporters and curious bystanders, anxious to discover what was happening inside.

He called for his men to clear a path inside, then indicated for everybody to follow. If he would make this work for him, he needed it recorded.

They entered with no resistance. The guards had vanished. Only the hapless manager remained.

'I have been informed that a person is being held here against their will. Where are your inmates held?' he asked the shaken fellow.

He gulped. 'Whoever is here is in the basement. We are not allowed to go down there,' he mumbled.

'What are you talking about? This is an orphanage. Who looks after them and feeds them?' Moses roared.

'Special staff come in twice daily to care for their needs.'

'Enough of this nonsense. Show me where these people are kept,' he demanded.

'I can't. The door is automatically locked as soon as it closes. Only the staff can enter,' he pleaded.

Charlie stepped in. 'I am with these ladies,' indicating the crew standing alongside him. 'I tampered with the locks to make them inoperable. These people would not want to have prying eyes to see what was happening.' At the same time, his men were manhandling the lady outside. 'I took care of it so they could not be locked. If you follow me, I can show you,' indicating the cellar entrance.

They stepped into the lower level, but it was hard to make anything out with the dim lighting. Suddenly, the place was illuminated by bright halogen lights suspended from the ceiling.

Sun Yee On stood beside a large switch box she had located and engaged the main switch.

The sight that confronted them shocked everybody to the core as the place came into focus.

# 12

It was like a scene from a blockbuster movie.

People flooded everywhere after seeing the scenes on live TV, wanting to satisfy their morbid curiosity.

The road was being hurriedly cordoned off, and police were escorting everybody unconnected with the operation behind the barrier.

Seeing all those young people being held in an unconscious state with nobody present to attend to them sent Commander Moses into a rage. He immediately declared this a major crime scene, and everybody connected was detained.

He then turned to Sharlene, who was recording all of this. 'Who is the best person to deal with something like this?' he asked.

She pointed at Christina. 'This doctor here, she is responsible for discovering this place,' and introduced her.

Christina briefly explained how she had uncovered this place and mobilised her friends to help. He decided not to ask her why she did not call the police first, realising she would know about the rife corruption, deciding to take things into her own hands, something he grudgingly respected.

Instead, he asked her, 'Where is the best facility that could handle something like this?'

'Because we have no idea how long these people have been sedated. They will have to remain in this state until they can be assessed. I would suggest The Ethekwini Hospital. They are large enough to handle this quantity of patients,' Christina responded.

Moses began barking instructions for ambulances to be dispatched at once. His underling asked, 'How many?'

He threw his hands in the air and yelled, 'All of them!'

Over the next few hours, the event was broadcast live on every news channel in the country. It had already attracted the attention of international news channels, with Sharlene Ndlovu presenting all of the crucial transmissions. She had remained at the site to report on the situation as it was happening.

Behind her broadcast position were ambulances transporting the victims to the hospital. Christina had demanded that Commander Moses ensure that the charts attached to each person were closely guarded as this was the only information they had regarding their treatment and the potential recipient, which could lead to whoever was behind this terrible crime.

Aurora and Sun Yee took Commander Moses aside to discuss handling the situation.

It was Sun Yee who spoke. 'You have a golden opportunity to do good here and, simultaneously, place yourself in a position of considerable power. I know because I have been in the same situation. Please don't ask how because I can't answer that. But I can tell you that with this power comes much danger. We have stirred up a hornet's nest here. An operation like this requires a lot of brains, expertise and, most importantly, clout at the highest levels. If I am correct, and we are sure we are, expect blowback, trust no one. We are as invested in this as much as you are. So I suggest we work together, agreed?'

He looked her in the eye, and then at Aurora. 'Could not agree more,' extending his hand.

Aurora joined them and then turned the conversation to their next move. 'The first problem is protecting Doctor Christina Herrero. She is the link to what has gone down here and will surely be a target.'

'Agreed, and thanks to her good friend, Sharlene, she has become an international celebrity for uncovering a "Human body farm". The problem is the people behind this are almost certainly outside this country and out of my reach. This should keep whoever is behind this at bay for the moment. I will still provide police protection.'

'Out of your reach, but not ours,' Sun Yee replied.

He fixed her with a puzzled look. 'Just who are you guys, and whom do you work for?'

Sun Yee looked at Aurora, who nodded. 'We work for ourselves together with three brothers and their friends. We help people who can't get help through normal channels. On the other hand, we are not restricted by borders and, occasionally, the rules,' she replied with a sly smile.

'In fact, they are over here on another task. They would be very interested in helping with something as heinous as this.'

He shrugged. 'It looks like I can use all the friends I can get!'

# 13

Desmond and the lads had checked into The Beverley Hills Hotel in downtown Durban and were sitting in their suite, discussing their next move while watching the girls' escapades unfold on national television.

'Looks like they have everything under control. Time for us to get back to business,' Bill said as he turned the TV off.

'What's the latest from Vince?' Des asked.

'Okay, this is where it gets strange. Vince has discovered he has been kept in what can only be described as an "open prison", supposedly for political or favoured individuals who want to give the impression of paying for their misdeeds yet still carry on with somewhat everyday life. This is where this so-called ASTRA is held. The weird thing is that he is imprisoned without a charge. The only thing he could find out was that if he left, he would be immediately arrested and deported back to Iceland.'

'Iceland?' echoed Des.

'Yes, the name and nationality he is being held under are Axel Sigurdsson, with an Icelandic passport.'

'So, what's the plan?'

Bill looked at them. 'I reckon we should go and have a chat with this guy.'

'What if he doesn't want to talk to us?' Des queried.

'He might if we offer him a way to get out and not be deported, something I assume he would like to avoid, considering he is sitting in a jail he can walk out of.'

They pulled into the car park of The Institute for the Rehabilitation of the Misguided, which was emblazoned across the entrance, looking more like a top hotel than a jail.

They were greeted by a pleasant receptionist dressed more like an office worker than a correctional officer. When Des commented on this, she giggled, 'We are allowed to choose our attire when we come to work, so long as it is not provocative, as this facility houses male inmates as well.'

'We would like to speak to one of your inmates. Their name is Axel Sigurdsson. If you could tell them we would like to discuss the possibility of their release,' Des requested.

She went to the computer and quickly found the name. 'If you wait here, I will see if the inmate agrees to speak to you. You understand we have no authority to compel them to do so,' she explained.

'Of course, shall we wait here?' he asked, indicating some seats along the side.

'Yes, I will have him asked at once,' she replied as she picked up the phone.

'Some place,' commented Des as they sank into the comfortable chairs.

'I would love to be sent to prison here. If I told my pals back in Russia about this place, they would be on the first plane over,' Sergei added.

'Axel will see you,' the girl announced after about fifteen minutes.

They were escorted through the building, and to their surprise, there were no locks or bars to be seen anywhere. 'You could walk out of here anytime you liked,' Bill remarked.

'This prison is modelled on a system championed in Sweden with great success, especially for people who have committed what society describes as "soft crime",' Des informed them.

Since being together with Maria, she had convinced him to try Google rather than relying on movies, where he had previously. Since then, he believed everything his mobile told him.

They arrived at a door that an officer opened and invited them to enter. 'Your visitors are here,' he announced, and they were greeted by the sight of a tall Nordic girl with almost white-blond hair and striking features who stood to greet them.

'You are a girl!' Des blurted out in his usual fashion.

'Last time I looked,' she replied, 'are you always this observant?' she asked sarcastically.

Bill took charge. 'Your name confused us, our error; please excuse us,' he added quickly, trying to regain their composure at the sight of this beautiful woman.

She nodded, indicating for them to sit. 'You are not the first to make this error; I guess my parents wanted a boy. Now, they said something about getting out of here?' she said, fixing them with an intense stare.

Bill proceeded to explain how Des's father had been scammed out of eighty-five thousand euros, and they had decided to take action. After an investigation by another member of their group, they discovered that the fraud originated here in South Africa.

'So the three of you have come all this way to try and recover 85,000 euros. It seems you must have money to burn, throwing good money after bad. These small-time crooks never get caught; if they did, you would probably find they have already spent the money. These people are petty crooks and usually kids,' she replied.

'Euros,' mumbled Des. They all looked at him in confusion.

'I was saying it was euros, not dollars,' he continued as he saw the look of confusion on their faces.

Lesley continued as if he had not spoken, 'In any case, what brings you here today, and what makes you think you can get me out of here without being deported?'

Bill explained that they were a group that tried to help people who could not get help through "normal" channels.

'You are new age Robin Hoods,' she laughed.

He grinned back, 'Something like that. So when we discovered you were here, our search for the top hacker led us to you.'

'You think I stole your friend's money?' she asked in shock.

'No, of course not. We were told that if anybody could help us locate this person, it would have to be ALPHA, so here we are.'

'You are wrong on so many fronts. Let's begin with my name. It is Axel, and not a male, as your chauvinistic traits led you to believe. And it is those idiots here that have people believing I am this ALPHA. That is why the government back in Iceland is anxious to talk to me; you have come to the wrong place,' she snapped.

Des piped up, 'The girls who make up a large part of this "group", as you call it, would disagree with your chauvinistic comment.'

'Pity they are not here to back you up,' she retorted.

'They are, in fact, here. It is because they are here trying to rescue a kidnapped girl that we decided to tag along and try this,' he replied angrily.

She froze as her whole attitude changed. From being only vaguely interested in the conversation, they now had her attention.

'Are you talking about the incident that commandeered the TV yesterday?' she asked.

Bill stepped in to try and defuse the situation. 'Yes, they were contacted by a friend to help with a problem that the authorities could not be trusted with. Somebody had contacted them to help rescue her from that place. Now they are trying to find out who is behind her abduction.'

Axel looked him straight in the face. 'Well, you can tell them to stop looking. I am the one behind her abduction!'

# 14

A few days later, they gathered at the clinic where Christina was treating Eve, as they had decided to call the girl under their care.

'As far as we're concerned, she is the first one we have saved, so until we discover her real identity, she needs a name,' she explained.

'Is she awake yet?' Sharlene asked. She had been invited along with the rest of the rescue crew.

'That's why I asked you all here today. We're about to attempt to bring her out of the induced coma, and I felt the outside world should witness it.'

She led them to the room where Eve was being treated. It was a cubicle sealed off from the outside area, which was bustling with activity. The smell of disinfectant filled the air, and the sound of movement and machinery filled the room. Technicians and nursing staff were monitoring various pieces of equipment.

The contrast inside the cubicle was profound. They immediately noticed the near silence, except for the gentle hum of the fluorescent lights.

Christina addressed them, 'You can speak, but keep your voices constant and low. Although Eve is unconscious, her brain will receive sound, as we have no idea what condition she is in mentally. As we bring her out, we want to keep the environment as neutral as possible. So when I administer the adrenaline, she should start to regain consciousness. If she shows distress, I will put her under again. This is trial and error. She has been held in this semiconscious state for a very long time, so we are not sure how she will react.'

She approached the motionless figure of Eve and began to administer the adrenaline.

Eve was dressed in a surgical gown, and her hair spread out on the pillow, forming a halo of dark brown against her pale skin. Her breathing was steady, and rapid eye movement (REM) could be observed behind her closed eyelids, indicating that something was happening. The others stood outside the curtain surrounding her and Christina, watching everything on a large monitor that displayed images from the camera mounted above her bed.

Over the next couple of minutes, Eve slowly began to awaken. Her eyelids started to flutter, and slight movement could be detected from her lips. Just as Christina turned to check something on a monitor, Eve's eyes sprang open, and she gasped aloud as if she had been holding her breath for a long time. The sudden movement startled Christina, who turned to make eye contact with the girl for the first time.

Regaining her composure, she continued with her tasks, allowing Eve to make the first attempt to communicate. Eve's eyes followed Christina as she kept her occupied. Then she spoke.

'Where am I?' she asked in English, with a completely neutral accent, as if she had learned to speak from a computer.

Christina responded calmly. 'You are in a safe place. You're under observation because you've experienced a sort of setback,' she tried to explain without shocking the girl.

Once again, Eve glanced around, then focused on Christina. 'Who are you?' she asked in that strange voice.

'My name is Christina Herrero. You can call me Chris. I'm your doctor until we establish exactly who was treating you. What can you remember about what happened to you?'

Once again, there was no reply, just a curious expression on her face as she looked around.

When she remained silent, Christine tried a different approach. 'Now that you know my name, can you tell me yours?' she asked.

Eve looked at her and replied, 'No.'

This response shocked Christina. 'Why can't you tell me your name?' she asked.

For the first time, the girl's voice seemed to carry a trace of emotion as she replied. 'Because I don't know what it is. I can't remember anything!'

# 15

**TEL AVIV, ISRAEL.**

Abdiel Mizrahi stood at the floor-to-ceiling window that overlooked Tel Aviv from the top floor of the building that his company, Masadalink Pty, owned. He could barely contain his anger after receiving the latest news from Durban. The raid on the orphanage and the disappearance of the girl were baffling. A knock on the office door prompted him to turn.

'Come in,' he grunted, as he looked at his brother.

His brother was seated in his specially constructed chair that supported his gaunt frame, attached to the oxygen machine that was trying to help his damaged lungs to function. He starkly contrasted himself, who looked more like an IT nerd than his brother, who, when well, had looked like he was chiselled out of stone.

His right-hand man, Eitan Zoari, entered. 'Any news?' he asked him.

Eitan was tall and muscular in appearance. His background was Israeli special services, and since he had been dismissed under a dark cloud, he had worked with slavish devotion when Abdiel took him under his wing. His response was tense.

'The tech people have traced what happened. Somebody hacked our private servers and sent a message under the guise of coming from you directly, asking Miungisi to move Z652 from the main facility to the one in Durban. I assume this was to make it easier to snatch her.'

'Have they discovered who is behind this?' he asked.

'Not a chance,' he replied, 'they say whoever did this is at a whole other level. They have run into a brick wall.'

'Remind me to compliment this son of a bitch just before I get you to blow their brains out the back of their head,' he raged. 'You realise my brother was scheduled to have his transplant next week? Do I have to remind you of the importance of this?' he continued, indicating his brother's frail condition.

Eitan just nodded and waited for him to continue. He knew his boss well and knew it was better to say nothing.

'This makes no sense. If she was the target, why snatch her the night before? Why not pick her out when they raided the place the next day?'

Eitan replied, 'It would seem from what the IT people can figure out, whoever this was has been inside our systems for quite some time. When they looked at Z652's file, they saw that whoever hacked IT seemed interested in tracing the donor for the kidney transplant to Levi last year. It looks like this might be some blackmail scheme.'

'That moron Miungisi might be involved. Perhaps he found out about my brother's donor and decided to pull this stunt. He has been complaining about his cut for some time now.' Abdiel suggested.

Eitan shook his head. 'I can't see him trying anything like that. First of all, he is not that clever. He is just a thug. Plus, where would he get the expertise to hack our system? Whoever did that is not the person you would associate with him. The country is full of hackers, but not at the expertise required for something like this.'

'More questions than answers,' he raged. 'I want you over there as soon as possible. Just do what you have to, but we must locate that girl. Levi will fly in next week on the company jet. Make sure that she is available for the operation, understood? At the same time, locate who has those other "units". The clients they are being prepared for could require a body part at any time. Remember, they are very influential and important people, and staying alive is vital.'

After Eitan left, Abdiel went over to his brother and caressed his head. 'Don't worry, little brother; I will take care of things. You concentrate on getting well.'

Levi grasped his arm with his feeble grip and nodded, the mask and his lack of breath preventing him from talking.

As he looked at his wrecked body, he saw no resemblance to the rugged, burly man he was when they were starting some years back, and he was the one who took care of all the nasty stuff. Their fledgling human trafficking business was just getting started, and his ruthlessness was essential to keeping the women and the competition in check. Something Abdiel had no stomach for. Levi's cruelty knew no bounds until he began to get sick. Luckily, they recruited a young Eitan Zoari, who gladly took over his brother's role.

His sickness had led his brother to uncover an untapped market: organ supply and demand. When his brother was diagnosed with chronic heart and lung disease and the hospital informed him that because the damage had been caused by his regular drug habit, he would not be eligible to be included in the heart/lung transplant program, which the prospect of would be slim in any case, but the only chance for survival. He quickly discovered that his money and influence were of no use. Organ transplants were rigorously controlled, and the only organs available through the black market were kidneys, usually arranged by "brokers".

For a transplant of any kind to succeed, the donor would have to be tissue and blood-type compatible, which further complicated the situation due to him having the rarest blood type, AB-negative, which is held by only 0.6 per cent of the population.

This is when the light went on in his head. He realised he had a steady supply of the product required passing through his hands daily: The lost souls from his human trafficking business. Almost all were orphans or discards from broken families and were rarely missed. Plus, many were male and not in as much demand as the girls. So he devised a plan with a group of corrupt doctors in Africa, as this was a source of many of his victims.

They set up a clinic for orphaned and war-torn victims and, alongside that, started funnelling candidates as potential donors into secret facilities he had built under the complex.

In a short time, thanks to his company's shady dealings in the murky world of cryptocurrency, which had become the mainstay of his company due to a fortuitous theft that had changed the game for him, his IT people were able to serendipitously put out on the dark web that a new business had opened, offering hope for people in desperate need of a replacement organ.

The response was incredible, and in the year since they had established, they already had over two hundred units ready and waiting.

Eight months ago, the impossible happened. They found a suitable donor for his brother. When she arrived at the clinic, he made sure that her origin was not recorded, just that she had been rescued from some cult and somehow had arrived at their door.

As soon as her blood type was established, she quickly disappeared into the underground facility. Five months later, his brother had a successful kidney transplant in an African clinic. But now he was sinking again and was doomed if he did not get his transplant soon.

He paced up and down the palatial office, mumbling to himself. 'Shyster, I will find out who is behind the kidnapping of my brother's lifeline.'

He cursed under his breath in Hebrew.

# 16

Desmond, Bill, and Sergei arrived back at the clinic to be informed by the others that Eve had awoken. When they were told that she could not remember anything and became distressed, Christina gave her a mild sedative to allow her time to come to terms with her predicament.

'Well, our situation may have crossed paths with yours,' Desmond began.

He explained how the hacker they had visited, a woman named Axel Sigurdsson from Iceland, turned out to be the one who arranged for Eve to be transferred to Durban and also acted as the whistle-blower who contacted Christina.

He raised his hand for quiet as the room exploded with questions. 'Hold on; we will tell you what she was prepared to divulge. It seems she has another agenda. During her investigation of these individuals, she discovered that one of them had received a kidney from Eve. When she realised that the girl was being prepped for a full heart-lung transplant, she understood that it would result in her death. Further investigation led her to uncover a business set up to provide organs for wealthy individuals who were willing to sacrifice orphans. So she decided to kill two birds with one stone by hacking into their system and arranging for Eve to be transferred to the facility in Durban. She realised it would be much easier to stage a rescue there than at the main hospital in Johannesburg, where most of the "donors" were housed.'

Christine burst in. 'So she is the one who has been in contact with me!' she exclaimed.

'We asked her that, and she said she looked for an organisation that aids in rescuing victims of various conflicts, and your name came up repeatedly,' he replied.

'Did she say who the girl was?' she asked.

Bill stepped in. 'You have to remember that this was not why we approached her. Rescuing orphans is not her agenda. Her reason for saving this girl seems to be related to her own goal. I would guess the people behind this horrible scheme are somehow involved.'

'So what does she want?'

'Her problem is that if she leaves this holiday camp of a prison where she is being detained, she will be deported back to Iceland, something she wants to avoid. And before you ask, she was not prepared to divulge the details. So she has agreed that if we can resolve that problem, she is willing to help us with Dad's situation. And, by the way, she assures us it will be, and I quote, "a piece of cake".' He went on, 'As far as Eve and the other victims are concerned, it appears that whatever her agenda is, it involves bringing down this scum. So we agreed to help each other. Now, we have to figure out how to get her out without her being deported.'

They discussed this new revelation and tried to figure out how they could free her from jail.

'I know just who can help us,' Aurora cried, looking at Sun Yee.

She grinned and nodded in agreement before continuing. 'Our new friend, Commandant Moses Khumalo.'

Aurora explained how he had become involved in their publicity scheme, resulting in the rescue of all the orphans at the Durban clinic.

'Why should he help?' Desmond asked.

Sun Yee answered, 'We convinced him that now that this has become international news, the police officer who brings down this vile business could become a national hero. It could be his ticket to success. I think he sees himself as potentially the next Nelson Mandela,' she joked.

Charlie responded, 'Well, that's settled. Let's see what he has to say.'

# 17

Axel Sigurdsson stepped out into the bright African sunlight to be greeted by Des and Bill. Two striking-looking women accompanied them. The tallest had a European appearance, standing at least six feet tall and exuding a stunning beauty. The one with her was Asian and, despite her slight frame, radiated an aura of confidence. Looking into her eyes sent a cold shiver; it felt as if she could peer into his soul. An African man in a police uniform accompanied them. Axel feared that she had walked into a trap, but the tall girl stepped forward.

'I am Aurora, and this is my friend Sun Yee On, and this is Commandant Moses Khumalo. He has arranged your release and assured the authorities that he will take full responsibility for you remaining in South Africa,' she said, and introduced everyone.

Axel nodded, realising her options were limited, and without speaking, she stepped into the waiting car.

From there, they all headed to Christina's compound where they could discuss the situation and address all the questions. They gathered in the garden, where the staff prepared a barbecue for them. After everyone had been introduced, Axel met Christina for the first time.

She was delighted to meet the person who had approached her, embracing her and whispering, 'You are an angel sent from Heaven.'

Embarrassed by the display of affection, Axel began to bluster as she explained that she had no idea how to help Eve and had reached out to her in hopes that something could be done with her influence.

Christina profusely thanked her, saying, 'If you had not intervened, this girl would surely have been dead by now, and worse than that, this operation would have continued unnoticed. Lord knows how many have already died.'

Axel listened as they explained how they had carried out the rescue of the orphans. 'What is the situation with their recovery and returning them to their homes?' she asked, concern evident in her voice.

Moses replied, 'They were transferred to Ethekwini Hospital, where they are slowly being brought out of their sedated state. Sadly, the chances of them having any surviving relatives are slim. The few who could remember details said that their families were all dead. It was obvious that whoever was procuring them was careful to choose only people who would not be missed. Thanks to Christina and her friends, the ensuing publicity will ensure they are well cared for. Thanks to you guys, the operation has been shut down.'

Axel interjected, 'Sorry to be the bearer of awful news, but that was not the main base of operations. I didn't investigate as much as I would have liked. The longer I stayed in their system, the greater the risk of being discovered.'

Aurora interjected, 'You haven't explained why you were investigating these people. I assume from what you've said that you stumbled across this information while searching for something else?' she asked.

There was a moment of silence before Axel spoke, 'I will help you find those people, but my interest in them has no bearing on what is happening here and does not directly affect this country. As agreed, I will assist you as best as possible. However, as Mr. Khumalo knows, if I touch a computer in this country again, I will be in big trouble. That's how I ended up in this situation in the first place.'

Khumalo spoke up, 'I think, under these circumstances, we can turn a blind eye. We must shut down this operation as soon as possible before more lives are lost.'

'In that regard, from what I could see when I was tracing Eve, this operation hasn't been in operation for very long. I'm not sure how long it takes to cultivate a suitable donor.'

'So perhaps they are still in the development stage,' Axel added.

Christina burst in, 'Axel is correct. If they offer a personal "donor", it would require full medical details of the recipient. So as a suitable donor is located, many tests would have to be carried out before the transplant could take place.'

Des asked, 'So do they ship the organ by mail or deliver it by another means?'

Christina looked at him as if he was on drugs, prompting Chaz to intervene. 'Ignore him. I'm afraid in his case, the lift doesn't go to the top floor. Please continue,' Chaz said.

Des grunted in disgust, 'I was only asking,' as Christina continued.

'The best option would be to bring the recipient here. Transporting an extracted organ would attract too much attention and risk it being confiscated. Remember, this practice has improved significantly since Christiaan Bernard performed the first human heart transplant in 1967 here in South Africa,' Christina explained.

Aurora stepped in, 'Then that's how we take them down. Remember, they need Eve's organs urgently. So let them lead us to her!'

Everyone gasped in response, except for Sun Yee, who knew what Aurora was thinking.

# 18

After Aurora and Sun Yee outlined their plan to draw out the people behind the operation, it was decided to use the clinic as their base of operations as they had the security of Moses' police to protect them from retribution.

Moses explained what they were facing. 'The African Mafia that was behind keeping the orphanage here in Durban and presumably the one in Johannesburg secure from prying eyes is called 'The Sysue mafia,' which translates to "The Angels", something that could not be further from the truth. They're a scourge and are well protected as many of them are related to people in positions of power. The guy running them is a particularly nasty character who learned his trade when he was one of the infamous Winnie Mandela gangs. His name is Miungisi Moyo, which means fixer, and that is how he came to be in control of the mafia. When Nelson Mandela was released, and Winnie was found wanting, the gang dismantled. Miungisi stepped in and arranged for them to be folded into the Sysue, where he quickly rose to the top thanks to his ruthlessness.

'His favourite was the necktie, where they placed a petrol-soaked tyre over the head of the victim and ignited it. If we can connect them to this operation, they will lose all support from their powerful cronies. With the international attention to this terrible crime, they will drop them like hotcakes.'

'Well, they will also have to be invited to the party. That is the best way to hang them all together,' Charlie added, which brought a gasp from some of the group who were not used to the unusual methods the Savage brothers employed.

'About time to get serious,' added Des. 'So what about Dad's problem?' he asked, with his unique mindset.

'Are you crazy? Lives are at stake here. These orphans are set to be cut up and sold off, and all you can think about is Dad and his stupid mistake,' Charlie roared at him.

Not to be deterred, Des continued to argue. 'Don't forget if he had not screwed up, we would probably not be here to help. I don't want his situation to be ignored. You know him; if we don't do something, our lives and sanity will be at risk.'

That shut Chaz up because he knew Des was right.

Axel came to the rescue. 'Will you guys stop arguing? Your father's situation is the least of our problems. I will be able to locate the culprit in no time. All I need is his telephone. Now, can we get back to the real problem?'

Sheepishly, Des muttered something, but a sharp glare from his brother shut him up.

Chaz stepped in. 'Since Aurora and Sun Yee were the ones who arranged the rescue of Eve and the other victims, they should head up the operation. Sometimes there are too many chiefs and not enough Indians, so let us leave them in charge,' as he turned to the girls. 'Over to you, ladies. We await your instructions.'

Aurora turned to Axel. 'I think it's time you filled us in on how you discovered this operation.'

There was silence as she cast her view around this strange bunch of people. Her instinct was not to trust people due to what had happened in her past. But something about them made her feel that perhaps if she was to succeed in her quest, now was the time to start. She nodded in agreement and began to explain.

'The people you are looking for are the same people I have been searching for since March 2018. My reason for this search is something I would prefer to keep to myself for the time being. Enough to know that I am as interested in bringing the people behind this down as much as you are. The fact that they are behind this horrible idea only makes me more determined.'

Aurora responded. 'Whatever reason you have for searching out these individuals is your business. Just help us locate the main facility before they have time to react. And if there is any way we can help you, just let us know.'

Axel nodded in agreement. 'Okay, let's get me on to a computer, and I will show you who is behind this,' she said with a cheeky smile on her stunning face.

She had only been on the computer for what seemed like a minute. Her fingers flew across the keys in a blur, with her sparkling blue eyes fixed firmly on the monitor in front of her.

'Got it. This is the backdoor I placed in their system. They have discovered it, but I still have a record of what I have discovered.'

On the screen was the name of a company, 'Masadalink.' She scrolled down to display two names, Abdiel and Levi Mizrahi.

'These are the people you are looking for. They are brothers, and they run the company together.'

'What do they do?' Sun Yee asked.

Leslie went on to explain that they ran a cryptocurrency exchange where people could buy and sell Bitcoin and other forms of currency.

'So, they are a legitimate business?' Charlie asked.

'It depends on how deep you dig. While investigating, I discovered that they were involved in money laundering on a massive scale and some other shady practices. I discovered that Levi was gravely ill and needed an organ transplant when researching the brothers. That was when I discovered their side business, which seemed to have grown out of Levi's predicament. So when I found his donor, the girl you call Eve, I arranged through his man in Africa. Some guy called...'

She scrolled down further, she found what she was looking for. 'Here he is, Miungisi Moyo. As I said, I arranged for her to be transferred to the facility in Durban under the guise that the order had come from Abdiel himself. And you know the rest.'

'So where are these guys?' Des decided to get in on the action.

'They are in Israel,' Axel replied. 'From what I could see, a huge amount of the type of business they are involved in—human trafficking and IT crime—operates out of there,' she added.

Aurora pushed her further. 'So how do we locate the main facility?'

'That's easy. It is on the outskirts of Johannesburg. The brothers sponsored a hospital for the young affected by the many conflicts. It is called Mount Masada Hope. From what I could see, part of it operated legitimately, with its primary purpose hidden from view.'

'Then what's stopping us from reporting its existence?' Aurora queried.

Moses stepped in. 'Easier said than done. Miungisi is well-connected. He has connections at the highest levels of government. Remember, he began his career as a member of "Winnie's Boys", many of whom became involved in the emerging government of the new South Africa. Unless we can expose them and get the press involved, there is no chance of getting any official action. All we would do is drive them further underground.'

Sun Yee started to outline their plan. 'Well, I suggest we get them to find us first.'

'How do we do that?' Moses asked.

They all gathered around as Sun Yee and Aurora began to explain. "We've got a plan for that," they said together.

# 19

As they were going over their plans, events were already beginning to develop elsewhere. Eitan Zoabi was climbing into the back of a stretch limousine, black with heavily tinted windows.

'Welcome, my friend,' the booming voice of Miungisi Moyo greeted him from his seat facing Eitan.

Discarding his welcome, Eitan jumped right in, gruffly demanding information. 'Have you located the subject?' he snapped.

Taken aback by his attitude, Miungisi, who was not used to being spoken to like this, was about to respond angrily until his survival instinct jumped in. He knew that the Mizrahi brothers' company, Masadalink, was used heavily by his cronies in government. They had so much financial success that he could not upset them, so he swallowed his tongue and replied.

'So far, nothing. Whoever took the subject knew who they were coming for and have vanished without a trace. We are waiting for them to contact us with their demands.'

'How can you be so sure they will contact you?' he demanded.

'Whoever raided the facility the following day had a completely different agenda. They were all about rescuing orphans and were very well organised. They made sure the free press was there to witness their release. It has people in government running for cover. If it comes out what those people are being kept for, the ripples will be felt around the world. Heads will roll,' he warned.

Eitan waved his hand, dismissing his comments. 'We are aware of that and have already taken steps to calm the situation. We received inquiries from some of our clients, asking if there was any truth to the story that humans were being used as spare parts depots, which we denied, of course. But the location of the main facility must be kept hidden. On that note, Abdiel's brother is arriving for his operation in four days. Whatever happens, we must protect the facility until we can complete his transplant. This means you have less than four days to find Z652,' he warned.

The limousine pulled up to the heavy gate, which opened automatically as they made their way up the long driveway to the mansion owned by his employers. Sandton was one of the most desired suburbs of Johannesburg, and this property was considered the jewel in the crown.

Once inside, he quickly called Abdiel to bring him up to speed as to what was happening. When he was finished, he waited in silence, knowing his boss often took minutes to formulate his thoughts before replying. Finally, he spoke.

'Eitan, you are the only one I trust in that godforsaken place. The only thing that matters is locating the item and having them ready for my brother in four days. Do whatever you have to do. After completing this, I don't care what it costs. When he is safely back in Israel, I want every trace of the facility destroyed,' he instructed.

'What about the inhabitants?' Eitan asked.

His chilling voice came over the secure line. 'Everything!' he instructed and hung up.

## 20

'You want me to dress up as a woman!' Desmond roared when Sun Yee On outlined their plan.

Trying to calm him down, she patiently explained their plan again. 'If we are going to draw the people out, we have to give them an incentive, and the only thing that would entice them to this country is by providing what they are looking for. So we propose to offer the girl to them for a large ransom. We must convince them that we are kidnappers looking for a payday,' she explained.

'What has that to do with me dressing up as a woman?' he cried in despair.

'We have already explained that to pull this off, we must make them believe we are serious. So we will propose delivering the girl to where they are doing the transplant. That is where they will have to be holding the other victims,' Aurora explained.

'How do you know that?' he blustered, looking to the others for some support without much response.

Christina stepped in. 'Desmond, the only place they can do these transplants is where the donors are kept. We can't let the girl fall into their hands again, so we need to substitute somebody in her place. And you are the perfect candidate.'

This drove him even crazier. 'In case you have not noticed, I am a man, so how am I the perfect candidate?' he pleaded.

It was Aurora who responded. 'It is the hair; you are the only one of the group with long hair,' pointing to his flowing locks that hung to his shoulders. 'Because you are supposed to be a patient and prepared for a delicate transplant, it would be necessary for the subject to be kept in a sterile state. So you would be completely sealed in the protective covering. The only part of you that would be visible would be your head. Your face would be covered with an oxygen mask, and some head covering. Your hair being exposed will add realism to the illusion. Remember, as far as they are concerned, you will be sedated and, therefore, unable to be questioned. We can't use Aurora, as she will deal directly with them, and I am an Asian chick,' pointing to her almond-shaped eyes.

Charlie stepped in. 'Enough, Des. This is right up your alley. We are winging this, and until we can implement our plan, you will have to improvise, something you are a past master at. Remember how you handled the lost treasure in Spain and Australia. You dismantled the nuclear device all on your own. You are the only one of us that can handle this part of the operation; if anybody can pull this off, it is you,' Chaz said, playing to his pride.

'I suppose. As usual, all the shitty jobs fall to me. Okay, I am in,' he said.

Charlie continued. 'If I were them, I would be very cautious. They will want to verify that this is the right subject. If they want to inspect the tattoo on her inner thigh, we are screwed,' he added.

'Correct,' Aurora replied. 'So we must verify with a blood sample.' He looked at her in confusion. 'They will never accept that unless they can verify that it came from the "girl",' pointing at Des. 'And that is what we will insist on, but only if we do it while they observe. We will not permit them to touch the subject to protect her from harm. Remember, they only need her organs. I am sure they will agree. They will expect us to be just as suspicious,' she added.

'But how will you give them the blood?' Chaz asked.

'I will extract it in front of them,' she replied, bringing a startled response from Des.

'Great, if I don't bleed to death, I could find myself without a heart and lungs if this plan does not work out,' he snarled.

Sun Yee butted in. 'Enough talk. Let's stir things up, as The Umbrella crew would say,' spurring everybody into action.

# 21

Miungisi was using all of his contacts to try and locate who was responsible for snatching the item. He was still smarting from the dressing down he had received at the hands of the Israeli, Eitan Zoabi.

He sat at his desk, contemplating how he could punish this guy for daring to talk to him that way. Yet he knew that as long as his employer was pouring money into the pockets of select politicians, his hands were tied. But he was a Zulu and, as such, had a long memory. He knew if he were patient, an opportunity would present itself.

His thoughts were broken by the sound of his private mobile ringing. Very few people had this number, and none were calling. He cautiously pressed to accept the call.

'I presume this is Miungisi Mayo,' a heavily altered voice came over the speaker.

'Who is this?' he demanded. 'How did you get this number?'

There was a pause.

'Too many questions. What is important now is that you listen. We have what you are looking for, and we know that time is of the essence, so this is what will happen. I will outline what we require for the exchange of Z652.'

There was another pause.

'You still there?' Mayo yelled, afraid to lose a golden opportunity.

The silence seemed to him to go on forever, then the voice spoke again.

'We just wanted you to realise that we are in complete control. What we have is irreplaceable, so any wrong move by you or the Mizrahi brothers will result in the item being disposed of. By now, I am sure that Abdiel will have contacted you or sent somebody to act on his behalf, probably his henchman. Eitan is his name, I believe, a very objectionable character, Israeli, so warped he was even too much for Mossad. None of that is of concern to us. We will call back in one hour. Have whoever can make decisions there as we will explain how the transfer will happen and how much it will cost. And be assured it won't be cheap.' The call disconnected.

Back at Christina's place, Axel disconnected the voice-altering equipment and swung her chair around, propelled by her long legs.

'So then, let the games begin.'

She had hacked into Abdiel and Miungisi's email accounts. They both had high levels of security, but to a hacker of her ability, they might as well yell it from the rooftops.

From there, she discovered the identity of the Israeli, Eitan Zoabi. And more importantly, that the sick brother was flying in on the company jet in two days. When they found that out, Chaz responded with a suggestion.

'If we can discover when it is due to arrive, it will give us time to prepare things at the main facility,' he pointed out.

'I am on it,' Axel replied as she resumed her search.

While she was at that, the others discussed the next step of their plan. Aurora began to outline their approach.

'The only way we can be sure of bringing down this operation without risking lives. She is our ace in the deck, Eve. I am sure that the resulting publicity from our little stunt scared them. If it was not for their need for Eve, I believe they would have disposed of all evidence and vanished. We must bring it down while the brother is here for the transplant. They won't risk a gunfight while he is present. I suspect they will surrender and expect to bribe themselves out of trouble.'

'What's to stop them from putting up resistance?' Des asked. He had not been taking much notice of the plan since he discovered he was to play the role of the transplant victim.

Exasperated at having to repeat it, Aurora replied with one word.

'Publicity.'

## 22

Eitan listened to the telephone call recording they had received for the umpteenth time. He couldn't understand how the extortionist knew the identity of the people involved and even his first name, along with his Israeli nationality. At least it confirmed his and Miungisi's suspicions that money was the motivation behind this. That made him feel somewhat relieved. He was well acquainted with this realm, and their main concern would be the transfer and their safe escape. This was where most kidnap ransom exchanges went wrong. But he didn't care. They would pay whatever was demanded, and once the transplant was completed, he would hunt them down and eliminate them.

Seated in front of Miungisi, both of them glanced at the clock on the corner of the desk. It was ten minutes past the scheduled hour. Being kept waiting was something they were not accustomed to.

The sound of the phone jolted them, even though they were expecting it. Miungisi answered, 'Hello,' and the altered voice echoed through the speaker, 'Put the Israeli on.'

Eitan replied. 'I am here. Who am I speaking to?'

The voice responded, 'Not necessary; we will not be forming a lasting friendship. It is enough that you know we represent a group called 'The Umbrella Crew,' and we are highly resourceful.'

'Now to the business at hand. I assume you are recording this, so it will not be repeated. The conditions for the exchange are non-negotiable, so no conversation will be necessary.' There was a pause for effect, and then the voice continued. 'We know that the recipient is arriving in Africa in two days. You will advise us of where the transplant procedure will take place no later than twenty-four hours before the exchange is to occur. We will transport the victim in a specially-designed vehicle to ensure the item is in perfect condition. Our physician will accompany the item, and nobody else will be permitted to touch or interfere with it in any way. This is to ensure that we can conduct our business and that our operatives can return safely.'

'We know that you plan to allow the transfer and then kill all those involved or perhaps kill the item itself, as all you require are the organs. So, to prevent any unfortunate circumstances from occurring, the item will be fitted with an explosive device. It won't be significant, but enough to render any part of her useless.

'Now, onto the most crucial aspect, the money. The value of the item in good condition ranges from $800,000 to $1 million. However, since this item is scarce, it will be priced accordingly at $50 million in cryptocurrency. Our specialist will accompany the item and oversee the funds transfer, which Masadalink will no doubt be arranging. Additionally, two of our representatives will ensure that all instructions are followed. You must follow their instructions precisely. By now, you are aware of the consequences. We are businesspeople, and if you behave the same way, perhaps everything will go well, and we can wish your brother a speedy recovery. We will contact you again within twenty-four hours to discover the destination and final instructions.'

With that, the line went silent.

They sat silently for a moment, digesting what they had just heard. Miungisi spoke first. 'They seem to have thought of everything. Even if we discover who this Umbrella Crew is, we can't touch them.'

'Correct. They are very clever but made two fatal errors. First, allowing the ransom to be paid in crypto will play right into the boss's hands. That's his game. He'll have it back before they can spend a dime. Number two, now we know who they are. After they have delivered the girl to my brother and the explosive device is removed, all bets are off,' Eitan replied with a smug smile on his face.

'How do you know they won't set off the device anyway?' Miungisi muttered.

'Because there's no upside to it. As far as they're concerned, they have what they want, and we have what we want. So why inflict pain? That's something a psychopath would do,' Eitan replied, fixing Miungisi with an accusatory stare. He held it until Miungisi finally glanced away, fumbling to put his phone away.

Eitan didn't trust Miungisi one bit. He was a loose cannon, and as far as Eitan was concerned, he was just one more problem he would have to deal with, along with whoever was behind all this.

*Who was The Umbrella Crew?* Eitan wondered, smiling to himself as he looked at the perplexed Miungisi. He realised that the only true psychopath in the room was himself.

## 23

Axel hung up the phone. 'I love this, making these scum squirm. You guys are the best.'

It was Charlie who addressed the elephant in the room.

'I'm glad that you're enjoying this, and we appreciate your help. But as far as we're concerned, we still have no idea of your motive for all of this. Considering we're all risking a lot, clarity about your intentions would help relieve the stress,' he said, waiting for her response. She sat for a moment, lifted her head, and began to speak.

'I guess you deserve an explanation, so I think I'd better start at the beginning.'


**ICELAND, REYKJAVIK, 2018.**

Gunner Sigurdsson couldn't shake the feeling that he was being stalked. His wife had laughed at him when he suggested he was being watched, telling him to lay off the booze, which was funny as he didn't drink.

He had been on the night shift for some time at the Advinia data centre. This suited him as he preferred his own company, and as the security guard of this facility, he was the only one working at night. But for the last few days, he had been battling a terrible bout of flu. However, he was feeling worse as he entered his home after a long night. It was March, and it was dark for nineteen hours a day at this time of year. Glad to be home, he was greeted by his daughter, Axel, who had recently returned from the USA.

As she hugged him fiercely, he couldn't believe this beautiful creature could be his daughter. From an early age, it was apparent she had remarkable intelligence, and from the age of six, she embraced computer technology with a vengeance. It was quickly discovered that she possessed an almost savant ability to read binary code. She could decipher it as if reading a children's book. That, coupled with an IQ of 165, resulted in her being offered a scholarship to MIT in the USA, where she graduated with Honours in Advanced IT at seventeen. NASA and the military quickly headhunted her, but Cybercrime approached her. This is what piqued her interest. Primarily, it would pit her against the most intelligent crooks in the hacker community—a challenge she embraced. But after two years, she began to miss home and decided to take a break.

'How's my favourite daughter?' he asked, returning the hug with a kiss on the forehead.

She pushed him away, laughing. 'I'm your only daughter,' she corrected as her mother entered, wiping her hands with a towel.

Helga had met her father when, as a student from the USA, she decided to take a holiday to Reykjavik. She met Gunnar, and within six months, they were married. To Axel, they were a perfect example of two people meant to be together.

'Look at the state of you. You look like you're about to drop dead. Off to bed with you, and I'll bring you something to make you feel a bit better,' she assured him as she shooed him off to bed.

Axel smiled as she watched the two lovebirds who were her parents. They fussed over each other as she helped him upstairs.

A little later, her mother called Axel. 'Please bring this up to your dad, will you? It's warm milk with a sedative in it. Don't tell him that, or he'll worry about waking up for work.'

She nodded in agreement and did as her mother asked. As she sat watching her father finish the drink, little did they know that this simple action was to change their lives.

# 24

Gunnar managed to make his way to work despite waking up late. Even though he knew he was incapable, he was determined to maintain his perfect work record. As he returned from his first circuit of the facility, not long after arriving, he again felt that he was being watched. But before he could react, a wave of nausea came over him, accompanied by diarrheoa. Whatever his wife had given him disagreed with his stomach as another wave of nausea passed over him. He realised he was about to pass out and decided to head home to recover a bit.

As he stepped out of the toilet in his house, he felt faint and decided to lie down for a few minutes, where he immediately fell asleep. He sat bolt upright as he awoke to realise it was nearly 8 o'clock. He rushed to his car only to discover somebody had slashed his tyres. Realising his predicament, he called headquarters to explain what had happened. When he mentioned the slashed tires, his superiors became alarmed and told him they would send someone and for him to wait where he was.

A couple of hours later, he was jolted awake by banging on the front door. It was the police. They confronted him with the news that the data centre had been broken into and 600 Bitcoin computers and the hardware to operate them had been stolen. They were valued at $2 million, but their real value lay in what they were designed for. These computers, each the size of two cartons of cigarettes, could produce a bitcoin every ten minutes—each untraceable. To those who knew how to operate them, they were a free money-printing press.

It was billed as the cybercrime of the century, especially as Iceland has the lowest crime rate in the world. For the people of this peaceful land, it was an affront, as this cyber industry that had sprung up had been the saviour of the country after its disastrous failure during the Global financial crisis.

This was all thanks to an enterprising German, Marco Strege, who arrived in 2014 and began setting up data centres in the disused hangars abandoned by the US military. His reason was simple: Iceland was the perfect location for the centres. First, there was the climate. The low temperatures and icy winds blowing through the large hangars kept the delicate computers at ideal operating temperatures. And then there was the abundance of cheap energy provided by geothermal and hydroelectric power.

Numerous other enterprising companies followed suit in no time, rescuing the economy. So the reaction from the public was immediate. Axel's dad came under suspicion immediately due to being missing when the robbery occurred. He was brought in for questioning and was released without charge, but the doubts remained.

Although there was little or no crime in the country, that did not mean they did not know where the bad guys were. Within a couple of days, they detained Thor Stefansson and tried to locate another guy, Hafthar Logs Hlynsson. Thor was charged, and to their surprise, he admitted to the crime but said he was not the mastermind. He had been contacted by a mystery man he could only identify as Mr X. He insisted he had no idea who he was and also said they did not know what had happened to the computers. He was sentenced to a few years in prison for his part but escaped to Sweden. To this day, to Axel's knowledge, the computers have never been recovered.

Axel had to watch her parents crumble before her eyes. In this country where crime was a deadly sin, the shame destroyed them, especially her dad, who was a very proud man and insisted on blaming himself.

Finally, one day he went for a walk on a dark winter night. When he did not come home, an extensive search finally found him sitting at the entrance of the deserted data centre as if guarding it. He was frozen solid!

# 25

**DURBAN,**
**PRESENT DAY**

'So from that point on, I dedicated my life to bringing whoever was responsible for my father's death to justice.'

Axel paused to take a breath. This allowed the shocked listeners to digest the incredible story she had just told.

Charlie broke the silence. 'I am sure that I speak for everyone here when I say that the tragedy that has befallen you and your family goes to the core of what we are about. Helping those that the system has let down. The people that get crushed and nobody stands up for. Well, from this point, you are not alone. Whoever it is behind what has happened to you and your family is firmly in our sights now.'

Axel burst out in tears, and Aurora rushed to comforter her. As she calmed down, she began to speak. 'While I was investigating, the person I believe was behind the robbery, and still is operating the stolen computers, is the same person whose brother needs Eve's organs.'

Desmond jumped in. 'So the people you discovered are behind the human puppy farm  scheme are the same people you are looking for?'

Axel nodded. 'I believe so. I discovered this terrible secret when I got access to their main computer and went fishing for clues. So the only thing I could do to help was to reach out. Luckily, Christina came to the rescue, and thanks to Desmond and his friends finding me, I now find myself with people I feel I can trust.'

She broke down in tears again, hugging Aurora.

It was Des that snapped everybody back. 'I don't know about you guys, but as far as I am concerned, destroying everything this mongrel has is the very least I will be satisfied with. Now. How about putting a spanner in the works starting with the operation here? Is it okay with everybody if we start destroying his business here first?'

Axel wiped her eyes. Sitting upright, she released Aurora, giving her a hug in return. Then, she firmly replied. 'For sure Let's take these bastards!'

# 26

**TEL AVIV**

'I can't find anybody that knows anything about a crew calling themselves The Umbrella Men,' Abdiel snarled into the phone to Eitan.

Eitan did not bother to respond, instead continued where he had left off. 'They insisted on Bitcoin and would bring their person to effect the transfer.'

'Are they *meshugge*, crazy? They want the payment in crypto? Do they not know what I do?' he raved. 'They can use whoever they like; I don't care if they think they can cover their tracks; good luck to them. I will eat them for breakfast. Forget the money. I will have it back before they can touch a dime. Have they contacted you yet?' he yelled in his high-pitched voice.

Eitan could not believe Levi was his brother. They were in stark contrast. Abdiel had no taste for the dirty side of the business. Something he would never say to him. But he himself and Levi at least had something in common, both sadists with a hatred for women. So the steady supply of victims they had access to from the human trafficking business gave them plenty of helpless females on which to feed their perverted tastes.

But his boss's devotion to his brother was extraordinary given how opposite they were. All his brother wanted to do was to party and break heads. On the other hand, he was the brains and the reason behind the success of the business. It was this effort to secure a donor at all costs and perform the transplant, which, from what he could gather, had very little chance of success, was putting the whole operation in jeopardy.

'No, but I must be ready to respond as soon as they do. I believe these people are serious and would not hesitate to dispose of the girl if they feel threatened.'

There was silence for a moment, then Abdiel spoke. 'I agree. Our first consideration is assuring the unit is available for my brother. He will be arriving shortly and will be transferred to the main facility. They have already been informed to prepare for the transplant. Please give them the location as soon as these Umbrella People contact you. Do exactly as they ask. Then dispose of them. The priority is assuring the exchange goes ahead.'

'That is easier said than done. We first have to figure out if the explosive device attached to the girl is real. If so, I will have to play by their rules and take care of them at a later date.'

Abdiel grunted. 'Just do what you must to get my brother and whoever is in the same place for the transplant. After that, kill every last one of them.'

Eitan looked at his phone, shaking his head as the call disconnected. With his military background, his first instinct was to abort the whole thing. Something about it felt wrong. Although it appeared that whoever was behind this was making fundamental errors, he still thought he was being played. Considering this was all to attempt a transplant operation with very little chance of success, as far as he was concerned, the good money would be slim to none. But he knew Abdiel would stop at nothing to try and save his worthless brother.

With a smirk, he began to plan to outsmart whatever these "Umbrella People" were planning as he relaxed in Miungisi's luxurious hideout.

# 27

'Got it!' yelled Axel, causing everybody gathered there to drop what they were doing and turn.

'What?' Aurora asked. She stopped trying to arrange Desmond's long hair to prepare him for his task, much to his disgust.

'The location where the transplant is to take place,' Axel replied.

'Where is it?' Chaz asked.

'Well, I looked at all flight logs over the last few days and located a private jet from Tel Aviv landed this morning and was met by a medical helicopter that transferred a patient to a hospital between Johannesburg and Pretoria,' she replied.

'How the hell did you do that?

She grinned sheepishly. 'I hacked into the main computer at Oliver Tambo International Airport and poked around until I found what we were looking for,' she replied.

'Our dad would love you; you could single-handedly control every scam. You with your incredible skills and him with his devious mind,' Des retorted.

'Are you sure this is the right place?' Chaz asked.

'The hospital is called Masadahope Hospital, kindly sponsored by Masadalink, and the helicopter and the jet are also owned by a couple of shell companies owned by them. So, yes, I am sure this is the place.'

Charlie decided to add his voice. 'Fantastic work. This will give

Moses time to coordinate his end and Sharlene to plan how she wants to respond. But let us not get ahead of ourselves. These guys are bound to be planning a response. A lot will hinge on how we present the explosive device; without that, what's to stop them from just luring us in and killing the lot of us? And don't think for a second that would bother these guys. Remember, they are chopping people up for parts.'

Sun Yee jumped in. 'I have been working with Moses on that very thing.'

She was the only one on the crew with knowledge of explosives, thanks to her training as a Chinese spy. She continued with what they had planned, 'He assures me, and I agree, that they will recognise it as authentic. It will be attached to the inside of the ceramic transport bed. When we place Desmond, or should I say "Eve" inside this clear plastic bed, he, or I should say "she",' hurriedly correcting her error. 'If we make the mistake of using the wrong gender when this stunt gets going, we are all dead!'

All of this was only causing Des to feel more uncomfortable by the minute, now standing in his jocks while the women tried to make him look as feminine as possible. To accomplish that, they had bound his upper body to try and compress his manly chest. Fortunately, he would be transported in a surgical gown that would only expose part of his/her forearms.

Sun Yee resumed, 'As I said, it will be attached to the inside of the bed. They would know from experience that any interference could detonate it. It will also be apparent to them that it is armed, and only when the display advises that it had disarmed would they feel safe. Anyone who has dealt with this type of IED would know it was always controlled electronically. If they believe we will risk ourselves blowing up rather than fail, our plan can work.'

Chaz took over. 'Looks like we are about ready, all agreed?' He got nods of approval from all. 'Okay, Looks like it's time to make that call. Axel, not to put pressure on you, but it is in your hands to make them believe we are serious.'

She fixed him with a stare. 'Oh, I am as serious as a bullet to the head. Time for us to create some havoc,' she said, as she reached for the phone.

# 28

Eitan grabbed the phone before Miungisi could reach it. The familiar altered voice broke the silence as he held it to his ear. The sound brought a chill to his hardened shoulders. He sensed a brittle determination behind the voice, a determination he had heard only a few times in his life. It was the same voice a suicide bomber would use. At that moment, he knew something profound was driving whoever was speaking.

'Same as before. I will not repeat any instructions. I am aware you are recording, and your friend, that piece of shit Miungisi, is trying frantically to trace this call. He is wasting his time. I require the destination within twenty-four hours. We will be transporting the item in a ceramic bed. The reason for this is twofold. One is to maintain the unit in perfect health and prevent you from trying to try before buying. The subject will be sedated and on oxygen. To identify the unit's identity, she will be accompanied by our physician. Nobody will be allowed to touch the subject.'

Miungisi could not contain himself. 'But how will we know?'

'Interrupt again, and the next thing you will receive is proof that the unit has been destroyed,' the voice continued.

'In the presence of your physician, our attendant will extract a vial of blood from the unit while they observe. They will then be able to check the "Item" is correct, as they will have samples on file. Plus, as it is a scarce type, I believe that will satisfy.'

'That sounds to be foolproof. We agree,' Eitan replied, as he realised the voice was waiting for a response.

'The physician and two other personnel will accompany the unit. One will be the person to oversee the transfer of the funds. Make sure that you have somebody from Masadalink present to effect the transfer. And finally, the person who will ensure that all our requirements are met. When that person is satisfied, our people will depart. Thirty minutes later, the explosive device will be deactivated. And before you ask, in this matter, you will have to trust us. We know your boss's reach. We have no reason to renege on this arrangement. When you provide the location, we will inform you one hour before our arrival. Are we agreed?'

Eitan replied quickly. 'That is agreeable, and we are ready to provide the location,' as he relayed where the facility was located.

There was silence for a moment then the metallic voice replied. 'Then we are ready to proceed. One question. Will we use the hidden entrance below the hospital to meet?'

Eitan could not believe his ears and could not contain himself. 'You already knew the location?'

The voice replied. 'And so much more, Eitan, so much more,' as the call disconnected.

'Brilliant!' Chaz exclaimed as he clapped Axel on the shoulders. 'Letting them know we knew the location should have them second-guessing themselves. Anything to give us an advantage as we enter the lion's den.'

On the other end of the call, Eitan handed the phone to Miungisi. 'These guys are sharp. Unless we can get a lead on them in the next twenty-three hours.' He glanced at his watch. 'We will have to get them after the delivery is completed.'

Miungisi stood. 'Don't worry. I will have enough people there that we will be ready whatever their escape avenue.'

Eitan was not so confident. What puzzled him was that they only asked for $50 Million. Whoever was behind this was displaying excellent capability so far. They seemed to know so much that they must have realised this was a drop in the ocean for Mizrahi. His was one of the biggest unregistered cryptocurrency exchanges with a reported capital of $200 billion.

*What are they after?* he wondered, as he picked up the phone to report to his boss.

# 29

Twelve hours later, both sides were preparing for the exchange. Moses had joined them, and Bill, Sergei, and Sun Yee were reviewing their part of the plan.

They were joined by Sharlene Ndlovu, who now had the full support of her network. She had been invited only when she had agreed that their plans would stay in the room. Like the rest of the rescue team, she would have to wait until Aurora pressed 'Go', as she would be their contact inside and wired for sound so she could connect with the outside.

Desmond was as ready as he could be for his part. The thought of being inside a plastic cage disguised as a young girl while being partly sedated to ensure he lay as still as possible was freaking him out. Ask him to charge into a cell full of lions, or this? It was apparent what his choice would be.

Christine was trying her best to assure him it was harmless. 'You will have a plunger in your hand to depress if you feel you need to be revived quickly,' she informed him.

She positioned the catheter attached to his arm, which had been carefully shaved and his nails manicured to add to the illusion. All of them were fake, except the stimulant he had at his disposal.

'This is the one that I will extract the blood sample,' she said, pointing to the catheter on his left arm.

It appeared to be inserted into his arm, but she had inserted a small sack of the correct blood she had collected from Eve. It was covered by some false skin which, without a careful examination, was indistinguishable to the naked eye.

'They will never suspect; you can trust me,' she assured him.

'Fine for you to say. I will be surrounded by the enemy lying in a plastic container dressed as a woman dressed only in my underwear,' he moaned. 'I can tell you if anybody tries to cut my lungs and heart out, they will get the shock of their lives,' he added.

They had a special guest watching the proceedings. Eve sat comfortably in a chair, observing the operations with great interest. Since Christina revived her, she had made a remarkable recovery. Her complexion had recovered to exude a healthy glow, and all her vitals appeared okay, but her memory was still blank.

The last thing she remembered was fleeting glimpses of people in white coats and being surrounded by others in the same predicament as she had been. When she remembered this, she became distressed, wanting to know what had happened to those people.

They had assured her they were safe and well cared for. Later, Aurora explained to her that they were endeavouring to secure the release of the remaining captives. Through all this, they had ascertained that English was not her first language and that she seemed more comfortable in French, which they discovered when her laughter at a French program led them to discover she spoke at least three languages, with French being the dominant one.

The way she spoke and her level of knowledge indicated an excellent education. Her understanding of the world, in general, seemed to be unaffected, but any recollection of her past was gone. Christina explained that if her abduction involved a lot of violence or trauma of some sort, it could have caused her to block all memories of the event.

'In cases like this, often in time, as they recover, their memory begins to return. The most important thing, for now, is just for her to feel secure. For this reason, I explained what had happened to her and explained that I had approached a friend for help to rescue her. This was only possible with the help of some special people. Now, together, we were trying to bring the people responsible to justice,' Christina said.

When she heard this, she immediately wanted to meet the people involved. Chris agreed and introduced her to everybody.

They all treated her like one of the group and explained what they were planning. When asked her age, she quickly answered, saying she was going on twenty, which would agree with her appearance. She looked like a young girl about to blossom into a woman. Aurora and the other girls soon formed a bond with her. She behaved shyly with the men but did not exhibit fear, which would be expected for a girl of her age.

When Desmond was introduced to her, and when she was told he would be her substitute for the sting, she could not help herself and burst out laughing, which only added to his discomfort.

Charlie called everybody together. Moses joined him as he began to speak.

'This is it, folks—time to put rubber on the road. Shortly, Moses and I will be heading off to Johannesburg to hook up with his men. Sharlene, I believe you are preparing to do the same so you can coordinate with your crew. I don't have to tell you that timing is everything. Miungisi and his mafia will be there in force. The last thing we want is a gunfight. With some luck, we,' indicating Moses, 'will have located where they will be set up. We don't believe many will be inside, so if all goes to plan, we will catch them with their pants down.'

Des spoke up, 'So how are we supposed to get there?' he asked.

'You and the three girls will be arriving by helicopter as long as they follow our instructions, and we confirm that Mizrahi's brother is there; his name is Levi,' Charlie replied. 'Then we can put our plan into action.'

There was silence for a moment; then Des piped up, 'So the four of us will fly into the lion's den. I will be encased in a glass case disguised as a girl, accompanied by the three girls armed with only a computer. Sounds like one of our plans. What could possibly go wrong!' he replied sarcastically.

There was some nervous laughter, then Sergei spoke, 'Don't worry. I will be there with Sun Yee and Bill as backups. But I bet we won't be needed.'

Words he would probably regret!

# 30

The Bell 429 helicopter, piloted by Solomon Nkosi and his son Shaka, brought the aircraft gently into a landing on the pad at the rear of Masadahope Hospital.

Axel had called Eitan with the final instructions.

'Our transport will land on the helipad. You will meet them with only enough personnel to transport the item and the three accompanying personnel to where the verification will be done. Next, your person will assist in transferring the Bitcoin to the value of $50 million. When that is completed and verified, our tech person will return to the helicopter, and they will remove them to a safe location.

'Three, the item and the personnel will be escorted to where Levi Mizrahi is located. We presume this is where verification will be made, and also the transplant. When there, our people will instruct you on the verifying procedures. During that time, the device will be disarmed. We must warn you that a simple tracking device attached to both beds will prevent any attempt to interfere or move Mizrahi to a safe distance. Any movement while the device is disarmed will destroy both "items",' the voice instructed, emphasising the last word.

Axel had contacted Charlie to let him know they had agreed to everything. 'A little too easy. I am sure they will be ready to act if they see any opportunity,' she cautioned.

'Agreed. The first danger point will be until we get Des and the ladies alongside Mizrahi. If we get to that point, they will not do anything to endanger him,' he replied.

'Good luck. They are calling me to the helicopter,' as she broke the connection.

Aurora could see a handful of men hurrying towards where they had landed as the rotor began to spool down. Pushing the side door open, she jumped out, followed by Christina and Axel. Ducking down, they moved outside the slowing rotor.

'Stop there!' she shouted to the approaching men. One stepped forward.

'We are here to assist you as instructed,' the hard-looking individual replied.

'Who are you?'

'I am the person you have been talking to. I represent Mr Mizrahi. My name is Eitan Zoabi.'

'We must verify that you and your people are not armed,' she responded.

He just indicated for her to proceed with the inspection; she quickly verified they were unarmed, simultaneously noticing the naked hatred in Eitan's eyes. Stepping back, she fixed him with a defiant stare, which only seemed to infuriate him more. She was sure that this one had some trick up his sleeve.

They transferred the bed with the cleverly disguised Desmond inside, which was remarkable and did not attract undue attention.

The transfer went without a hitch, and they found themselves inside a vast underground complex. Making their way deep inside, it was evident that no expense had been spared. Off to the side, they could see laboratories where medical staff were busy at work.

They entered an ultra-modern operating theatre where the transplant would take place.

Aurora took charge. 'I believe that before we continue, we will provide a blood sample for verification. Our physician will now extract the sample from the item,' continuing to use the phrase. 'Are you ready to verify?'

Eitan indicated to one of the doctors in attendance to step forward.

Christina carefully opened the side of the bed and inserted a syringe into the catheter, which she had positioned already in Des's arm. She began to slowly extract the blood she had hidden in a small sack cleverly hidden under a skin-like patch that was invisible to the eye.

'Enough?' holding up the vial for the other doctor to see.

He nodded in agreement as she handed it over and closed the side again, but not before giving Des a reassuring squeeze.

An audible click could be heard as the lid closed as Aurora pressed a switch hidden in one of her nails, activating the device on the casket. Eitan glanced at Aurora to see if she was responsible, but her face was blank.

They all stood patiently as the doctor ran a comparison and returned quickly to verify that the sample was correct.

*Now to the critical part. The money*, Aurora thought as she introduced Axel.

'This is our IT specialist who will assist in the transfer,' she said.

Eitan stepped forward. 'That will be me,' as he indicated a desk set up with a bank of computers.

As Axel began to prepare, he looked at her with obvious disdain. 'Are all of your crew females, or is that guy on the phone your bitch?' he asked with a sneer, not realising he was talking to that very person.

Aurora interjected, 'Enough chit-chat. We are not here for a bonding session. Don't forget what this female is holding in her hand,' waving her hand as if pressing a button.

She was doing this because she could see Axel becoming nervous.

She need not have been concerned. As soon as Axel was seated in front of the computer, she became another person. After a short time, she turned to Eitan.

'These are the accounts you are to transfer the Bitcoin to,' turning the screen towards him.

He connected to Abdiel, who was waiting in Tel Aviv to take care of the transfer.

Sitting in his office, Abdiel smiled when the instructions came through. He would make the transfer but attach a trace, so as soon as his brother was safe, he would bounce the coin back.

*Who does this idiot think they are dealing with?* he mused, clicking frantically at the keys.

'Done,' Axel announced a short time later as she closed her laptop.

Aurora again intervened. 'If you could now escort this female back to the transport,' she instructed icily. 'As soon as they inform me that she is safe and the helicopter is back, we can proceed with the final step.'

Eitan indicated to one of the men standing there, who indicated for Axel to follow him.

A short time later, as soon as she had boarded the chopper and was safely away, she texted Aurora and called Charlie, who was waiting with Moses.

'All done, we are $50 million better off. Now we need him to take the bait.'

# 31

Charlie disconnected the call and turned to Moses. They were sitting in a heavy military vehicle located in a secluded street with a view of both entrances to the hospital. They watched the helicopter transporting Axel to a safe distance, where they would wait in case an urgent extraction was required.

Moses' men had located what they believed were all of Miungisi's thugs and had been in position for some time now, ready to neutralise them when he gave the word.

Inside the operation theatre, things were proceeding at a frantic pace. In a flurry of activity by the medical staff, a space was cleared, and a bed was wheeled in, and for the first time, they laid eyes on the frail creature that all this horror was about.

Sitting upright, attached to a ventilator, was Levi Mizrahi. Despite his frail appearance, his eyes darkened with the evil that lurked within. He berated the people attending him in his hoarse voice behind the oxygen mask. It was impossible to understand him, but his desire to survive at any cost was apparent from how his gaze settled on the casket containing what he believed was his saviour, which brought an evil smile to his pale, shrunken face.

They were positioning him beside the bed containing Des as preparations for the transplant began with urgency. As Eitan issued orders to the medical staff, Aurora went to the beds and attached a small device to each. Turning to him, she indicated them, then spoke.

'These transmitters will alert us if you decide to get clever when we are gone and move this creature to a safe distance,' pointing to Mizrahi. 'I do not need to tell you what will happen if you attempt this,' holding up the detonation device.

The doctor who seemed to be in charge interrupted and inquired in a heavy accent if he was permitted to prepare Mr Mizrahi for the operation.

Aurora shrugged. 'Do what you want with him. But do not attempt to touch the item until you are informed that the device is disarmed,' nodding toward Eitan.

He had become more agitated as he began to see his chance of intervention was slipping away. 'What happens now?' he asked.

At that point, Aurora held her hand over her earpiece and listened. 'Our transport is about to  land. Time for us to say our farewell,' as she indicated to Christina that she was about to give Moses the signal to go.

Then all hell broke loose!

The bursts of gunfire from outside caused instant havoc. Time seemed to stand still for Aurora as she saw Eitan dash for the desk where the computers were and reach under the desk producing an Uzi and pointing it directly at her.

Before he could fire the weapon, she used the only available option. Without hesitation, she depressed the switch hidden under her nail, exploding the device attached to the casket!

# 32

Kagiso Malandele nudged his long-time friend in the ribs.

Gatshia Diyase grunted. 'What?' he snapped at having his nap disturbed.

They had been staunch friends since they met in Soweto when they were orphaned and found themselves fending for an existence. The relatives they had been sent to had no interest in them as they were in the same position. When Nelson Mandela became president, a wave of euphoria swept the nation. Still, despite his best efforts, the old enmity between the different tribes soon raised its ugly head, and, on the great leader's death, the country descended into chaos.

The two boys were typical of the challenges that faced the country's youth. They had survived on their wits and the petty crimes they committed as orphans. Their favourite target was drugs, not for themselves but to provide for the rising middle-class that had developed a taste for pills. This is what brought them to where they were today.

Kagiso had been the one that had put his eye on the hospital. Usually, their target was pharmacies or wealthy houses. But his taste for the latest fashion sports shoes worn by his heroes on TV drove him to look for bigger targets. This was why they were scoping out the hospital, as he had explained to his friend.

'I think there is some drug lab in the hospital basement. They only have traffic at night. The entrance we discovered looks unguarded; there is a small window to the side you could easily slip through and open the door from the inside. We could make a killing.'

He had convinced his pal. 'I am not that small,' Gatshia complained, conscious of his small stature.

Kagiso ignored his comment. 'Come on, let's go. It is starting to get dark,' he urged as the sun slipped below the horizon.

They had been checking the place out for a few days and discovered little activity most nights. This night had been much the same except that earlier, a helicopter had delivered some people that had gone inside, but soon somebody had come out and departed in the chopper. Since they left, there had been no activity.

They crept silently to the point where they could see the entrance which they targeted was obscured by thick foliage.

'Looks clear,' he whispered to his pal. 'Follow me,' indicating for them to head for the bush in front of the entrance.

When they got there, Gatshia paused. 'I will lead the way. As soon as we get there, it is over to you,' giving Kagiso a nudge.

They crept forward and crawled through the thick undergrowth, poking their heads out to see if the coast was clear. They were confronted by a colossal guy standing with his back to them, relieving himself against the side of the building. Gatshia could not help himself as he jumped up, letting out an unmerciful scream, which startled the guy as much as them.

He turned, and when he saw them, at the same time as they saw an Uzi lying across his chest. They all panicked. The kids froze for a moment, then, to their horror, saw him fumbling with his zipper while trying to grab his gun. This turned out to be a bad idea.

In his confusion, he depressed the gun's trigger, firing a burst of gunfire across his body, which took most of his right leg and a large portion of his groin off.

The sight of this and the inhuman screams of the stricken man, writhing on the ground, was all it took to spur the boys into action. They took off in a panic with their tails between their legs.

In the armoured vehicle, Charlie jumped at the sound of gunfire. 'Shit. Something has gone wrong,' he cried.

Moses reacted immediately, shouting into his radio to his men. 'Go! Go! Take them down now. All units respond,' he instructed.

Charlie, Moses, and the remaining troops bailed out of the vehicles and charged toward the entrance, fearing the worst for their friends inside.

'Murphys law again, something has gone wrong,' Charlie cursed under his breath.

# 33

The device attached to Des's bed exploded, but instead of destroying everybody, it burst out with tear gas, something they had planned in case of an emergency.

As it started to fill the operating theatre with a debilitating, noxious cloud, obscuring everything, Aurora, who knew what was happening, dropped to the floor where the gas did not settle.

On the other hand, Eitan had no idea what was happening. As he tried desperately to clear his vision, he waved his gun around frantically, looking for a target. Then, to his horror, through his distorted vision, what appeared to be a large, masked figure shrouded in white emerged from the cloud and launched itself at him.

He only had time to fire his gun once before the apparition smashed him to the floor. He felt a sharp sting in his shoulder and immediately descended into darkness.

'Fuck, he shot me!' came a muffled voice came from the masked face of Desmond.

He struggled to his feet and shrugged off the sheet that had followed him as he jumped from the bed. He dropped the syringe that Christina had provided for them to sedate their intended victim and looked at where he had been shot.

At the same time, as soon as the device exploded, Christina seized the oxygen mask from Levi's face and rushed to Aurora's aid. By this time, the gas was dissipating, aided by the efficient ventilation system, and as the gas cleared, to their horror, they saw Des standing there in his shorts with blood pouring from a wound in his arm.

'You've been shot!' Aurora cried as she rushed to his assistance.

'It's not like the movies, where they say it's only my arm. It feels like it's on fire. This hurts like hell,' he groaned through the mask.

'You can take the mask off now,' Christina instructed as she inspected the wound.

'You won't die. It just cut a nice groove in your upper arm,' she said as she wrapped a temporary bandage to stem the bleeding.

Aurora took charge. 'We have to get out of here. Something has gone wrong. Charlie must have been discovered. Let's get to the helicopter. Let's hope they have got the message and are responding. Come on, let's grab the package,' she said, pointing to Levi, who was sitting dumbfounded at what had transpired.

'I am not going anywhere with you. Do you know who you are dealing with?' he snarled in a croaky voice.

'I will take care of this.' Des stepped over to where he was lying and grabbed him, pulling him upright with his good arm. Then he lifted the frail frame effortlessly over his shoulder. When he started to struggle, Des gave him a clip on the jaw, knocking all the fight out of him. 'Okay, lead the way.'

Aurora led them out to the entrance to the helipad. When they emerged, it was chaos everywhere. Gunfire could be heard from around the facility. It was impossible to discern who was shooting at whom, but to her relief, she could see Shaka, Solomon's son, waving at them frantically to hurry. He was standing at the door of the helicopter. It was in the process of spooling up, ready to take off.

They made a frantic dash with the fizz of bullets flying everywhere. Des got there first and flung the unconscious Levi onto the cabin floor, and then the girls jumped in and helped the hampered Des in after them. Shaka jumped in, yelling at his father to get them airborne.

As the helicopter ascended into the night sky, Aurora grabbed the radio they were using to contact the ground and yelled, 'Come in. Is anybody there?'

To her relief, Charlie's voice came back. 'Are you guys okay?' he asked.

'We are all clear, and we have the package. What happened?' she asked.

In the background, he could hear his brother yelling, 'Don't forget to tell him I have been shot!'

Before he could respond, Aurora came back. 'He has a small flesh wound. Christina is taking care of it,' she replied, much to Des's disgust.

'What happened down there? That was not what we planned.'

'No idea, somebody started shooting, so we had to act. Have to go now. Things are heating up down here. I will fill you in over a drink when we get back,' he replied cheekily.

'I will hold you to that. Where is Sun Yee? Is she okay?' she asked, concerned for her partner.

'She is just doing her thing. God help anybody in her way. She still thinks you are inside. Don't worry. We've got a plan. Over and out.'

He hung up the call as he watched the helicopter vanish into the inky darkness of the African sky.

# 34

The fighting around the hospital had intensified. Moses had insisted that his people had to deal with the rescue operation and the containment of The Sysue Mafia alone. He had pointed out that if it were discovered he had outside help, it would hurt his ability to control the government blowback.

'You just go and control your mad friends,' referring the Sun Yee and Sergei, who had bolted toward the entrance to the underground facility, glaring at Charlie. 'Have they secured the package?' he snarled as he directed his men to surround the hospital and contain everybody inside.

'Yes,' replied Chaz. 'They have him in the helicopter.'

Moses sighed in relief. If they had not captured Mizrahi, their plan of using him as the reason they raided the place and their scheme would have been doomed.

'I reckon now would be a good time for our friend Sharlene to appear,' Charlie suggested.

'Agreed, time to release the press hounds, ' Moses replied, preoccupied with the ongoing assault.

Chaz called her number, which she answered at once.

'What happened? I was expecting you to call before beginning the assault,' she yelled.

'Murphy's Law,' he replied, not bothering to explain what that meant. 'Light the place up and make sure that it is going out live. We need maximum coverage.'

She laughed. 'People on the moon will be watching.'

He thanked her and, with a chuckle in response, returned to the fray. 'Good. Have to go now. I have a couple of heroes to contain before they ruin everything.' He hung up and jumped from the truck, dashing towards the action.

Moses's men quickly took care of Miungisi's men, who offered little resistance to his professional soldiers as he hurried to the entrance where they had seen Aurora be escorted earlier. He could see that fighting was still intense there. He headed to the door which Aurora and her friends emerged from as they made their dash to the chopper.

Creeping through the undergrowth, he was startled by the sight of one of Miungisi's men lying on the ground with one of his legs hanging off. Approaching, he could see he was dead and on closer inspection, he could see that the wound was self-inflicted.

*This must have been the idiot that started the shooting*, he thought as he pushed the door open and went inside.

He could hear voices and headed in that direction. He arrived at what had to be an operating theatre, and as he peered in, he could see Sun Yee ordering what had to be medical staff into a side room.

'Need any help?' he asked.

She turned .'No problem here, but there is no sign of Aurora,' as she pointed her gun threateningly at one of the terrified staff.

'Relax, she is safe. Oh, and by the way, the others got away also,' he replied sarcastically. 'They escaped in the helicopter just after the fighting erupted'.

She glanced at him sheepishly, embarrassed at showing her emotions. 'Good news.' she replied. 'Have you seen Sergei?'

'Last I saw of him was when he followed you. Where did he go?' he asked.

She pointed outside. 'When we were going in, he spotted who he thought was Miungisi. He looked like he was making a break for it, so he went after him.'

Charlie exploded. 'If he is caught, it could blow things wide open. Moses was emphatic that the only one that could be involved was Christina. Which direction did he go?'

She shrugged just as Moses and a group of his men entered. 'Sun Yee had everything under her control. She will explain everything. I have to go and tidy up a little problem,' Charlie explained as he made a dart for the door.

Moses watched him disappear, turning to Sun, 'Sergei?' he asked. She nodded.

'Some little problem,' he groaned.

# 35

Miungisi realised that something had gone seriously wrong.

As soon as the gunfire erupted and he saw the strength of Moses' forces emerging from the darkness, he knew his rag-tag crew would have no chance against them and so decided to make his escape, making a hasty retreat to the secret lift which connected the facility below with the main hospital.

As he emerged, the place was in chaos, with people rushing everywhere in terror. He exited the hospital by the ambulance ramp and hurried down the slope to the automatic door. Pressing the button, it quickly rose where he was greeted by the sight of the biggest white man he had ever seen.

'Are you that *Naaier* Miungisi?' the figure asked, using the Afrikaans word for fucker.

'Get out of my way, or I will kill you,' he roared as he charged at this giant, colliding with full force.

But before he could inflict any damage, the guy slipped to the side. As Miungisi hurtled past, he delivered a punch under his right arm straight into his liver.

He had been in many fights before but had never been hit with anything like that. He dropped to the ground, writhing in pain as the guy stepped in and finished him with a mighty blow to his head, connecting it with the earth and putting his lights out.

'Always with the talk. Hit first, talk later,' Sergei advised the unconscious figure.

Charlie emerged from having skirted the building to be greeted by the sight of Sergei standing over the prone figure of Miungisi. As he rushed over to him, before he did more damage, Moses and a group of his men appeared, followed by Sharlene and camera people ready to record.

'Stop there,' he ordered her. 'No filming until I get your friends out of here.'

She quickly complied, aware of the importance of them not being discovered here.

Sergei hauled the semi-conscious Miungisi to his feet. 'What do you want me to do with this garbage?' he asked, his disgust evident.

He was hoping Moses would play the Roman emperor and give the thumbs down so he could dispatch him from this mortal coil. To his obvious disgust, Moses ordered one of his guards to take him into custody.

As he handed him over and he was marched away, Moses turned and spoke. 'A quick death from you would have been preferable to where he is going. Believe me; his suffering has only just begun.'

This brought a smile to Chaz and Sergei's faces.

'Now, could you make yourselves scarce? Head back to my command post. You can watch the whole thing unfold there. I believe it is being broadcast live on Sharlene's network. And already my people are posting on the internet. Enjoy your show!' Moses suggested, with a smile on his face.

The command post was a hive of activity as they coordinated Moses' instructions. The hospital was surrounded, and Miungisi's men were being loaded into police vehicles, ready to transport them.

A series of huge spotlights illuminated the hospital, and there were personnel everywhere. Sharlene had set up a position to begin her interviews with all this activity as a backdrop.

From their body language, it was evident to the Savage brothers and crew that an incident of this magnitude was a once-in-a-lifetime chance. This was a career-maker for both of them. But she was well up to the task. She had Moses ready to begin.

'I am here with Commandant Moses Khumalo of the security and terrorist squad. Could you tell the public what is taking place?'

Moses cleared his throat. Then began to speak.

'We received information from a source in one of the aid agencies that an illegal organ transplant operation was to occur here tonight using organs from a living donor who had been abducted from an orphanage. Fortunately, we arrived in time to prevent this. While undertaking this operation, we uncovered a secret facility below the hospital where many people were supposedly held against their will for this purpose. We have discovered that these people were being prepared as "spare parts" for people who could afford them. The person being prepared for the transplant is the brother of a prominent businessman; information is very scarce at this time, but as we uncover more about this terrible situation, we will keep the public informed.'

'Can you tell us what has happened to this individual?' Sharlene asked.

'They have been moved to a secure location and are being cared for by professionals. That is all I can tell you at this time for security reasons,' he replied.

'Do you know the nationality of the victims at this time?'

'I am sorry, that is all I can tell you now. The situation is very fluid, as you can imagine. We will keep you informed as more information becomes available,' indicating that the interview was over.

Sharlene faced the camera. 'As you can see, the situation here at ground zero involves many departments besides the criminal aspects. Outside aid agencies have been rushed to assist the victims. I have unconfirmed reports that the discovery and rescue of orphans being held captive at a facility on the outskirts of Durban led to this raid. We will remain here to bring you all the latest news as it comes to hand. This is Sharlene Ndlovu reporting live from Masada Hope Hospital,' as the cameras panned around the bustling scene.

'Couldn't have gone better!' Charlie roared. 'It was just as Sharlene had scripted, and I would imagine there are a lot of nervous politicians watching this and shitting their pants simultaneously.'

'What should we do now?' Sun Yee asked.

'Head back to Christina's place, get a drink, and plan our next move,' he replied.

# 36

Two days later, they gathered at Christina's clinic for Moses and Sharlene to update them on how the investigation was progressing.

Moses began with his report. 'As we suspected, the operation was overseen by a surgeon named Amara Abioye from Nigeria. A particularly nasty piece of work who had to flee her home country to avoid investigation into some illegal operations she carried out. We only had to threaten her with deportation for her to start singing like a canary.

'As we suspected, she was approached by Abdiel Mizrahi sometime back when he searched for a donor for her brother. Although she says the idea for the "Human Farm" was his. But considering this was the sort of thing she was wanted for, I believe it was her idea.

'No matter, she and her two other accomplices will be the ones facing the courts. She also provided us with the names of the officials receiving kickbacks to look the other way. We have managed to round up most of them, except for two who decided to take the easy way out and eat a bullet.'

Chaz interrupted, 'Isn't that a bit extreme? They probably would have gotten away with jail time.'

'Prison here is not like where you come from. Given a choice, especially as many of the inmates they would be incarcerated with would have a particular hatred for politicians, a quick death would win out every time given the choice: death or prison,' he explained.

Christina took over. 'Thanks to Sharlene's brilliant work bringing the story to the world, it has had an instant effect. Our hero

Commander Moses has been given complete control over the whole investigation with sweeping powers to investigate every corner of the establishment. I imagine many people are looking over their shoulders.'

'As for the poor victims of this scheme, the ones we released earlier have been transferred to where the others were held. On inspection, the facility was of the highest standard and ideally suited for treating them.'

'Have you managed to locate where they are from?' Aurora asked.

'Nothing yet. We are concentrating on getting them back to a regular routine. Remember, they had been partly sedated for some time and need to adjust before questioning them. Moses had his IT people go through the records found attached to their beds. It will take some time as we don't have personal details, just their tattoos.'

'Anything we can do to help?' she asked.

'At the moment, the government is covering all the costs. But something as big as this could take much time, and I am afraid that when the story gets replaced with the next big thing, I am worried the funds will dry up,' Christiana replied.

'She is right. Much as I would love to keep this story on the front page, eventually it will run out of steam,' Sharlene added.

'If money can fix it, it isn't broke,' came a voice from the corner.

Everybody turned to Axel, who was engrossed in her computer.

'What are you talking about?' Aurora asked.

'Are you forgetting the $50 million we just got from Mizrahi?'

She looked puzzled. 'I thought you said he would transfer it back as soon as he traced it. That was the plan, wasn't it?'

Axel put a cheeky grin on her face. 'Yes, as I suspected, that's what he did. But he is not as clever as he thinks he is. Remember, cryptocurrency exists in code. What he transferred back is a duplicate of his file. The only problem for him is that it is worthless. So now we have that Bitcoin at your disposal. Will that tide you over until we figure out how to clean this lowlife out of all his money and hopefully destroy him for good?' she asked.

Christina cried out with delight,' Will it help? It will be a lifesaver for these orphans. Are you joking?'

'But what happens if he tries to redeem them?' Chaz asked.

'That would be a problem. That's why I asked for payment in Bitcoin. It is still the largest of the currencies and the likely one for him to hold on to. I have been tracing it since he took it back, and it is sitting in a warm wallet. I expect he will transfer it to a cold wallet if it is part of his real stash,' she replied.

The confused look on their faces forced her to explain.

'Just think of the wallets as money boxes. The warm ones are connected to the internet, where they can be vulnerable. For a crook like him, he would put the bulk of his holdings in a cold one. Again this time, think of a safety box in a bank. Nobody but the owner would have access.'

From the looks on their faces, they were not much the wiser.

Des was the one to ask the right question. 'Forget all that mumbo jumbo. Can you catch the guy?'

Axel turned to face him. The confident expression on her face spoke volumes.

'What do you think?' as she turned back to her computer screen.

# 37

The snow was falling like a dense white cloud. She felt as if she was floating. The sky above was like a dark-blue carpet dotted with glittering lights. As she reached out, she found, to her surprise, that she could almost touch them. The snow surrounded her in every direction. The treetops were just below her as she flew across the sky.

She was flying.

Below, the world stretched out in every direction, covered in its blanket of white. Yet she felt the sensation of danger emanating from under the surface. Again, the feeling of foreboding and fear started to rise. She tried to shake off the feeling. She knew that she loved the snow, and even though she only had on a nightgown, she felt no cold, she was just enjoying the sense of freedom.

She suddenly found herself sheltering in a dense forest. She had burrowed into the snow, and despite that, she felt the danger approaching. She began to run, but hard as she tried, all that would happen was the feeling of sinking deeper into the clutches of this darkness that pursued her. She tried to scream, but no sound came out of her mouth. The more she tried, the more snow she swallowed. Panic seized her as she struggled to reach the surface. She pulled herself to the surface, and just then, she heard a voice in the darkness that unearthed the deepest fear in her heart. A voice she recognized but still did not know.

'Got you!' it said in a sound that seemed to come from around her. Then Hell ascended.

An ear-shattering scream startled Christina as Eve sat bolt upright in her bed. Her face was a mask of terror and she began to shake violently. Christina darted to her side and began to try to calm her.

'It is just a dream, don't be afraid, you are safe now,' she said.

The nightmares had become more frequent, and the psychiatrist who was treating her assured them that it was normal for people with amnesia from some event their mind had blocked.

Eve began to calm down as she awakened. Clutching Christina's hand in fear, she began to blubber.

'It was the same, I am in the snow, and something is trying to capture me. I know they want to kill me,' as she began to cry. 'Why can't I remember who I am?' and she descended into sobs of tears.

Chris embraced her. 'Remember what Olive said,' referring to her psychiatrist.

'It is your subconscious trying to make sense of what you have been through. Please don't push it. She says this sort of thing usually resolves itself as you become more comfortable with your surroundings.'

Eve began to relax a bit. Since she had awakened here, what seemed a lifetime ago, she had been interacting with the gang, who were treating her as if she were one of their own. Her health had returned quickly, no doubt due to her excellent condition.

Even to her, it was obvious she was from a different background than the others. The lack of any sign of hard work on her hands and her general condition made it apparent that she was well cared for. While all of the orphans were in great shape—no doubt to preserve their value—they all showed signs of a hard life, contrasting her general condition.

'Why don't you join us? We are just about to eat and discuss what we will do next,' Christina suggested. Eve nodded in agreement. 'Just let me check your dressing,' referring to the wound where her kidney had been removed.

'Is there something wrong?' she asked.

Christina dismissed her concerns. 'Not at all, just tidying up some of their sloppy work,' as she finished her inspection and escorted the beautiful young lady to dinner.

The conversation at the table was animated and relaxed as they discussed their options. Des was in top form, revelling in being the first of the Savage brothers to have gotten a bullet wound. Charlie was usually the one to get damaged, evident by the thin scar that ran through his right eyebrow, a result of an altercation in his youth. The next one, Vincent Savage QC, usually avoided the physical stuff, leaving that to his brothers.

'That's not a bullet wound. I have cut myself worse shaving,' Chaz ribbed him.

Not to be outdone, Des retorted, 'Perhaps you would look better if you shaved your chin instead of your eyebrow.'

When the laughter subsided, Charlie put his hand up. 'Okay, time for us to start planning, and it is over to Axel.'

'As you know, my aim, and now it is the same for all of us, is to not only take down but destroy Abdiel Mizrahi,' she declared with venom. 'The plan we hatched when we asked for the ransom was to allow me to implant a trace into the deepest part of his fortune. So far, that is working perfectly, and the fake $50 million is sitting in a warm wallet he controls. I will gloss over a lot of what I am doing if that's all right?'

There were nods of agreement as she continued.

'In principle, his business is a marketplace for cryptocurrency. But unlike a bank, the security depends on the credibility of what it is trading. I believe he is running a Ponzi scheme, from what I have been able to uncover.'

'Just like Bernie Madoff!' cried Des, unable to contain himself.

'Correct. But for those who don't know what it is, think of the old saying, "Taking from Peter to pay Paul."'

'So, how do we take him down?' Aurora asked.

'Well, right now, there will be a lot of nervous investors having seen his name mentioned regarding what has gone down here. What brought down Bernie Madoff was not his doing but rather the global financial crisis. What we need is to keep the pressure on. When the money deposited becomes less than the withdrawals, his only choice is to use his reserves. If that happens, there is a chance I can clean him out.'

'So what do you intend to do?' he asked.

'I have already begun. I have also used some of his $50 million to short sell his stock.'

'Okay. Sorry, but you will have to explain that,' said Des.

She thought for a moment about how to explain. 'It is like I am betting that his company will fail. And what do rats do?'

'They jump ship!' Des yelled, delighted that he got that part.

When the laughter subsided, their attention was drawn to Eve, who continued to titter with laughter. They saw that her attention was on the TV, which was tuned to international news. It was this that was making her laugh. They were all struck silent. It was the French news!

Christina stepped over to her. 'Do you understand this?' she asked.

'*Oui, il est très marrant.*' Then she stopped, '*Merde. Je parle français!* I speak French!'

As she began to panic, Christina comforted her, 'Relax. It is just you beginning to remember your past. Nothing to be concerned about.'

Christina took her back to her room to rest as she began to relax.

Aurora turned to the others. 'That adds another part to the puzzle. I suggest we leave that to Christina while we apply pressure on the person behind this.'

# 38

**TEL AVIV**

Abdiel Mizrahi slammed the phone down and then switched it off to give himself a second to compose his thoughts. It had continued ringing since the news broke about the Johannesburg fiasco. Worse than that, somehow they had uncovered his involvement.

He had been fielding calls ever since with concerned clients worried about their money. He had convinced some of them that it was all a mistake, but the withdrawals kept coming in.

As well as that, he had got a call from a friend in the government that the Israeli Mossad had taken an interest and was preparing to investigate. The last thing he wanted was them on his tail, considering their history.

He slammed his fist into the desk, dislodging a computer screen that smashed onto the floor.

He cursed himself for allowing himself to be talked into that crazy idea. But that bitch of a doctor was so convincing, and saving his brother was paramount to him. Now he had no idea where he was, and to make matters worse, he had lost all contact with his go-to man, Levi.

He was a computer geek at heart. He had yet to taste the seedy part of the business. He had always left that up to his brother, and since he became sick, that task fell to Eitan.

*Who was behind this?*

He wondered if it was a parent or relation of one of the items but discounted that for two reasons. All of the donors came from refugee camps, plus the sophistication of the group behind the extortion could not have come from that source.

Yet they needed to be cleverer. He had recovered his $50 million within a few hours of the transfer. He wondered what their reaction would be when they discovered their loss. On the other hand, the presence of the police and the press coverage indicated that whatever they had planned had failed.

He realised that he would have to implement his escape plan if things deteriorated.

When he obtained the stolen crypto computers from the Iceland theft, they would become his safety blanket; the Bitcoin they had been producing daily since then had swollen his stash to over $22 Billion, plus whatever he had fleeced from his gullible investors would ensure that he was set for life.

He had learned his lesson from watching people like Bernie Madoff and the young Barry Cotton, who had died in mysterious circumstances in India, taking the password for his cold wallet with him. He had no intention of following in their footsteps. For that reason, he had prepared a safe where his money could secure him for the rest of his life.

But he could not put the thought of his beloved brother out of his mind. How could he effect his return? He needed Eitan Zoaria's expertise.

Where the hell was he?

# 39

## JOHANNESBURG, NIGHT OF THE RAID

Eitan struggled to sit upright. He was completely disorientated by the effect of the sedative that guy in the mask had injected. What saved him from being fully incapacitated was that the needle had passed through his heavy shirt, absorbing a large amount of the dose. The gas had cleared, and he could hear the gunfire and noise of the battle outside. Shaking his head to try to clear his senses, he realised they had been entirely played.

Cursing under his breath, he struggled to his feet. He quickly realised that he was in no condition to be involved in the fight, and when he looked around the deserted operating theatre, he saw that Levi was also gone.

He could hear the sounds of people approaching. Looking around for an avenue of escape, he immediately dismissed the routine exits, and then, out of the corner of his eye, he spotted a chute used to dispose of soiled clothing.

Without hesitation, he threw himself into the opening and slid into the darkness to be deposited in a pile of dirty linen. He lay still, listening for any sounds, but all he could hear was the sound of fighting in the distance. It seemed to be decreasing, so he decided to try to escape, creeping to the door at the end of what must have been the laundry. He peered out. From his vantage point, he could see the entrance for the ambulances. To his surprise, he could see Miungisi in a stand-off with the largest human being he had ever seen.

As Miungisi attacked the monster, he moved as quickly as any fighter he had seen. He delivered a killer punch under his opponent's right arm into where the liver was sitting. This was a killer blow to be hit by someone of his size and skill. Not to be deterred, he finished him off with a staggering blow that Eitan suspected would have left him a cripple.

*Who are these people?*

He cursed under his breath as he remembered the girl that resembled Wonder Woman. The one that had exploded the bomb, which resulted in him being attacked by that apparition that had arisen from the bed.

Now suddenly realising that he had been fooled by having someone disguised as the donor. 'I will find you bitch, and then we will see how clever you are,' he mumbled under his breath as he crept away in the darkness.

He made it back to his safehouse after a few scares. To his surprise, he saw that it was the police who had raided the hospital. Was that a coincidence? Had they foiled the plans of the extortionists? With the presence of the news networks also, he could not see how that could have been their doing. Was the situation retrievable?

He began to plan his revenge, and with that in mind he reached out to his employer.

# 40

Abdiel snatched up his satellite phone as it began to vibrate. Only one person had this number.

'Eitan?' he gasped in anticipation.

'Yes,' came the reply.

'What went wrong?' he asked.

'Everything.'

'Is my brother okay?' he demanded.

'If you stop asking questions, I will tell you what I know,' Eitan responded, going on to explain what had taken place.

When he finished, there was silence, and then Abdiel responded.

'Whatever has resulted in the authorities raiding our setup in the hospital brought immense heat to bear on my operation. My clients are getting scared, and the Mossad is getting interested. I will probably have to implement our escape plan. Can you still get out of the country?'

'Yes. They have no idea who I am,' he replied.

'Do you think you can locate my brother? You know I will pay whatever is needed.'

Eitan did not hesitate. 'I will find him if he is alive. In any case, I have a score to settle with a particular female individual,' he replied.

'Good. Keep me posted, and let me know if you need anything.'

Eitan agreed as he disconnected the call. As he sat contemplating his next move, something on the TV caught his attention. The presenter, Sharlene Nuvolo, a well-known personality, seemed to dominate the developing story and was discussing it with the doctor in charge of their care. They were talking about the facility's rescued people and how they responded. Something about the doctor struck a chord in his memory, yet he couldn't recall what. Then something she was saying caught his attention.

'Most rescued people are being treated in the facility where they were held. The most vulnerable had been transferred to her clinic where she could observe them personally,' the doctor informed the presenter, who continued to inquire about the future for the victims of this tragedy.

His attention went to the doctor as her name flashed across the bottom of the screen. Dr Christina Herrero, it said. She was the director of a private clinic and had been involved with many aid groups dealing with the country's many refugees.

When the interview ended, he went online to locate her clinic and discovered it was only a short drive from his safehouse. At once, he knew where Mizrahi's brother was probably being held. He decided to investigate.

As he drove past, he saw that the facility was surrounded by police security, as well as army personnel guarding the outer perimeter. This presence convinced him that this was where Levi Mizrahi was being held. He wanted to avoid hanging around as every vehicle passing was closely observed. Any rescue mission was out of the question. He would need another plan if he were to succeed.

He returned to base and contacted Abdiel with what he had discovered. When he outlined what he had uncovered, Abdiel was delighted with the news.

'This is what I hoped. I am sure they are keeping him under wraps while they investigate. That should give you some time to devise a plan. I am counting on you.'

Eitan cautioned him. 'Don't get your hopes up yet. The place is completely locked down. Everybody is screaming for the people behind this to be caught. Your name has been mentioned on some of the talk shows.'

Abdiel cursed. 'That's the last thing I need. The negative publicity is crucifying the company's share price. Plus, some cretin has started to short the stock. My clients are deserting in droves,' he continued to rant.

'I don't understand one thing you just said. I will leave you to deal with that problem. I have my hands full with things over here,' Eitan said. He did not want his boss to fill his head with stuff he did not understand.

'You are right. I will take care of things here. Concentrate on figuring out how to recover my brother.'

'Are we going to be all right?' Eitan asked, concerned for his financial future.

The reply came quickly, 'I already explained to you from the beginning that I had an escape plan. I hope you remember what I explained to you. So far, I have held back the tide. But if things get much worse, I will go dark. If that happens, you know what to do?'

Relieved, he replied, 'Sure. Don't worry, boss. I will find Levi and get him back. Talk soon.' They disconnected the call.

At both ends of the conversation, two worried men began pacing as they tried to figure out how to extract themselves from the disaster unfolding around them. And more importantly, who the hell was behind it all?

# 41

The Umbrella crew were busy planning their next move, or more to the point, they were all waiting for Axel to tell them what that might be.

'Well, my shorting of his stock Is beginning to have an effect. Plus, the internet is alive with people clambering for news of who was behind something as abhorrent as preparing humans as spare parts. They want to know who is responsible and the sick people who "Reserved" a living person for that purpose.'

Chaz cautioned, 'Let's not forget our goal: Take down Mizrahi. Let's focus on that. I am pretty sure anybody involved in the scheme will be sitting down with their lawyers trying to figure out how to avoid going to prison. We can leave that to the authorities. Agreed?'

He got nods all around at that point, and Bill Heart intervened.

'It looks like you guys have everything under control. They need me back in Mallorca. Vincent has been in touch with me. Plus, Maria is missing her mum.'

Des was unhappy that his 'unofficial' girlfriend was departing, but knew it would let him focus on helping his brother.

'When are you going?' Aurora asked.

'Christina's dad has provided his private jet. He was only too happy to help. It is tomorrow. We will leave at noon,' he replied.

'No worries, I will drop you at the airfield. I could do with getting a few things in town,' she offered.

With nods of agreement, they turned back to Axel.

'Sorry for the interruption. Let's focus on your plan. Please continue,' Chaz urged.

'No problem,' she replied, with a flick of her blond hair. 'Well, as I said, the internet is buzzing, so I have been helping it by launching some fake cyberchats. Before you ask, it's better if I show you.'

As she clicked a few keys, a young man who looked like a Wall Street banker appeared on the screen and explained why he believed that Masadalink was in trouble. The puzzled expressions on their faces prompted her.

'Watch,' she said, and clicked again.

This time, some professor from LA complained about the company. She continued to click away. Each time another different person appeared.

It was Des that the penny dropped first. 'They are all fake,' he cried.

'At last, someone that gets it, the internet is just an illusion if you believe what you see. These videos are all produced by a computer program. No real people are involved.'

Charlie jumped in again. 'I think we should leave Axel to do what she is doing. Do you think this will bring him down?' he asked as he turned to go.

She paused before replying. 'I am sure that his company will vanish very soon. But that won't achieve very much if we want him obliterated completely. The problem is he will surely have planned for this eventuality.'

'How do you know that?' he asked.

'Because that's exactly what I would do,' she replied.

# 42

The women remained in a huddle, considering their next move, while Des and Chaz went to see if Moses had any luck locating the Eitan character.

'So how do we proceed? What will he do next?' Aurora asked.

'He will have a bolt-hole set up. Some country where money talks. Somewhere he feels untouchable. That is where he will control his money, which I believe will be in Crypto in his hard wallet. It is untouchable. He knows the liquidators of his company will seize all his physical assets. It is tough to hide assets in this interconnected world. He will write them off. In any case, I am sure they would only amount to petty cash to him.'

Discouraged, Aurora asked, 'So how do we get him?'

'We will get him because we have something he values more than anything—his brother. Just look at his efforts to find a cure for him, to the point that he got involved in the organ harvesting business trying to help him. Which almost assured the demise of his company. The Ace we have in our hand is that we have his brother. I believe he will do anything to get him back.'

Aurora turned to Christina. 'How is he?' she asked.

Chris looked at her and replied. 'He is cared for,' with a dismissing tone.

Aurora shrugged, putting her odd reply down to her dislike for who he was.

'So how do we use him?" Aurora asked.

Axel smiled as she replied. 'We ransom him again!'

For the next few hours, they discussed how they would approach this problem. Sun Yee came up with the answer.

"We will find a way to convince him, ' she assured them.

# 43

They broke up for the night for much-needed rest, leaving Axel to continue working on her keyboard.

They all congregated for a buffet breakfast the following morning to find her still working.

'Don't you ever sleep?' Sun Yee asked.

'I have conditioned myself to catnap; it seems enough. When I am in some program, it is like another world. When I am there, I feel very comfortable and at peace. When I am finished, I feel relaxed,' she explained.

Sun Yee responded, 'It is the same for me when I meditate. I have been told that when we go to the place in our mind where we can be alone, sleep becomes unimportant.'

'Well, from us humans that need sleep, don't expect any sympathy,' replied Aurora.

After breakfast, Chaz, Des, and the four women started to plan how they could provide proof that Levi survived and, more importantly, that they still had his donor.

'They will need proof of life, so we will have to make a video of both parties alongside a daily newspaper with the date.'

'That could be a problem,' Christina blurted.

Charlie nodded. 'Of course. We would not use Eve. We will have to use someone else.'

'You can forget me. I am never dressing up as a woman again,' Des interjected as he pointed vigorously at his bullet wound, which he believed was not getting near enough attention.

'Eve is not the problem,' came the response from Christina.

A confused Chaz asked, 'Then what?'

'We can't provide Levi,' was the reply.

'Why?'

'Because he is dead.'

There was silence for a second, then everyone started to speak at once.

'Quiet! Let Chris talk,' Charlie roared. 'Tell us what happened.'

Christina cleared her throat.

'What happened was that he had no chance of surviving any operation, especially one as radical as a double transplant. He was in bad shape when we got him back to the clinic. We managed to keep him alive for almost a week, but he died two days ago. I decided to keep quiet until we had time to discuss it. Sorry for not telling you before.'

She began to sob gently. Aurora went to comfort her. At the same time, Charlie began to digest this new information.

'You did the right thing. If Axel is correct and all this guy wants is his brother, then that is our only advantage. Word of this must not get out.'

Before they could discuss how to achieve this, Bill Heart arrived to say his goodbyes. When they finished giving messages to all their friends back in Mallorca, they headed out to a Range Rover the Herrero family had provided.

They loaded the car, jumped in, and were just about to leave when Sun Yee called out, 'Wait for me. I could do with a bit of retail therapy at the mall.'

Aurora muttered without turning her head as she jumped in beside her, 'Guess she is human after all. Meditation not enough?' she queried, talking to some imagined person.

That was enough for them to burst out laughing, glad for the release after the last few days. As they pulled out, they were followed by an armed convoy, which Moses had insisted on.

Their enjoyment distracted them from their ordinary vigilance, and they failed to notice that they had picked up a tail.

# 44

**TEL AVIV**

Eitan's excited voice assaulted Abdiel's ear. 'We've got them!'

'Stop shouting. What are you talking about?'

Eitan calmed down. 'I got lucky. I have located that Amazonian bitch from the shakedown,' he breathlessly explained. 'I have been watching the clinic that I believe Levi is being held. Yesterday a car carrying some people left, escorted by military police. I followed at a distance. They went to a private airstrip when one of the passengers, a male, boarded a private jet. After, the car with its escort went to a shopping mall where two females got out and went shopping again, escorted by security. When I got close enough, I recognised the tall one. She is the one that exploded the device that gassed me. She was with a small Asian-looking woman. In any case, I followed them back to the clinic.'

Abdiel got excited. 'I believe you are on to something. It would appear that this clinic and the gang that blackmailed me are somehow connected. And from what you describe, very well connected, judging by the military presence.'

'Correct, the security here excludes any chance of a frontal rescue. it would be a blood bath,' Eitan cautioned.

'Then what should we do?'

He paused before responding. 'If I am correct, expect another ransom demand. Remember, this is about money. Do they know you have taken the money back?' he asked.

'Yes,' he replied. 'But I will immediately replace it as a sign of good faith. I will pay them whatever they ask. Whoever is behind the hacking is good. But I am better,' he boasted. 'I will have it all back as soon as my brother is safe.'

'Good. I could need some additional muscle. In the meantime, I am working on an alternative plan. Can you make some hard cash available?' he asked.

'Consider it done. It will be sent to the bank we are using for our escape plan. Things are getting to the breaking point here. Everything is ready as planned. I have already activated our bolt-hole. So be prepared for me to go dark. After that, our contact will only be through a satellite phone. Please find, my brother,' he said, as he disconnected the call.

Eitan hung up. He relaxed over a coffee in a shop that had a nice view of the complex where he was convinced the Umbrella crew were holding Abdiel's brother. Now all he had to do was find a way to entice them to come out and play.

As he blew gently on the hot coffee, a glimmer of a plan began to form.

## 45

'Come here; you guys have to see this,' Axel shouted from where she was hunched over her computer screen.

'What's all the commotion about?' Des yelped.

He was watching the screen, trying to uncover the mystery of computers, as he had not seen anything in the jumble of numbers to prompt her reaction.

'We just got another $50 million. That's what all the commotion is about!' she retorted.

That got everyone's attention, as they clustered around.

"From where?' Charlie asked.

'That's just it. It is from Mizrahi. I have no idea what he is up to?' she replied.

They all started to discuss the possibilities, which continued for a few minutes trying to figure out what this guy was up to, when Des interrupted,

'Am I the only one that can see what this guy is doing? Correct me if I am wrong, but he still believes he got his money back from the first payment?'

Axel nodded. 'Well, that tells me is that he thinks he is cleverer than he is. I believe this payment is his way of atoning for "taking" it back before,' he replied smugly.

Charlie replied, as the penny dropped, 'You are right; he must believe we have his brother and is trying to mend fences. Trust the devious mind of my brother to figure it out,' bringing a grin to Des's face.

Aurora spoke up. 'So want do we do?' she asked him.

Chaz deferred to Des. 'You figured it out. So what is our next move?'

Des puffed out his chest, delighted with the attention. 'Easy, we do as Chaz suggested. We ask for more money, but we better have something to offer him before we do that. For example, proof of life. Which will have to include an Eve stand-in. A female one!' he hastily added.

'That makes a lot of sense,' Chaz added as he turned to Christina.

'Is there any way you can improvise something that would fool them? Remember, it is only until Axel can implement her plan to clean him out.'

Christina put a grin on her face, replying. 'I will figure it out, even if I have to bring the bastard back to life!' which brought a trickle of laughter, relaxing everyone.

'Okay, we will leave that with you. Meanwhile, Axel, you continue to prepare. Anything to add?' directing the question to Moses, who was operating his operations from here.

'All good here', he replied.

'Then I think it is time for us to stir the pot again. Can you still contact him like before?' he asked Axel.

She nodded.

'Okay, this is what I want you to say,' as Charlie outlined the call.

# 46

**TEL AVIV**

'Is this Abdiel Mizrahi?' the metallic voice asked.

'Yes,' came his gruff reply.

'Then there is no need to remind you who this is and how to proceed.'

As he realised who it was, he could not help blurting out, 'I am well aware of how the Umbrella people operate.' He wanted to show whomever they were that he was smarter and already knew who they were.

'Good,' was the sharp reply. 'Then you would know it was stupid to try and shaft us for our money. I am glad you are clever enough to know that the least you could do was to return it after your crazy attempt at snatching your brother. It is a miracle that he survived.'

Axel had to turn away to stop herself from laughing at how easy it was to play to this guy's pride.

'Is he okay?' Abdiel blurted out.

The emotionless voice continued to apply pressure. 'Only thanks to the doctors who are treating him. It is only because of them that he is still in a position to avail of the "item" we can provide him with, that I don't have to remind you he so desperately needs.'

'What do you want?' he demanded.

'This call was to re-establish negotiations. As you can imagine, our leaders are very angry with your actions. I can assure you the cost will have to be substantially increased.'

He began to plead. 'The rescue attempt was not my idea. I will pay whatever you ask. Just deliver my brother and the donor safely. Just tell me what you want.'

The disguised voice did not reply for what must have seemed to him like an age. Then the reply came, 'Stand back and stand down,' followed by the call disconnecting.

'Stand back and stand down?' Chaz asked Axel in bemusement.

'I know. I heard some stupid politician saying something like that. He was an idiot. So I think this guy might relate to it,' Axel replied with a giggle.

Just then, Moses started to wave to get their attention. Little did they know that what he was about to say would change everything.

He held the phone in his hand and said, 'Some people are outside. They claim they are Eve's parents!'

## 47

The reaction by Christina was immediate. 'How is that possible? We have not released any information about her specifically.'

'I can answer that,' Axel replied. 'It may be because Moses asked if we had any information about the rescued captive's identities. I provided him with the records we recovered. "Eve" could have been included. Remember, there was only the identifying tattoo and, in some cases, a small photo. I have noticed lately that the internet was conducting its search. Perhaps that is where they saw something that made them believe we had their daughter. Many people are looking for lost children. I would imagine it is a long shot,' she added.

'Well, why don't we ask them? After all, they have travelled here hoping it is their daughter,' Des asked.

Christina responded, 'In her condition with such a severe case of amnesia, if we were to introduce people that think they are her parents and it's a mistake, it could set her back considerably.'

Charlie took charge. 'I agree. But we should still meet these people and see what they say.'

Chris nodded in agreement. 'Okay, let's hear what they have to say.'

Moses instructed whoever was on the phone to escort them in. A short time later, there was a tap on the door, and a soldier escorted a couple of middle-aged people inside.

The man appeared to be of European origin. He was of medium stature and appeared in good physical health. His hair was steely grey, cut militarily. He gave the impression of somebody of authority. The woman was a sharp contrast. She had the appearance of somebody from the tropics. At first glance, she was similar to a young Sophia Loren. Her eyes were bright with anticipation as they came forward to be greeted by Commandant Moses, who introduced himself.

'Before we begin, I would like to introduce Dr Christina Herrero. She is in charge of caring for all the people concerned.'

She came forward to greet the couple. As they shook her hand, the man began to speak. To her intrigue, although he spoke in English, he had a distinct French accent.

'Allow me to introduce us. This is my wife, Aubriella Palmet Blanchet. I am Eliott Blanchet. My wife has included her former surname out of respect for her heritage. She hails from Martinique,' he explained in a voice that reminded them of how Eve spoke.

'We are pleased to meet you. Have you journeyed far?' Chris asked.

'We flew in from Paris, where we live. As soon as we saw the photo of our daughter, we got on the first flight out,' he explained.

Christina turned to address the lady. 'We understand how you must feel, but you must understand these people have been through an extremely traumatic time which has affected them all differently,' as she tried to broach the subject of Eve's amnesia.

The man intervened. 'You will have to excuse my wife. Her English is not perfect,' as he translated into rapid French, which brought tears to her eyes immediately as she questioned him.

'She is asking if she has been harmed,' he asked.

Chris led them to where they could sit and continue the conversation. 'First, I would like to introduce you to the people involved with the rescue of the individuals.'

They all introduced themselves, and after Chris arranged for refreshments to be served, she began to explain the situation.

'The first thing I can assure you is that Eve is in good health.'

Eliott interrupted, 'Who is Eve?' he asked.

Christina recognised her error. 'Sorry. We have no idea what the names are of the people we have rescued. So when we don't know, we give them a name. In this case, we have called her Eve,' she explained.

He turned to his wife to explain. She began to chatter excitedly. He stopped and asked, 'Why did she not tell you her real name?'

There was an awkward silence before Chris replied. 'If this is your daughter, whatever she has been through had a profound effect on her memory. I am afraid she has amnesia and can't remember anything before her capture. Her mind is a complete blank as to her past,' she explained.

This time the woman must have understood and, in broken English, asked, 'Can we see her? I am sure she will remember us.'

'Before we can do that, we must confirm that you are her parents. Can you tell us what happened to her and how she disappeared? If she is not your daughter, and you were to meet her, it could cause her mental harm,' she explained.

He turned to his wife and spoke to her for a moment. She nodded, and he began to tell their story.

# 48

**SAN MORITZ, SWITZERLAND,
1 YEAR AGO**

Estelle Palmet Blanchet cursed her bad luck. She knew it was her fault for trying to ski that black slope. They had told her it was too difficult. But did she believe them? No, of course not. Her foolhardy attitude had put her in this position as she massaged her leg where she had been stitched after colliding with a tree. The doctor had insisted that she rest and not try to travel. So going home was not an option, just as well; she could hear her dad telling her that, for the umpteen time, she was 'A risk taker!'

'Probably true,' she mumbled, massaging her injured leg.

Finally, she got so bored that she decided to hobble down to the bar where all the skiers gathered for their après-ski drinks.

She knew many of the young people gathered there. Being from a wealthy family, she had been coming here since an early age. Her father was an excellent skier and used to accompany her when she was younger. But lately, he had been busy, which suited her. At eighteen, she wanted to spread her wings, and the opportunity to come alone was a new experience. Although she was still young, she knew how she looked and how men admired her. She enjoyed the attention, so when the young man approached her, although he was much older than her, at least in his late twenties, she had no interest.

But soon, she found him fascinating, unlike the young men who usually clustered around her, making childish remarks. He had an air of confidence and was interested in her background and family. When he asked about her injury, he showed concern and explained that when he was in the army, he was part of a ski squad and suffered many similar injuries.

As the evening wore on, she became more relaxed, so when he offered her a drink, she did not want to look like a kid and admit she was not allowed alcohol. However, she had tried a few times with her friends and smoked a few joints. So she agreed.

When he returned and handed her a cocktail, she took a sip and smiled. 'It tastes sweet; what's in it?' she asked.

'Nothing extreme, but it will help to take your mind off your injury,' he replied.

'It must be working. I am feeling better already,' she replied.

He smiled. 'That's exactly what is needed,' Eitan Zoabi replied.

When the doctor from the clinic where she had been treated for her wound contacted his boss to say she had found a suitable donor, Abdiel dispatched him immediately. The doctor in question was one of the medicos they had reached out to in a search for a suitable donor for his brother.

Her name had come up frequently. She was Dr. Amara Abioye and had a reputation for obtaining organs from dubious sources. She had told them about Estelle and how, when she had run blood tests on her, she had the rare type that his brother needed.

Eitan tried to caution his boss, explaining that she was not some homeless refugee without a family to search for her. This girl had to be from a wealthy family to holiday in a place like San Moritz. But his boss would not be deterred, especially when his brother was concerned.

'I don't care if she is the daughter of the Queen of England,' he raged. 'Do what you have to, but bring her back. I have the jet prepped and ready. I want you on it at once.'

So Eitan found himself sitting with this girl, preparing her for a trip into hell.

'I am starting to feel a little woozy,' she said as she finished the drink.

'Perhaps you shouldn't push it. I am sure you are anxious to get back on the slopes tomorrow.'

She nodded. 'I agree. Thank you for a lovely evening. I hope we meet again,' she said as she got up a little shakily and said goodnight.

He watched as she said her goodbyes to her friends and returned to her chalet.

When she got there, she began to feel like she was feeling out of touch with reality. By the time she got undressed and was in bed, the room was spinning. After what seemed like forever, she fell asleep, yet still felt like she was in a dream. She had the impression she was being carried. She could see Eitan's face floating above her line of sight. There was snow everywhere, yet she felt warm. Something told her she should be frightened, but she felt helpless to do anything. It was as if somebody had taken control of her thoughts. Then everything dissolved into darkness.

Eitan pulled the car alongside Abdiel's private jet and carefully transferred Estelle inside. He had sedated her again after he had taken her from the chalet. The drug the doctor had given him to put in her drink had messed with her head. As he was carrying her, she began to rant and rave. At that point, he had to administer an injection he had been given for the plane trip, but it must not have agreed with her as she began to foam at the mouth. He was terrified that she would die before they landed. Dr. Amara had accompanied them and assured him she would be fine.

'It won't affect the quality of her organs,' she informed him heartlessly.

He looked at the doctor with disgust. He would gladly have cut her up for pleasure at that moment. But she had negotiated a deal with Abdiel to fund a plan to provide suitable donors for people who wanted to be assured of a donor if needed. She was a bottom feeder. Only after the money, at least he was honest with himself. These people meant nothing to him, especially the women. Always stuck up and thought they were better than him. Just like his whore sister, who had begged for mercy as she was bundled into a van.

'She deserves what she has coming,' he replied, prodding the unconscious girl beside him as the plane became airborne.

# 49

**PRESENT DAY.**

Eliott Blanchet concluded what little they knew about their daughter's disappearance.

'A search was mounted, but she had vanished without a trace. She was last seen the night before her disappearance relaxing with her friends in the bar and was seen going home alone to her chalet. One of her pals went the following day to see if she needed anything. But her room was deserted, and her bed seemed to have been slept in. There was no sign of a struggle, plus all of her clothes appeared to be there.

At first, they thought she had wandered outside and got disoriented, but finally, the police were contacted. We flew out the next day. But nothing turned up. The police expected we would receive a ransom call if she had been abducted. But again, nothing. We engaged private detectives, but they turned up empty. We had all but given up hope until we were contacted by people who knew her and saw her picture on the website with all the people recovered by yourselves. And now we are here.'

Eve's mother began to sob again, and her husband comforted her.

Christina decided to explain the situation. 'We treat this girl with such caution because she has suffered an extreme mental episode. You may wonder why we question you so much. It is because we can't ask her. With trauma like this, she mustn't be forced. Too much pressure on her to recall what happened to her could have the reverse effect, sending her into a catatonic state.'

'Are you saying we can't see her?' her father pleaded.

'No. I want you to understand that there is every chance she won't recognise you. And it is important that you don't force the issue. Can you handle that?' she asked.

They nodded vigorously. 'Anything. We just want to see her.'

Chris paused. 'She usually joins us around this time. We encourage her to join in our search for the ones responsible. Let us assume she does not recognise you at once. I will introduce you as parents who are looking for their daughter. I will use your real names. But don't expect miracles. Things like this can take some time to resolve themselves.'

They waited anxiously for Eve to arrive. Christina had gone to fetch her, and as they appeared and her parents caught the first sight of their daughter, her mother could not help herself from gasping when she appeared.

Eve did as she usually did and greeted everybody. When she arrived at her parents, she looked at Christina, puzzled.

'This is Eliott and Aubriella Blanchet. They are here searching for their daughter. They were hoping we could help,' then waited for her reaction.

Eve looked at them with a sad expression. 'That must be terrible,' she commiserated.

Her mother could not contain herself and blurted out, '*C'est le pire moment de ma vie*. It is the worst time of my life,' she cried.

'*Tu parles français! Je viens de découvrir ça moi aussi*. You speak French! I have just discovered I speak it also,' she replied.

Christina could see that this was confusing her, so she intervened.

'They will be staying with us for a short time. Perhaps we can chat together later. But right now, I have to speak to them in private. You and the others carry on while I show them where they are staying.'

Eve said her goodbyes as her parents reluctantly followed Chris.

A cry from Axel startled the group. 'It is working!' she yelled. 'Come and look.'

They crowded around to see what she was talking about. 'What?' Des asked.

'The share price of Masadalink has tanked,' she replied. The puzzled looks prompted her to explain, 'When we started to short the share, some hedge funds followed suit, which started many people to get concerned about their crypto investments, resulting in a rush of withdrawals. That must have been the death knell. If I am correct and this is a Ponzi scheme, he can only run. And guess what? His interface just went dark.'

'So what does that mean?' Charlie asked.

'It means that the first part of the plan is working. At this moment, I would bet that Abdiel Mizrahi is sitting comfortably in his new residence with his spoils secured in a hard wallet, locked in some safe place.'

'Are you saying he has got away with all the money? By this time, he could have it in some Swiss bank account,' Des cried.

'You are not listening. He would not have any of his money in traceable currency. Regardless of the stories you read about Swiss bank accounts, they are not as secure as before. The reach of governments to look into banking practices in any country makes it very hard to hide currency. He will have the bulk of his assets in crypto. Of that, I can assure you.'

'So, how do we find him?'

'Leave that to me. I will have him when he reaches out to the outside world,' she replied.

'Then what do we do?' Des asked. He was chomping at the bit to get into action.

'I've got a plan for that,' she replied with a sly grin.

# 50

Eitan was sitting in the coffee shop, still keeping watch on the clinic. The only movement he had seen was the African soldier who was obviously in command, who came and went frequently.

On the daily newscast, which had blanket coverage of the events, he discovered his name was Commander Moses Khumalo of national security and that he had been put in charge of the investigation. He still needed to learn how this guy was involved with the crew behind the extortion. As he sat there, his phone rang.

'Can you talk?' Abdiel asked.

'Hold on. I am just stepping outside,' he replied as he nodded to the waitress and stepped out into the car park. 'Go ahead.'

'As I suspected, things have come to a head sooner than I expected, so I am going dark. You already know how to proceed. My problem is that I am waiting for them to come back to me about my brother's exchange,' he explained.

Eitan decided that it was time to take charge. 'All right, it is time to take the initiative. Please leave it to me. I will make contact. But I am sure eventually they will want to talk to you.'

Relieved, Abdiel replied, 'If you think you can do that, fine. But do you think they will talk to you?'

'I am certain. There is an Amazonian bitch that would be happy to talk to me. I will be in touch. Enjoy the sun,' he finished the call. He stood for a moment, then started to dial a number he never thought he would. 'Fuck it,' he muttered as it began to ring.

'Hello, Command post,' a stern voice answered.

'Put me through to Commander Moses Khumalo. Tell him I have important information about the recent events involving The Umbrella organisation.'

'Hold the line,' as he was placed on hold. He knew by this time they would be scrambling to trace this call, which was useless as it was a satellite phone.

'Putting you through now,' the voice informed him.

A booming voice answered. 'Who is this?' he demanded.

'Commandant Moses, I presume you are trying to trace this call. You can't trace this phone. So let me save us a lot of time. I want to speak to the leader of The Umbrella Organisation.'

'I have no idea who you are talking about,' Moses replied.

'I will save us both time. I am speaking about the The Wonder Woman lookalike that gassed me.'

On hearing this, he glanced at Aurora. She looked to Chaz, who nodded for her to take it. She moved closer to the speaker. 'What do you want with me?'

'At last, I have the voice of the first woman to trick me,' he replied mockingly.

'You must be mixing with the wrong type of women, shit-for-brains,' she snapped back.

'Quite a smart mouth. But better we stick to the business at hand. We can carry on this private conversation when next we meet face-to-face.'

Before she could respond, he carried on.

'Thanks to your efforts, Masadalink has shut its doors. But I am sure you already know that. My employer, of course, is innocent of any crime and will defend this. But in the interim, he is removing himself to a secure location. The contact connections you have for him are redundant. Until he has established a secure connection to the outside, he asks that you contact him on the number of this device. By now, your clever tech guy has hacked.'

Axel nodded in response. Eitan took the silence as a nod for him to continue.

'Commander Moses, I will leave this device at a secure location to save time. Any calls to it will be bounced around long enough for us to have an hour-long conversation. All my boss wants is his brother's safe and secure return.'

'Does that include anybody else?' Aurora responded.

There was silence, and then Eitan came back.

'I do not know what arrangements Mr Mizrahi has discussed with you. I will await your call to proceed with whatever you decide,' and he hung up.

# 51

'Well, that was interesting. It would seem they believe this Umbrella crew business that the internet is talking about,' Charlie responded.

'Or whatever name is the flavour of the day,' Des retorted. 'More to the point, how did they know we're here together?'

'I can answer that,' Axel replied. 'With all the activity I have been creating, it was only a matter of time before they connected the dots.'

'How do you know that?'

'Because that's what I would do. The only difference is that I would have found you within hours. In any case, I needed the company to collapse to follow the money trail.'

'But I thought cryptocurrency could not be traced?' Chaz asked.

'Correct. Technically, you are right. However, you must remember that cryptocurrency is data. Massive amounts of it. And when you move a lot of it quickly, it leaves a signature if you know where to look.'

'Let me guess, you have found it.'

'As soon as his company went dark, data flow into one country increased by a thousandfold. That country was Aruba. It is an old Dutch colony island, one of three. Technically, they are still under Dutch control, but they have self-governed for a long time.'

'Can you locate where he is holed up?'

'Let's not get ahead of ourselves. Stick to the plan. We need to proceed with the sting. How are we coming with the proof of life?' she asked Christina, who was engrossed in something she was reading.

'Sorry. I was looking over my notes from speaking to the Blanchet family. I just encountered something odd.' Turning her attention to Moses, she continued, 'Her father had the police report from Switzerland on his phone. What was that doctor's name supposedly running the show for Mizrahi?'

He turned to his computer and quickly searched, 'Amara Abioye,' he replied.

Christina just held up her notes for all to see. The doctor who treated their daughter for her ski injury was noted on her chart as Dr Amara Abioye.

'Well, sure looks like she was a lot more involved than simply overseeing the care of the victims,' Charlie responded.

At the same time, Moses was on the phone giving orders for her to be picked up.

'Is she not under arrest?' Charlie asked.

'She was. But she had the best lawyer in South Africa representing her. She was released on a bond of one million dollars and surrendered her passport. But don't worry. I have had her under surveillance. She won't be getting out again anytime soon,' Moses assured them.

Three hours later, she was escorted into Moses' office. As soon as she was seated, Moses became his most charming.

'I am sorry for inconveniencing you again. I know you have been most helpful with locating relatives of the victims.'

'I did not know anything about that. As I told you, I believed we were helping them escape,' she responded indignantly.

'That's okay. We would like you to try and help us identify one of the captives,' he explained.

A concerned look flitted across her face. 'I am not sure I can help. I was mainly involved in the administration.'

'Let's take a look, shall we?' he said as he escorted her into the clinic. They entered a room with a large mirror covering almost the whole wall. 'This is an observation room. This is a one-way mirror where patients can be observed without disturbing them. When activated, we can see into the other room where the patients are kept. In a moment, I will switch it on. Just let me know if you recognise the person on the other side. They will be in the company of doctors, but nobody can see you,' he assured her.

Amara glanced at him, but his expression gave nothing away.

'Are you ready?' he asked. She nodded reluctantly.

He activated the mirror. She was immediately greeted by seeing Eve sitting and chatting with people she did not recognise. Her expression froze at the sight of her victim as she struggled to regain her composure.

'No, sorry, I don't recognise anybody,' she replied hoarsely.

'Then how do you explain treating her in the clinic in Switzerland for a leg injury less than a year ago? And how do you explain your signature on her treatment card? Also, this is your file from Interpol. They are anxious to discover why you vanished the same day this girl was kidnapped.'

He placed the documents from the police report in front of her. She could not stop shaking and began to bluster all kinds of denials.

'Place her under arrest and take her to the interrogation room,' Moses instructed two female guards who had been waiting outside.

'No question she knows the game is up. She almost dropped when she saw her. She hasn't admitted it yet, but she will,' Moses assured the crew as he delivered the news.

'Well, there is no doubt that Eve is the Blanchet's daughter,' Charlie added.

Chris nodded. 'I agree. I will still run a DNA test. But I have no doubt. So how do we use this woman to our advantage?'

It was Charlie who provided the answer. 'Thanks to this, we have already solved one part of our proof of life problem.' Before they could question him, he continued, 'Moses, do you think you could persuade this person to cooperate with us?'

His expression said it all. 'She will do whatever you ask. The prison I can send her to is enough to convince her,' he assured them.

'Great. Christina, now all we need you to do is rig up the brother enough to convince this Amara woman that he is alive!'

# 52

It took little convincing for Amara to start talking.

She knew well what Moses could do to her life in the future. She admitted that she accidentally discovered the rare blood type while treating a patient. At that time, she had a side deal as a connecter in the organ donor business. She had been contacted by Abdiel Mizrahi, whose brother needed a kidney transplant urgently, but his rare blood type made his chances slim, even in the black market.

'So when I discovered this girl, I took the opportunity to achieve my dream,' she said.

Moses relayed this information back to the crew. 'And this is where the idea started to create a bank of suitable donors to be kept available for those that could afford it. Here in Africa is an endless supply, and to top it all, her justification for this was, and I quote, "I wanted to distribute the organs that were going to be wasted. And help the people that deserved them."'

Moses stopped for a moment to get his breath. Getting the information and making sure what she was saying was true had taken some time, but the threat of being handed over to Interpol with this crime hanging over her head had worked.

'She was smart enough to know her only chance was here in this country where a little money could change things. So when I told her I wanted her to help provide proof of the life of Mizrahi's brother, she immediately agreed, not at all surprised we were planning to ransom his brother and possibly the donor.'

'She is living proof that Idi Amin had children!' said Des.

Christina intervened, ' I may have solved the problem of how we bring the dead back to life.'

She asked them to come to a drawing board as she illustrated her plan.

'Will it work?' Chaz asked.

'I guess that depends on how much she wants to verify. A lot will depend on how she views what she sees,' she replied.

# 53

Amara Abioye was escorted from her holding cell to a comfortable room with armchairs, with soft music in the background. She was only seated a moment when a young white woman entered. Amara recognised her as one of the people who had been speaking to the young girl she was so shocked to see alive.

'Hello, I am Dr Christina Herrero,' she said, as she shook her hand. 'It is so nice to meet a doctor that sees the bigger picture.' Amara looked confused. 'Let's have coffee and talk. I need to speak to someone who believes in helping the right people.'

The coffee seemed to arrive by magic. 'Let me first explain why I need your help at this time,' Christina continued. 'I am under a lot of pressure from this Moses character to release the donor. But I will hold Moses off if I can convince Mizrahi to pay sufficient for his brother and the donor. This money will help the people who can pay for donors. At the same time, we can weed out those that would have no chance in the real world and help those that deserve saving. If we are to save Levi, we must act quickly,' now pausing to sip her coffee.

Amara was in shock. Not able to believe her ears. Was this woman really on her side? 'How can I help?" she asked eagerly.

Christina caught up with the rest of the crew after she had returned from her meeting with Amara.

'I can't believe it! She really believes in this stuff. She could not have been more helpful. We are recording the Proof of Life this afternoon. Wish me luck,' she said.

'Well, it looks like Des's suggestion was right this time. She accepted that we were crooks, so as he suggested, the best approach was convincing her that we think the same as she does. And it looks like it worked,' Charlie added.

Des smirked. 'Always putting the little brother down. What do you mean, this time?'

'Sorry, brother. You are right,' Charlie said. 'So Christina, what is the plan? How do you convince her Levi is alive?'

Chris replied, 'I have a plan, but I need somebody's help,' glancing at Desmond.

# 54

Christina collected Amara from her room, greeting her warmly as if they were best friends.

'Everything is ready. As we discussed, we will be filming, so be your natural self. All you are verifying is that we have the Donor and Levi and confirm they are safe and sound. Are you ready?' she asked.

'Lead on,' was her reply.

They entered the pre-op area in the operating theatre, where the doctors and nurses gathered before surgery. They were followed by a big man wearing an oversized white coat, making him look like a giant snowman. He was filming them with a handheld device.

'We will begin by showing you the donor again. Although you have seen her, this is so you can confirm with Mr Mizrahi. Are you ready?'

Amara nodded, then realised she had to speak. 'Yes,' she replied.

They went to a similar mirror as before. 'Ready?' Christina asked.

Amara nodded, and the mirror became a window. Behind, she saw Estelle conversing with a tall, athletic woman with a similar complexion.

'Is that the subject?'

'Yes, that is the girl I sourced in Switzerland. Her name is Estelle Palmet Blanchet, and as you can see, she is in perfect condition,' she replied.

Then they moved to a glass cubical where the glass was of the type that, with the press of a button, you could make it transparent or opaque. Christina activated the mirror where Amara was presented with a sight that took her breath away.

Levi was lying on a hospital bed with his back slightly elevated. He was connected to all types of monitors. An Oxygen mask covered his face. She could hear the pump functioning as she watched his chest rise and fall in rhythm with the pump.

'I wanted you to see how important it was that he receives the transplant as soon as possible. As you can see, we have him in a sterile area in his present condition. A simple cold would be enough to finish him,' Christina explained to the shell-shocked woman beside her.

'How bad is he?' was all she could ask.

'If you observe the monitors, he is stable at the moment. But he must proceed with the transplant as soon as possible to have the best chance of success. Do you agree?'

Amara stood there, switching between the monitors and the gently breathing Levi. She suddenly realised she had been spoken to, and the camera focused on her actions.

'Of course. Based on these readings, I agree that he is functioning well at the moment, but as the doctor has said, the sooner he is operated on, the better.'

'Thank you for that, Dr Amara. We are concluding the recording now,' giving the slashed throat signal to cut.

After Christina escorted Amara back to her room, she left her in her room to herself, explaining that she had to help with the video.

The crew watched it and gave their critique. But all agreed that it could work.

'You could have tried to be a little less healthy. The balloon under Levi's shirt could hardly keep up.'

They were kidding Desmond, who had provided the vital signs to operate the monitors.

'You can all piss off! Why am I always the one to get stuck with the shit jobs?' he complained.

But in reality, he was glad to have something to do. He was so bored that he had struck up a friendship with Estelle's dad and had been sitting and talking about anything other than his terrible situation.

They watched his daughter chatting in French with her mother without showing any recognition. Charlie brought them back to the moment.

'Okay, it is time we made a phone call.'

# 55

'Have you established contact with your employer?' the digitally altered voice asked Eitan.

This sound was starting to grate on his nerves. 'Yes,' he replied.

The voice continued. 'We are about to send you a video file. It contains verification of life for Mr Mizrahi's brother and the item. A reliable source will verify it. Before you ask who, you will be satisfied. She is one of yours. Tell Mr Mizrahi when he watches the video to heed her words. Time is of the essence, or all will be in vain. We will call this number tomorrow same time. Ensure he can be patched through and is prepared to pay heavily for his futile rescue attempt. Are we clear?'

Eitan had only one question. 'Who is this she?'

'The doctor that provided the item,' Axel replied, then cut the connection.

'Okay, the game is afoot.' Charlie announced. 'Everybody take a break, and we will regroup back here in one hour.'

Charlie took a deep breath and stepped outside to gather his thoughts. He was getting a bad feeling about all of this. He felt like a circus performer spinning plates on sticks, and they were starting to wobble because he was over-stretching himself. This situation they found themselves in had too many facets.

They were embroiled in what had started as helping a friend rescue somebody they thought was in danger, and now had turned into an international incident.

Then Des, as usual, in his quest to satisfy their dad, had chanced upon a computer genius on a personal vendetta to avenge her father, clear his name and at the same time destroy the person responsible, who by chance is also the person behind all this human organ business. If it were not for Des, who always seemed to be the catalyst for their adventures, he would not have believed it.

He glanced toward a window where he could see his brother in deep conversation with Estelle's father. Who was now starting to remind him a little of Peter Sellers in his role as Inspector Clouseau in *The Pink Panther* movies. Which made him smile. Des seemed to be helping this poor guy through a terrible time.

Then he realised something that had been niggling him. *Who is this guy that seemed to have it in for Aurora?*

Deciding to investigate more, he found her together with Axel in deep conversation.

'There you are. I was trying to understand how Axel intended to get the money from this shithead,' she explained.

'We can get to that in a moment. What can you tell me about this guy you ran in with at the hospital? He seems to have something against you?'

She shrugged. 'He was the one in charge, for sure; they all moved at his commands. He looked like an ex-military. He certainly was full of confidence. I guess he did not like being bested by a girl.'

'Why don't you ask that doctor? She is sure to know all about him?' Axel suggested.

'Good idea, let's go and see what she has to say.'

Amara was watching TV with a drink in her hand when they entered her room.

'We would like to ask you a few questions,' Charlie informed her.

'Where is Christina? ' she asked in a worried voice.

'She is busy. What we want to ask you is, who would you say was in charge of security for the operation here in Africa?' he asked.

Her face paled considerably. 'The Devil himself. His name is Eitan Zoabi. He is an ex-Mossad, but he was even too ruthless for them; at least, that's what Mizrahi said. And I believe him. That beast treated those poor people as if they were nothing. I am just glad you caught him. He terrifies me,' she said, hugging herself in fear.

They thanked her and returned to the operations room. Which also doubled as a general gathering area.

'I am not happy that this guy is still on the loose, especially if he is still here in Africa. I wonder if Moses has any news?' Charlie said.

He then called Moses at his office and asked him to join them.

# 56

Charlie explained the doctor's reaction to this guy, Eitan Zoabi, who they also believed was the guy on the phone that had shown such interest in Aurora.

Moses then rang someone in his department and gave them Eitan's details. 'This won't take long to check, so what do you have in mind?' he asked.

Charlie began. 'This guy bothers me. He managed to escape your security while still drugged, yet hung around instead of vanishing. This guy is the real deal, and the way he spoke to Aurora, I don't think she is on his Christmas card list. We must track him down before he returns the favour.'

'I believe I can help with that.' Axel cried, jumping up from her laptop. 'Always trust human nature. Fools always take the 'usual path'; I've got them. Mizrahi's new location and Eitan's satellite phone.'

Moses replied, 'Great news, but we already know how to locate the phone, but it has to be powered on.'

'Exactly, But Eitan got lazy and used the phone to contact his boss. When he did that, he invertedly gave me access to the location.'

'But how did you know when he was going to use the phone?' Moses asked.

'I just put in a link, a silent assassin, an old-fashioned wiretap, if you like, so when it was activated, it infiltrated the phone and piggybacked in on his signal.'

'You are a genius,' Charlie replied, in awe of her talent.

'I know. So, if he is true to form, after we call his phone for the new number to contact Mizrahi, I believe he will retrieve the phone for future use. Here is the location where the phone is at present. You guys can figure out what to do next,' as their phones dinged with the address.

'Leave this to me. We will put the place under surveillance; this guy must be taken down. I have just received his background sheet. He is one sick individual. No wonder he was involved in something as evil as this. He is blacklisted in his home country because of his treatment of prisoners. We need to get him while he is still here in Africa,' Moses said.

'How much time do you need to set this up?' Charlie asked.

'We can be ready in six hours.'

'Perfect. That will give us time to prepare for the next phase. Let's assume he believes the video is real and is prepared to pay. How much time do you need to put your plan into place?' he asked Axel.

'Providing we ask him for enough Bitcoin. If I am correct, the bulk of his holding will be in that currency. Remember, if he still has the stolen computers, that is what he produces. This will prompt him to open his hard wallet, where he will have the bulk of his wealth. He must have at least a couple of billion dollars in there. If we ask for a hundred million, that should open his wallet. Then I can activate the little surprise I sent when he stole his 50 million back that he thinks is real. With luck, he will never see his fortune again!'

## 57

**EVE**

Estelle awoke with a start. She'd had another of those nightmares, but strangely when she felt she was being carried or floating, she could hear the voice of that kind lady calling to her in French to come back. She could sense her reaching out for her.

Then as she opened her eyes, to her surprise, she found Aubriella sitting beside her, ready to comfort her.

She felt sad, not only for this woman but also for herself, who had no memory of her youth. They had formed a strong bond since she and her husband arrived. She had told her he had been in the army, and they had met while he was stationed in Martinique. When she questioned her about her missing daughter, she got a wistful look in her eye—describing somebody who seemed to have embraced life, adding that she reminded her of her daughter.

'Shall we see what's on television?' Aubriella asked.

They had got in the habit of watching programs in English and French to help her improve the little English she had.

They scanned the channels until she found an old movie with Edith Piaf, a famous French singer from the last war. As they watched, she began to sing one of her hits, 'Le Vi En Rose', Life in Pink. They joined in, singing along in French, following the lyrics in perfect harmony. Estelle could see her new friend looking at her strangely.

Aubriella whispered, 'You remember this song. It is from before you were born.'

Immediately she began to experience strange flashbacks. 'I remember somebody telling me that this song was supposed to refer to people looking at life through rose-coloured glasses.'

She could see her friend looking at her intensely, and then, in unison, they both put their hands up to their faces and formed fake glasses with their fingers around their eyes.

As her friend stared at her intensely, she found herself saying, 'We also used to make glasses like this.'

Then like a thunderbolt, she gasped. 'It was you!' then promptly passed out.

# 58

Aubriella was franticly trying to explain what had happened to Christina, who was attending to Estelle. Her parents and the others surrounded her while she monitored her condition and listened to what had transpired.

'Do you believe she remembered you?' she asked.

Aubriella nodded. 'It was a piece of music we listened to when she was little,' and indicated how they would make the fake rose glasses.

'It is usually some sound or sight that can trigger the memory. We have to be careful that she does not get an overload. That can sometimes trigger a relapse,' Chris cautioned.

'What should we do?' her father asked.

'The most important thing is to let her remember at her own pace. Don't prompt her. Allow her to deal with it herself.'

As they were speaking, she started to show signs of recovering consciousness.

'It would be best if there were only her parents here. I am not sure how she will react.'

Charlie nodded in agreement. 'Keep us posted as to her condition. We are just about to call Mizrahi. With some luck, Axel reckons that if he takes the bait, she will destroy him and his fortune.'

As they went about their plan. Desmond decided to keep her father company. 'Okay if I stay?' he asked.

Christina shrugged as she prepared for Estelle to recover. Just then, her eyes began to blink. Then she sat bolt upright with a yelp, her eyes darting in terror.

'Relax, you are fine. You have just had a big shock. Just take a second to gather your thoughts,' Christina advised her.

When she sighted her mother, she reacted at once. '*Maman*, Mom,' she whispered in French.

Her mother approached, and without hesitation, they embraced. Then she saw her father.

'*Mon Pere*, Dad,' as he put his arms around his wife and daughter.

After they hugged and held each other for a while, Christina intervened. 'You will have plenty of time to catch up later. Right now, we must assess how much you remember. Are you comfortable trying?' she asked.

Estelle separated from her parents while still grasping their hands, then nodded.

'Why don't you tell us what you remember? In your own words?' Christina encouraged the frightened girl.

She explained that her memory flooded back when she had recognised the Edith Piaf song. She said it was like downloading a movie at breakneck speed. She then went on to describe how her memory was patchy. She said there were blank spots.

Christina decided to push the issue. 'What do you remember about the events in Switzerland?'

She paused as if searching for words.

'I remember hurting my leg and the doctor treating me. Then later that night, feeling sorry for myself. I went to catch up with friends then... ' she paused as a horrified look crossed her face. 'That's when I met him.'

As she began to sob, Aubriella comforted her. She composed herself and continued to explain how this guy had befriended her and bought her a cocktail. She remembered going back to her room feeling very woozy. The next thing she remembered was being carried to what she thought was a big van. Then she was put on board a plane where he had spoken to her. She remembered his cruel words.

He said, 'You can forget the wonderful life, Princess. You are nothing other than an item now to be used for spare parts. This will help you to forget,' and injected her with something that made her pass out.

All she could remember after that was flashes of half-consciousness. She gasped and clasped at her side. When she felt the scar, she collapsed into tears again.

'I remember him laughing when he told me they were taking one of my kidneys!'

# 59

When Estelle calmed down, Christina paused momentarily, then began to speak.

'What I am about to tell you could get me disbarred from practising medicine. But you are entitled to know the truth.' She took a deep breath and continued. 'When they brought Levi Mizrahi here after his removal from the hospital...'

She could see the confused looks on her face.

'He is the reason you were abducted,' and went on to explain that she was a unique match for his blood type. 'When he arrived here, he was almost dead. I could see he only had hours left to live. So I decided to do something which is against everything we're taught in medicine. I removed your kidney and reinstalled it where it belonged. You are complete again. I have been monitoring the replant, and your body has recovered perfectly.'

There was silence for a moment. Then she was engulfed by Estelle and her parents, crying with gratitude for what she had done.

Elliot spoke, 'You are an angel. As far as we are concerned, our daughter was never operated on,' he assured her.

'Anyway, what's wrong with taking back what belonged to you in the first place?' Des added, which brought a laugh of relief.

Des left them to reconnect, excused himself, and headed to where they were preparing to make a phone call. He pulled Charlie aside and filled him in on what had transpired, including replacing the kidney.

'She did the right thing. Her secret is safe with us. I want to get my hands on that Eitan character,' he replied.

Des nodded in agreement. 'He better hope that her father does not get to him first. You need to check this guy out. He is an ex-French secret service. He was in charge of an "Action Group". Part of the DBSE, Directorate General Security. Involved in "Opêration Satanique". They were the ones that sank the Greenpeace ship, *The Rainbow Warrior*.'

'I remember that! There was hell to pay for that if I remember,' Charlie replied.

'Correct. Two of his men were captured and sentenced to ten years. But were released within a few months. He is retired now, but from what he has told me, he is still well connected.'

Just then, Axel interrupted. 'We are ready to make the call.'

# 60

They were preparing to call Mizrahi when Moses strode into the room and everything changed.

'I have some guy outside claiming to be your brother. He demands to be let in. He looks like some official.'

'Did you say demanded?' Charlie asked. Moses nodded.

Charlie looked at Desmond, and then they yelped together. 'Vincent is here!'

They charged out to greet him, with a confused Moses in tow.

'What are you doing here?' Charlie asked, trying to embrace his brother, who immediately avoided his effort.

'Mind the suit. This humidity is ruining it,' he declared, in his usual courtroom manner.

'Bill. You came back also,' Des cried as he rushed over to his de facto father-in-law.

'How could I not? When the three Savage brothers get together, I usually find myself in the centre. Also, Maria insisted,' he added.

Back in the operations room, Vince was introduced to all. When they came to Axel, he fixed her with a glare.

'So this is the young lady that is on a vendetta and, I might add, the main reason I have made this arduous journey.'

The puzzled expression on their faces prompted him to continue.

'If I am correct, your objective is to destroy this individual?'

When she nodded, he asked her to explain the plan. After she was finished. He started to pace as if in front of a jury.

'So to recap. You intend to extract a little more money in the hope he will connect his cold wallet to the internet, and you can activate a bug you have planted there. Is that correct?'

She nodded again.

'If I understand this correctly, then all the crypto in that wallet will be lost?' He did not wait for a reply. He turned to Des. 'What do you see wrong with this plan?'

Without hesitation, he replied. 'The money is gone!'

They all started to speak, but Vincent Savage QC was not to be interrupted. Turning to Axel again, he asked. 'Can you locate where this fellow is holed up?'

She nodded.

'Now, I am not a Crypto expert, but I believe all that protects a hard wallet is a rather large password known only to this Mizrahi. And you only have twenty tries, or the wallet is sealed forever. Correct?'

Again, he got an agreement. Turning to Charlie, he asked, 'If you were faced with this problem, what would you do?'

Without hesitation, he gave a swift reply. 'I would persuade him to tell me.'

'Exactly!' roared Vince.

'What are you suggesting?' Axel asked.

'We take all of it,' he replied, then added, 'We'll make a plan for that!'

# 61

'Before you start, I considered going after the money. But this guy has an army behind him, and Moses' authority stops at the border. We would need a professional crew to go after him,' Charlie interjected.

'Perhaps you already know somebody that would like to help?' Vince suggested, glancing at Des, who quickly picked up what he was talking about at once.

'You are talking about Elliott. I have been trying to get them to listen, but nobody listens to me,' he grumbled.

'You mean Estelle's father. How could he help? He is retired. All he wants is to reconnect with his daughter,' Charlie replied.

'Then let me ask you this: if you were him and were given a chance to confront the person responsible for what was done to his daughter, what would you do? No need to answer. You would do whatever it takes.'

Chaz nodded in agreement.

Vince continued. 'When Bill filled me in on what was happening, I did a search on this guy and came up empty. He is a black hole as far as information goes after the Greenpeace sinking and the subsequent blowback. He vanished from all records, along with the elite team he led. I had to pull some big favours to uncover what little I could. He and his unit are the tip of the spear, completely outside of any official department. They operate autonomously, not unlike Mossad. It is said they answer only to the highest reaches of government. So yes, I think he can help.'

Desmond decided to have his say. 'Vince is right. This is not how we handle things. Even if we succeed, as soon as he discovers his brother is dead, and if he can't get at his money, he will go *meshugge*, ballistic crazy. I am sure he is not without resources, and let's not forget his pal, Eitan. If we deal with this guy, we must put him down for good.'

'What are you suggesting, kill him?' Aurora asked, glancing at her partner, Sun Yee.

'We don't kill people unless they try to kill us first. But there is nothing wrong with introducing him to somebody that might not feel the same. I think it is time we do what we do best. Go on the offensive,' Charlie replied.

It was Sun Yee that decided for everybody. 'I have seen how these brothers work. I don't know how, but when they are together, things go bad for the people in front of them. I, for one, want to finish this guy for good,' which got nods of approval from the rest.

'So, what next?' Des asked?

'We ask Elliot if he is interested in chatting with the person that abducted his daughter,' replied Vincent.

It was decided that he would speak to him, joined by Des, Christina, and Axel, as she could answer any questions about this guy's location.

Vince continued. 'But first, we must buy some time. When you contact this guy, we must convince him that preparing his brother for transport will take time. We will need at least one week. You must convince him that his brother needs this time to be ready for transport.'

Christina spoke. 'I have been thinking about that. He will want the donor as well. With that in mind, I have a plan. It will involve using my new best friend, Dr Amara Abioye.'

When she outlined her plan, the audacity surprised and delighted them.

It was decided that while Vincent spoke to Elliott, she would prepare Dr Amara for her role in the plan.

# 62

They arranged to meet Elliot in the open courtyard where Des and he had been conversing. After Vincent had been introduced, he began by inquiring how Estelle was faring.

His sharp mind detected their mood. 'She is improving quickly now. Ever since she recognised that song, her memory has returned. Every day is an improvement. But that is not why you have brought me here today. You have something else on your mind.'

'You are correct. Perhaps I should begin by explaining what has brought us all together.'

Vince began to outline what had transpired since the rescue of his daughter and all the events that had brought them to today.

'So, if your father had not asked you to track down some online scammer, you would not have met this young lady,' Elliot said, indicating Axel. 'And the connection would never have been made as to who tipped off Christina about my daughter, Estelle,' pointing to his friend Des, who nodded sheepishly.

Vince continued to explain. 'When Desmond mentioned your unique background, due to my position, I was able to reach out and make some discreet enquiries. As you can guess, I was told very little, only that the subject of what you did was definitely off the record. Nonetheless, I believe you're ideally suited for what we are about to discuss. I want to start with a question: Would you be interested if we could put you in front of the person responsible for what happened to your daughter?

Elliot's expression hardened, and any sign of the comedic Peter Sellers lookalike vanished. '*Pointez-moi et appuyez sur la gâchette.* Point me and pull the trigger,' he growled.

Vince then went on to outline what they had in mind. Then paused for Elliot's reaction.

'I will need a few days to get my team here.' He then turned to Axel. 'Can you show me where they are hiding?'

She explained that she had traced them to a well-guarded estate on the Island of Aruba, showing him the maps she had obtained.

After he had inspected them, he replied, 'We will set up here to prepare. Then infill to a safe house we have near Caracas in Venezuela. From there, it is only a short hop across to Aruba.' He spoke as if he was arranging a picnic.

'Great news. If you need transport, Christiana's dad has a plane,' Des replied excitedly.

A sly grin crossed Elliot's face, and he made a joke for the first time since they met. 'That's no problem. France has a couple of them also.'

# 63

Dr Abioye was seated beside Christina. They were deep in conversation as they prepared for the satellite phone call to Mizrahi. They were like close colleagues discussing a problematic case.

'Are you ready to speak to Abdiel? He must believe you if we are to succeed,' Christina asked her.

'I am sure it won't be a problem. What you suggested makes perfect sense,' she replied, delighted that she was helping them in their scheme. That, coupled with the promise of Commander Moses forgetting her charges, helped her agree to help.

Christina nodded to Axel. 'Okay, we are ready?' she asked, and prompted her to place the call. It was answered almost on the first ring.'

'How is my brother?' was his first demand.

'I am putting someone on the line that will outline the plan,' Axel answered while handing the phone to Amara.

'Abdiel, this is Dr Amara. I am assisting Dr Herrero in preparing Levi for transport. They have asked me to explain how they want this to happen. Due to his delicate state of health, you will need an aircraft capable of accommodating the capsule he is being insulated in. You have seen it in the previous video.'

He interrupted, 'That is no problem. I have one standing by. What about the donor?'

Amara glanced at Chris, then continued, 'The doctor handling the treatment has decided that to avoid the difficulty of transporting a reluctant donor. They will remove the organs needed here and transport them in a sterile state. I agree, as this is the most common practice.'

'I don't care how you do it, as long as he has the new heart and lungs. So when do I send the plane?' he demanded.

She again looked at Christina for assurance, then continued. 'They are removing them in three days and will be ready to transport them together in seven days.'

He exploded in anger. 'What! A week. Why the delay?' he demanded.

Vincent stepped in. 'You are in no position to be making demands. This would have been concluded without your friend Eitan's futile attempt to double-cross us. Perhaps you would prefer we forget the whole thing and we give your brother to the authorities?'

Abdiel quickly pulled his neck in. 'Who am I talking to now? he asked in a subdued voice.

'My name is of no concern. All you should be doing is preparing for the transfer. I presume you are ready to pay the ransom?' he asked in his best barrister voice.

'Yes,' he replied.

'Then I suggest you don't mess things up again. You can contact us on this sat phone link to tell us when you are ready and where you want your brother delivered, ' and cut the connection.

Christina hugged Amara as Moses' guards prepared to escort her back to her rooms, where she was being held under house arrest.

'Well done. With his money, we will be able to pursue our objectives. I will come and visit you later, my friend,' as they separated and she was led away.

'Unbelievable. She really thinks you will kill that girl for money. She needs to have her organs taken out. The only problem is that she has not got a heart,' Des muttered as she vanished from sight.

# 64

Two days later, Elliot's men arrived. As they were introduced, everybody was told all team members were only known by a code name. There were five of them they were called: Red, Yellow, Green, Black, Silver.

They noticed they called Elliot 'Le Blu', the blue.

When Des tried to engage them in conversation, he was greeted with silence.

'Not very talkative,' he remarked. His friend Elliot explained why.

'They don't want to have to answer any questions,' and when Des looked confused, he continued. 'The reason is that they don't what to have to lie to you.'

So, from that point on until their departure, they kept to themselves, going over plans with Elliot. Most of their time was spent with Axel reviewing Mizrahi's place's layout.

'I can see that many of these maps are in real-time. How are you achieving this?' Elliot enquired.

'I "borrowed" some time from some satellites when they were in the vicinity,' she replied.

Moses, who was coordinating his search for Eitan with them, frowned. 'Just as long it is not the Americans.'

Axel's face reddened as she avoided his gaze, typing furiously on her keyboard.

Elliot interjected. 'Can you show me the latest,' he asked.

She quickly pulled up a map. 'This is from late yesterday. You can see a much larger number of people over the last week. Which coordinates with his arrival.'

Elliot nodded, then turned to the group. 'We need to go over the final details. Our team will infill tomorrow to be in position before the seven days are up.'

'So, what is our part?' Des asked.

'I am sorry, my friend, but we operate as a unit. Your presence would put the operation in danger. This is what we do. Let us do our job.'

There were grumblings from the crew, but he was insistent. Finally, Vincent took charge.

'He is right. You have done enough. Now leave it to the professionals. Elliot will recover the hard wallet and the password.'

Axel interjected. 'Would it not be better if I was there in case of any problems?'

It was Elliot that replied. 'Your help can be delivered electronically. You can do more seated here at your desk,' he assured her.

Reluctantly they agreed as Elliot and his men returned to where they were preparing for their departure.

The following day the crew departed with as little fuss as they did when they arrived. They were loaded into the staff bus to avoid prying eyes, which came and went throughout the day. Goodbyes were said, and they were given the thumbs up from everybody as they left dressed in staff attire.

During that and the following day, the rest of the crew amused themselves, discussing what they could do to prepare for the outcome of Elliot's raid. Nobody noticed that Aurora was preparing to march to the sound of a different drum.

# 65

Eitan was sipping his coffee as he watched the clinic, as he did every day.

He observed Commander Moses's squad leave to relieve the guys that were watching the site he had left the satellite phone in the hope that he would retrieve it. He smiled to himself. *Fool me once,* he thought. He was still angry after receiving the phone call from his boss telling the arrangements he had agreed to.

He cursed under his breath. Seven days! He was sure they had no chance of locating him, but every day here put him in even more danger. He did not trust this Umbrella crew one bit. Nothing was going in the right direction. If Abdiel's brother had died, they would be sitting in Aruba now, sipping Pina Coladas, commiserating with his boss on the tragic loss of his drop-kick brother.

He cursed again under his breath. He was just about to finish his coffee and leave, when out of the corner of his eye, he spotted the gates open again, and a dark-coloured Range Rover drove out and turned in the direction of the departing squad. The windows were heavily tinted, but the driving door window was open, and as the person inside began closing it, he gasped.

It was her! The Amazon woman that had made a fool of him. He gulped down his coffee and darted outside with his phone in his hand.

A gruff voice answered, and Eitan said, 'There is a dark-coloured Range Rover going in the same direction as the soldiers. Follow it, and whatever you do, don't lose it, I am on my way.'

He hung up and made a dash for his car.

On the other end of the call, a young African youth hung up his mobile, signalling to a similar-aged guy. 'We are on.'

Putting on his helmet and mounting a motorcycle, as his pal did the same. The white dude had hired them to keep watch on Moses' men. They quickly took off in the direction of the squad, as they always took the same route, and quickly spotted the Range Rover.

Inside the car, Aurora was feeling uncomfortable about what she was doing. She knew Sun Yee would be very angry, but she had convinced herself she could be of assistance if Eitan showed up. After all, she was the only one that had seen him face-to-face. The troops only had a grainy picture. This was her justification.

*What could go wrong?* she mumbled to herself.

Just then, a motorcycle swerved in front of her. It did not bother her as erratic driving around Johannesburg was commonplace. He was talking on his mobile, so she gave him a honk on her horn. He waved and sped up.

'Have you found her?' Eitan asked 'She is just honking for me to move out of her way.'

'For fuck sake, don't let her twig she is being followed. Get out of sight. I will be with you shortly.'

Aurora followed the convoy to the location of the phone, parking in a side street where she had a view of the house. There she settled down to keep watch.

Four hours later, the squad was completing their noon change. She was considering calling it a day when another guy pulled into the street and parked his bike in front of her car. He dismounted and removed his helmet, shaking his curly hair. He was quite young and had a big smile on his face as he approached. He gave a big friendly wave and held up what appeared to be a map.

'Can you help, please? I don't read English very well,' gesturing at what he was holding.

He stood away from the window, indicating for her to open it so they could speak. She lowered the window and the guy held up what he was holding so she could read.

'Hold it closer,' she said.

Instead, he held it for her to take. As she reached for it, he grabbed her wrists and dropped down, pulling her against the door. At the same time, the opposite window exploded, and the passenger door was wrenched open. She felt a gun barrel pressed against her head, and the horror of what she had done swept over her as she recognised the voice, mocking her.

'Got you now bitch!'

# 66

'Aurora is gone!' Sun Yee yelled as she rushed to where they were relaxing.

Charlie was the first to react. 'Are you sure?' he asked.

'I thought she was acting oddly, so I checked on her. She took one of the cars this morning and followed the men going to relieve the lookouts watching Eitan's phone.'

'Have you tried calling her?'

'Yes,' she replied, 'it just goes to message bank. There is something wrong, she would have replied by now. I spoke to Moses, but there has been no sight of her.'

'We can track her car. Which one was it?' Axel asked.

They quickly established which car, and Axel promptly located it by its sat navigation signal.

'It is parked very close to where the sat phone is,' pointing to the location.

Moses leapt into action and contacted his men there. They were back on to him within minutes. He hung up the phone with a grim look on his face.

'It does not look good. The car is there with the keys in it. The window is broken, and there are a couple of blood drops. Nothing to suggest serious injury,' he hastily added.

'Do you think it could be a mugging?' Vincent asked.

Moses gave an adverse reaction. 'Very unlikely. Too close to where there was a police presence. Also, if it was a mugging, she would not be abducted. Street gangs are only after the valuables. My guess is that somebody recognised her and snatched her.'

'Eitan,' snarled Charlie. 'That guy had had a thing for her since she put one over on him.'

'She could be anywhere. We can put a bolo on her, but I doubt they would try any normal exit point,' Moses pointed out.

'I can track her,' came the voice of Sun Yee, thrusting a small device into Axel's hand.

It was a memory stick. She quickly plugged it into her laptop, and a tracking signal immediately filled her screen.

'I have got her. She is travelling in a vehicle that is heading in the direction of Pretoria,' Axel cried.

'Send me the directions; we are on our way,' Moses said, as she headed for the garage, quickly followed by Des and Charlie.

In the garage, there was a new Audi S8 parked near the entrance. Sun Yee pushed him aside as Charlie was about to take the driving seat.

'I will drive. You navigate.' Her tone indicated she was not taking no for an answer, as the car roared out in pursuit of her partner.

# 67

Aurora had a bag thrust over her head and her hands and feet tied with duct tape. Bundled into the back of what felt like a van, they shot off at speed. She was accompanied by the guy that had tricked her. He sat in silence, not reacting to her struggles.

In the front, Eitan was not so calm. He was struggling to contain himself. He could not believe his luck. Grabbing the phone, he made a call. The person answered at once.

'How soon can you be ready to fly?' Eitan demanded.

'Both pilots are here, and the plane is fuelled. All we need to do is file a flight plan,' returned the voice.

'No flight plan. Just be ready to take off as soon as we arrive. Two passengers, one reluctant, so be prepared,' as he cut the connection.

He then called his boss, who answered quickly, surprised to be hearing from his man.

'I am on my way to the jet. Call them and tell them to do exactly as I ask; I am bringing you a present,' he instructed.

'What are you talking about?'

'No time now. Just be assured I have the answer to all our prayers,' and cut the connection. 'How much further?' he asked the driver.

'Thirty minutes,' was the reply.

Several miles behind them, Sun Yee was concentrating on keeping the powerful Audi S8 on the road. 'Any idea where they are heading?' she asked as she struggled with the wheel.

Axel's voice came over the speaker. 'The only thing I can find is a private airport catering to the corporate clientele.'

'That has to be it. Send me the coordinates. How far are we out?' she asked.

'At the pace, you are going. You should be there within the hour,' Axel replied.

As she accelerated, Des gripped the seat. 'At this rate, we will be there before they arrive. That's if we survive,' as they narrowly avoided colliding with an overcrowded taxi bus.

Charlie hung up. 'He must be trying to fly her out of the country. I will contact Moses to see if he can close the airport,' as he hung on for dear life as Sun Yee overtook a semi-trailer with inches to spare.

In the back of the van, Aurora could feel the vehicle begin to slow, then felt them turn into an entrance. A short time later, they stopped, and she heard the side door opening. The smell of aviation fuel told her where they were. Lifting her out, she was carried by two of them up the stairs of an aircraft. She was bundled into a seat, and the hood was wrenched off her head. Eitan's face greeted her.

'Hope your journey has not been too uncomfortable. Just relax. We will be airborne shortly, and then we will endeavour to make your trip a little more comfortable,' he mocked.

She could not respond as her mouth was still gagged with a strip of tape. She could hear him arguing with the pilot about taking off without a flight plan. Finally, they agreed they would contact flight control when they passed out of South African air space.

Eitan turned back to her. 'We will be on our way shortly. So, relax. I have many surprises in store for you when we get to our destination,' he gloated as the pilots went through their pre-flight check.

In the Audi with Sun Yee On, Charlie had just received a call from Axel.

'Moses has been trying to close the airport without much joy. He has ascertained that Mizrahi has a Gulfstream III standing by at the airport, but they have not indicated they are going anywhere. They see no reason to detain them.'

'Looks like you are on your own,' Moses said. 'Our troops are at least an hour away.'

'There!' cried Des as he pointed to the road leading to the entrance to the airfield.

Inside the jet, the pilot had completed his checks. 'Ready for take-off,' he informed Eitan.

He sat opposite Aurora, reaching forward and wrenching the tape from her mouth. 'As soon as we are airborne. We can chat,' he said as he tightened her seatbelt. 'Can't be too careful. You are precious cargo...' as the jet began taxiing to the runway's end.

Sun Yee slid the powerful car onto the airfield entrance and sped toward the hangers. Suddenly, Charlie gestured in the direction of the runway.

'Look!' he said, pointing at a Gulfstream gathering speed. 'That has to be them.'

Without hesitation, Sun Yee wrenched the car toward the accelerating Jet. Her intention was obvious. She intended to try and cut them off as they hurtled in pursuit of the departing aircraft.

Inside the jet, the pilot shouted back over the noise of the engine. 'Some crazy person is chasing us in a car!'

Eitan released his seatbelt and pressed his face to the window to see the Audi fishtailing alongside the plane. He could see the people inside peering at him. He waved in mocking defiance as the pilot rotated and the jet rose gracefully into the air, leaving the Audi with its tyres smoking and its occupants watching in despair as the graceful aircraft disappeared into the clouds.

Sun Yee screamed in her mind. Aurora was gone!

# 68

As they climbed to their cruising altitude, Eitan released Aurora's seat belt.

'Your friends came to see you off. Unfortunately, they arrived too late. Now please stand and take your clothes off,' he instructed.

'Not a chance, you sick freak!' she challenged him.

'Don't flatter yourself,' he replied. 'I have no interest in you in that regard. But you must have a tracking device, which is how your friends found us so quickly. For that reason, I will have to search you.'

She struggled to her feet, hindered by the plastic ties restraining her. 'Touch me, and I will kill you!' she screamed.

'No more than I would have expected from you,' as he shot her with a Taser.

The shock flung her back in her seat, leaving her quivering as she tried to control her body. He waited until she slowly recovered. Then he hit her again.

This time it took her longer to recover. 'We can continue to do this until I rip them off you. Or you can comply. Your choice,' he challenged as he hovered over her with the device.

Realising she had little choice, she again struggled to her feet. 'If that is what you want, then you will have to remove these,' indicating the ties.

He shrugged and slit the restraints with a knife he held in his hand. At the same time, he kept the taser ready.

She stood defiantly, her athletic body towering over him, then slowly began to undress provocatively. She was only wearing jeans and a light shirt and was standing in her flimsy underwear in seconds. She hooked her fingers in her panties, cocking her head at him, she winked, making him even more uncomfortable.

'That's enough,' he growled.

'So what now?' she asked, placing her hands on her hips.

'This', he replied as he stepped forward and drove his fist into her solar plexus, driving the air out of her lungs.

She fell back into her seat, gasping for breath. He moved in front of her and delivered a crushing blow to the side of her head, knocking her unconscious.

'That's just for starters,' he snarled over her stricken body.

# 69

Sun Yee and the brothers arrived back with the bad news.

'They got away,' Charlie informed the anxious crew, waiting for the information.

Sun Yee went directly to Axel. 'Have you lost the signal?' she asked.

'It vanished shortly after you arrived at the airfield,' she replied. She shrugged. 'That is to be expected. It has a narrow range. No matter, we know where she has been taken. We must go and get her.'

They all started to speak at once. It was Vincent that called for calm.

'This changes everything. As soon as they have her secure, we can expect a call from them with demands. He will want to exchange his brother for her.'

Des burst in. 'How the hell are we going to exchange a dead man?'

'That is what we will have to figure out. But first, we must inform Elliot of the developments in case he mounts his attack,' Vince replied.

Charlie had already acted and was on the satellite phone with him. When he explained what had just happened, he spoke with Elliot briefly, then broke the connection.

'He will stand down until we have more information. He said they were just about ready. He had a helicopter fitted with long-range tanks. I said we would get back to him when we had a plan,' he informed them.

'He can forget about excluding us now. This has become our fight,' Des declared.

Charlie nodded. 'So, what is the plan?

For the next hour, they went over their options without much success. Finally, Vincent called a halt.

'This is how I see it. We have only one choice: to convince Mizrahi that we will negotiate but only on our terms. We have to convince him that trying to move his brother before the agreed time would put him at grave risk. This will give us some time to devise a plan of action.'

Des jumped in. 'So what do we do, wait for him to call and see what he wants?' he asked.

'No,' Vincent replied. 'We go on the attack and contact him first with our demands,' and outlined the germ of a plan that was developing in his mind.

# 70

The Gulfstream descended into a private airfield just outside of Oranjestad, the capital of Aruba. It was used exclusively by the various wealthy elements that made up the ultra-rich inhabitants of the Island.

Aurora was awake, feeling the effects of the beating she had received from the animal sitting across from her. He noticed her stirring.

'We are just arriving at your final destination,' he informed her as he looked out the window.

They burst through the clouds to see the tropical island stretched out below. The island was not very big, with an area of only 69 square miles.

'Where is that?' she asked, pretending that she and the rest of the crew had not discovered the location of his boss's hideout.

'I guess there is no reason not to tell you. We are arriving at the tropical island of Aruba. I am sure you will not be pleased here,' he gloated.

'Are you going to permit me to get dressed?' she asked.

'Why? It is hot, and I am sure that the men he has guarding the place will enjoy seeing what you have to offer,' he said, as he stood over her.

'Prick,' she said.

He quickly advanced, and she saw he was about to hit her again. As his fist smashed into her face just before she faded into darkness, she heard him scream like a banshee from the kick she had delivered between his legs, crushing his crown jewels.

The Jet touched down gently and taxied to where a Toyota Landcruiser was waiting, surrounded by a group of tough-looking mercenaries.

Aurora was recovering from his blow and smiled when she saw Eitan struggling to open the door due to his extreme discomfort from her well-placed kick.

A blast of ultra-hot tropical heat flooded the cabin as the door opened.

'On your feet, time for you to put on a show.'

He stepped back from the door, wincing as he moved his legs.

She stood and made a swift movement, causing him to react, again causing considerable pain. 'Make a move, and I will zap you again,' he warned, holding out the Taser in defence.

Aurora stood defiantly and stepped out into the bright Caribbean sunlight. Her appearance brought gasps from the assembled men awaiting their arrival.

Ignoring the wolf whistles, she descended the steps, the hot surface burning her feet. Ignoring the pain, she made her way to the waiting vehicle.

They seated her in the back with a man on each side.

'Keep looking at me, and I will give you what I gave him,' she said, nodding in the direction of Eitan waddling towards the car.

This brought a grin to their faces. But they stopped ogling her and kept their eyes front.

Their destination was only a short distance from the airport, and she was observing as much as she could until they turned into a large estate. The security was intense, with men posted all around. They stopped before the entrance of a large house with a large building attached. It had the appearance of a secure facility.

Before seeing any more, she was escorted into the house, followed by Eitan. Her first sight was of Abdiel Mizrahi greeting her.

He was decidedly unimpressive, of average height and a receding hairline. He looked like a college dropout.

'Who is this?' he asked.

'This is the answer to our prayers. This is the wench that spoiled our rescue plan,' Eitan declared.

'All he has done is brought trouble to your door,' Aurora snapped.

'Shut up, or I will shut you up,' Eitan threatened.

A confused Abdiel looked her up and down. 'Why is she undressed?' he asked.

'This Umbrella crew are very clever. I believe she has a tracking device somewhere on her. I checked her clothes, but we will need to scan her and them before I return them.'

He then explained how he had seized the opportunity to snatch her.

Finally, Mizrahi calmed down. 'So, they don't know where we are?'

Eitan smiled as he glanced at Aurora. 'No idea. But we should check her as soon as possible.'

They arranged for one of their technicians to scan her, who, after a careful inspection, as he enjoyed the opportunity to examine this beautiful creature, finally declared her clear.

Then Eitan outlined how they could trade her for his brother. Abdiel needed more convincing. 'What if they don't want her?'

'Believe me, if you could have seen how she and her girlfriend behaved to each other. That Asian chick will do anything for her return,' he assured him.

Just then, the phone rang.

# 71

They had decided on their plan of action. Which, in turn, was an extremely long shot but true to their style. They believed it was their best chance of recovering Aurora.

'He has no intention of releasing her,' Charlie assured them. 'This guy has hung around when he could have vanished. Just for the opportunity of getting his revenge. He will double-cross us the first chance he gets.'

'Agreed,' Vince replied, 'So we will have to double-cross him first.'

It went back and forth for a while until Sun Yee On spoke. 'It makes no matter what you decide, I will be going, and I will find Aurora on my own,' which prompted Desmond to jump in.

'What is happening here? All this planning. Have you forgotten that in the past, our plans have never gone as they should have, but we managed to figure it out? Enough talk. We follow Vincent's plan and clean up the mess as we go.'

Which resulted in the phone call. It was decided that Vincent should do the talking as that was his thing.

He snarled into the phone in his best barrister voice as soon as his call was answered. 'Put Mizrahi on,' he demanded.

Mizrahi responded, 'I am he. Who are you?' he asked, responding angrily.

'Who I am is of no concern. What is of concern is that you have tried to double-cross us for the second time. Do you want us to dispose of your brother,' he threatened.

Abdiel quickly changed his tune. 'That was not my idea. My concern is only my brother's safe return,' he explained, fixing Eitan with an angry stare.

'Well, then, I suggest you get your Pitbull under control. Kidnapping our colleague has put the exchange in extreme jeopardy. Only her partner's intervention prompted this call. The committee had voted to terminate and to seek out those responsible. Reluctantly they have agreed. But be assured this is your last chance. If she is harmed in any way, your brother and the item will be disposed of. Then we will find you and kill you. Do you understand?' he roared in his best voice, using the Liam Neeson quote from the movie *Taken*, bringing nods of approval from his brother Des.

Mizrahi responded quickly. 'I understand. How do you want to proceed?' he replied in a much-subdued voice.

Vince paused for effect. 'We will proceed as planned with the exchange. The only change is that we will provide the transport, and our people will travel with your brother and the necessary organs at the time agreed. But before we can proceed, we will need proof of life. We wish to talk to the hostage on video link.'

Abdiel glanced at Aurora, standing there in her underwear, covered in bruises and quickly realised that if they presented her in that state, it could jeopardise everything.

'She is not at this location at the moment. It will take a little time to bring her here,' he said, playing for time.

'You have two hours,' came the curt reply. 'Don't screw it up. this is your last chance,' as he broke the connection.

It was Des who was the first to comment. 'Now that is what I call throwing the cat among the pigeons. Things should be getting heated over there right now.'

## 72

Mizrahi stared at the dead phone in his hand, then turned to Eitan in rage.

'You have put everything at risk thanks to this shit. I arranged everything, and now they want proof of life before negotiating. How can we present her in that condition? You idiot!' he roared.

Eitan went red in the face, trying hard to control his anger. 'This is what you employed me for. Before I grabbed her,' gesturing to Aurora, who wondered what had been said to anger Abdiel, 'we had no leverage. Now we have taken back control. Leave the negotiations to me, and we can get Levi and simultaneously put an end to this crew.'

Mizrahi shrugged, realising that what he said made sense. 'So, what do we do about her appearance? He is calling back in less than two hours,' glancing at his watch anxiously.

Eitan called one of the female staff over. 'Find her something to wear and get her cleaned up,' he instructed her. Then he turned to a couple of the guards that could not keep their eyes off her. 'And you pair, stop ogling, go with them, and make sure she does not kill somebody.' Handing them the taser, he added, 'Don't be afraid to use this. She may be pretty but believe me, she is dangerous.'

As they went about their task, he tried to calm Abdiel and prepare him for the video call.

Right on time, the phone rang two hours later. As soon as Abdiel answered, Vincent spoke.

'This is the link for video call. Are you ready to proceed?' he asked.

When Mizrahi replied that he was ready, they opened the link, to be greeted by the sight of Aurora dressed in a sarong. Abdiel's staff had covered the bruises on her face with makeup and somewhat fixed her hair. Although she was not restrained, a couple of guys stood on both sides of her. Her mouth was taped.

'Remove the tape. We need for her to tell us if she has been well treated,' he demanded.

'In a moment first, my man wishes to say a few words,' Abdiel said, reluctantly handing over to Eitan.

As soon as he appeared on screen, Sun Yee thrust her face in front of the camera. 'Touch one hair on her head, and you will live to regret it,' she said with a calmness that brought a shudder from those listening. Then she was replaced by Vincent.

Eitan continued, 'She will be fine so long as everything goes smoothly. But this is the last time you can see her until the exchange. I will take her to an undisclosed location that even Abdiel is unaware of. So, any idea you have of mounting a rescue operation will result in her demise.' With that, he stepped out of view.

'It would appear that the tail is wagging the dog,' Vince snapped.

'It would appear that my security man does not have much faith in you keeping to your word,' Abdiel replied with a lot more confidence than before.

Then Vincent played his trump card.

'Your brother may be your main concern, but I am sure that your fortune in your hard wallet is equally important to all concerned. So, I must inform you to be very careful the next time you try to access the funds. The person who disrupted your whole operation when you pulled your money back the first time, as they expected you would, have embedded a piece of code into your crypto account. So f you try to remove funds, it will activate a key that will make your password inoperative and prevent you from emptying it. Remember, you have only twenty tries. After that, the funds are lost forever, so I would advise you not to waste your time when you discover it is locked. So, you see, we have a standoff. Now, where is this exchange taking place?' pausing to let this news sink in.

Abdiel stood there frozen in shock. Eitan was equally shocked. This was where his money was also. He gestured furiously for him to stick to what they had planned. Regaining his composure, he replied, 'You will need an aircraft to fly to the Caribbean. We will give you the location a day before the exchange. That will be plenty of time for you to get here.'

Silence, then Vincent replied, 'That is agreeable. Now remove the gag so the girl can speak.'

Eitan reappeared into view, speaking to Aurora. 'Mention anything about your location or anything that has gone on, and there will be repercussions.'

She nodded in agreement as he ripped the tape off. She turned to the camera and spoke.

'Sun Yee On, time to bring back Li Yang and let her do what she does best,' she shouted as the camera swivelled away from her. Then the connection was broken.

Abdiel dashed to his safe, hurriedly twirling the knobs as it swung open. He grabbed the hard drive and was just about to open it when Eitan intervened.

'Stop. If what he says is true. You are better off leaving it until we have them here. They have played into our hands. They are overconfident. As soon as we have your brother, we can use all of them to force the release of the money. We have the upper hand.'

Mizrahi reluctantly agreed and returned it to the safe. 'What now?' he asked.

'I vanish with her. You can contact me, but you will not know our location. It is safer that way.'

With that, he and Aurora departed.

# 73

'Well, the stage is set. Now all we have to do is figure out how to convince him when you arrive that his brother is alive and well until we can recover Aurora. I guess it's time to go over our next move,' Charlie suggested.

It was Sun Yee who spoke next. 'You need to get yourselves over to Elliot as soon as possible. I am leaving at once for Aruba,' she announced, which brought cries from the assembled crew. She was not to be deterred. 'You guys forget what I used to do. I am going to locate Aurora.'

Charlie jumped in before things got out of hand. 'She is right. This is way out of our league. This is what she is trained for. Let her do what she does best. In any case, nothing is going to stop her. So let us focus on doing the impossible, making a guy that has been dead for days look hale and hearty.'

So, while Sun Yee arranged flights to Aruba, they got down to putting their crazy plan into action. Two days later, the transport plane provided by Christina's father landed on the outskirts of Caracas, the airfield that Elliot and his men had commandeered.

This was the location they were using for their staging area. Charlie, Des, Christina, and Sergei disembarked. Followed by a surprise addition.

Dr Amara Abioye scurried along on her short legs, delighted at the opportunity to be free of the charges facing her in South Africa, as she gently caressed the necklace Christina had placed around her neck.

'Something to remember me by in case you don't return,' she had whispered in her ear. Those words made her heart race at the possibility of her escape.

When Charlie approached Moses with the idea of using her, he was dead against giving her a chance to escape. But when he explained what he intended to do, Moses reluctantly agreed.

Christina had approached her and explained that they would be transporting Levi in the specially constructed capsule she had seen before. They would welcome her assistance, and she had immediately agreed to her new friend's request.

The crew were greeted by Elliot, whom they had contacted and explained their plan. At first, he refused. But when Charlie pointed out that Aurora was family and their presence was non-negotiable, he understood, considering his reason for being here in the first place. His only proviso was that they could not accompany his men.

Charlie had explained that they intended to accompany the package right into the lion's mouth. Elliot shrugged, 'It is true you Irish are crazy.'

Des chimed in, 'But we are lucky,' grinning from ear to ear, delighted to be back in the fray.

They spent the day preparing for their audacious scheme. At the same time, they waited for the phone call to inform them of their ultimate destination.

Later that evening, Vincent contacted them. 'You are on,' he said. 'Mizrahi called exactly on time and provided the coordinates of a private airport in Aruba. I told him he would be contacted shortly before you land. So, we have approximately 24 hours to pull this off. He sounded very anxious when I asked that Aurora be there to prepare for the exchange.

'He had blustered, telling me she was in proximity and would be brought to his place as soon as his brother arrived. I have no doubt that Eitan has no intention of releasing her. We have to hope Sun Yee can locate her before he discovers that his brother is turning a bit ripe.'

'Have you any news from her?' Charlie asked.

'Only that she had arrived. She said she would contact you and Elliot if she manages to locate Aurora.'

'We have to cross our fingers that she can, or we are in the shit,' Charlie replied.

# 74

Sun Yee On collected her backpack, and as she emerged outside into the bright Caribbean sunshine, she donned her sunglasses and glanced around for a familiar face. Spotting who she was looking for, she waved like a tourist recognising a long-lost friend.

She approached and embraced the young man, who appeared to be a guide.

'Great to see you again, Li Yang. I thought you were dead,' he whispered in her ear.

'I am. But had to come back for a special task. Did you get what I asked for?' she asked.

'In the car, it is an off-road vehicle. The roads outside the capital leave a little to be desired,' he replied, and escorted her to a Land Rover parked in the garage.

After she inspected the items she had requested, she thanked the contact from her past.

'Do you need anything else?' he asked.

'Just some good old Irish luck,' she replied, as she engaged gear and drove out on the main road in front of the airport.

She drove until she could find someplace to stop and set up the equipment she had requested. Pulling into the parking lot of a large supermarket, she found a spot under a canopy. It was not very busy, and to anybody interested in her, she looked like she was checking that she had everything.

First, she opened the disposable phone her contact had provided and connected to the maps app. Next, she activated a device she had prepared with Axel. It began to search for a signal. The longer it took, the more anxious she became. Finally, it beeped, indicating it had connected.

'Got you, my sweet. Hold on. I am coming,' she muttered under her breath as she started the Land Rover and roared off.

## 75

'If we wait any longer, they may get suspicious,' Charlie decided. 'Are you all clear about your roles?' he asked, getting nods from the assembled crew.

Charlie had arranged for Amara to stay at a separate location from where they were setting up. She needed to believe the exchange was real if they were to pull this off.

'If we are to arrive close to the time, we will have to get into action,' he said. 'Christina, we will leave you to deal with Amara's part in this.'

She nodded. 'Don't worry, I have her on a short lead.'

'Great, Des, you and Sergei go on board and prepare the brother for his home journey. You know what to do. The success of this depends on them believing he is alive.'

'On it,' Des assured him as he and Sergei headed off, both glad to be back in action.

'That's it. We will board in two hours. Which will leave us on the ground in approximately five hours. Does that work for you, Elliot?' he asked.

Elliot was sitting with his men, listening to what the brothers were planning. 'We will be on the ground before you and be in position. You will be connected to us by the embedded earpieces I supplied. We will be able to hear each other. Just press beside your ear where I showed you to activate,' he instructed.

'Are you sure they are undetectable?' he asked.

Elliot smiled. 'France's finest. No one will know,' he assured them.

Christina was the last to board two hours later, accompanied by Dr Amara. As they entered the cabin area of the transport plane, Chaz waved them in from where he was already seated.

'We are just going back to check Levi's vitals,' she explained.

They proceeded to the back of the cabin, where a door led into the transport section. As soon as they entered, they were greeted by the sight of Sergei standing beside the capsule, holding the body of Levi.

Because they could not use somebody to simulate his vitals over such a long journey, they had constructed a system housed in a compartment below the main body of the capsule. That duplicated the breathing rhythm of the balloon housed in his chest. The other vitals were on a loop transmitting from a program created by Axel, which was contained in a miniature computer disguised as a spare air tank.

Christina directed Amara to follow her. 'We will check the vitals before we depart,' she said.

Together they inspected the reading from the various gauges. Amara stared through the plexiglass. 'He looks so at peace. If not for his vitals and relaxed breathing, you could think he was in Heaven,' she commented.

Christina ignored her and instead asked, 'All readings are regular, agreed?

Amara nodded her head in agreement. She glanced around as they returned to take their seats and asked, 'Where is Desmond?'

Charlie replied, 'He decided to infill with Elliot and his crew.'

As they seated and the plane began to taxi, Christina turned to Amara. 'You have become a good friend, and I trust you. But I am afraid Commandant Moses does not feel the same way. So, for this reason, I must warn you that he was the one who provided the necklace I gifted you. As soon as we land, it will be armed. This is to prevent you from changing sides. We are being observed,' she whispered in a secretive way.

Amara glance nervously around the cabin, to be greeted by the steely glare of Charlie. Quickly averting her gaze, she whispered back, 'What can the necklace do ?' she asked in a panic.

Chris leaned in quietly to explain. 'The chain is made of titanium. It has a device in the clasp; any attempt to cut the chain or tamper with the clasp will activate it.'

Amara's mouth fell open. 'What will happen" she croaked.

Christina paused momentarily for effect, then replied in a matter-of-fact voice. 'The device will retract, causing the chain to cut off your breathing. So whatever you do, stay close to me.'

# 76

Sun Yee On was cursing at the slow progress of the trucks in front of her. She had forgotten that the primary industry here was the oil refinery. The signal was leading her to the northeast of the island, and the only major road that took her in that direction led to a prominent tourist destination. The area was dominated by a famous landmark on the northwest of the island called the California Lighthouse, which was named after a ship that had shipwrecked on the jagged coast on September 22nd, 1891.

The northeast was the most desolate part of the island due to the lack of beaches and, more importantly, no landing point for ships. This made it the perfect place for Eitan to hide with Aurora.

Finally, the traffic cleared enough for her to pick up the pace. She glanced at her watch, noting that the others would soon be about to depart for the exchange.

She was in contact with Elliot as he had provided her with the same earpiece he had given the others. She could speak to him directly, but for reasons of safety she could only listen to his conversations with the others. Finally, she reached the turnoff that took her toward the signal. To her dismay, it was little more than a goat track. Luckily, she had requested a four-wheel drive vehicle, or it would have been faster walking.

Nonetheless, she could not go much over 30kph without shaking out her teeth fillings. Her phone rang. It was Vincent, monitoring things from back in South Africa.

'How is your progress?' he asked.

The vibrations made it hard for her to speak. 'I am getting a shakedown as we speak,' she replied. Her voice vibrated with the violent bouncing of the car. 'There is no way he drove to wherever he is holding her. This road is a nightmare. How are the others progressing? Is Amara behaving?'.

'Christina had a hold over her until Aurora is secured,' he said, and explained about the device around Amara's neck. 'On that point, do you need some backup?' he asked.

'No, Vincent. For this type of operation, I am better alone. This is going to get nasty. I expect some reception. I doubt he would dare to hold her without help. Have to go now if I am going to keep this vehicle on the road.'

She cut the connection just as the Land Rover was launched into the air after hitting a massive hole in the track.

She cursed under her breath. This pace was painfully slow. Everything rested on her locating Aurora and affecting her release before they discover that the package they were delivering was only a dead body.

She began to push as hard as she could, at the same time wondering how the others were dealing with their challenges.

# 77

Charlie was wondering the same thing as the plane started its descent to its destination. He still needed to learn what reception was waiting for them. The arrangement was for them to have a vehicle big enough to accommodate the capsule and four personnel. They had instructed them that nobody would be allowed to assist with the transfer. This was to be handled exclusively by them. It remained to be seen if they would try and double-cross right away. They hoped that the threat of losing all his money would deter them long enough for Sun Yee to do her thing.

The jolt of the plane touching down snapped him back to the present. The aircraft taxied to where somebody directed them to an apron reserved for disembarking, bumping to a halt as the engines began to spool down.

The pilot emerged from the cockpit. Bill Heart had recruited him and his co-pilot. He had reached out to his contacts, and these guys came highly recommended.

'Okay, remember, no matter what happens, remain in control of the plane. Be ready to take off at a moment's notice. This operation can go south very fast. So be prepared for anything,' Chaz reminded the pilot for the umpteenth time.

The pilot nodded and then, with a sly grin, replied, 'Don't worry, mate. This is not our first rodeo,' he said in a broad Australian accent. 'By the way, Tyler's me name, Jack Tyler.'

'Okay, thanks Jack, let's do this,' Charlie said, indicating to Jack to open the door.

A blast of hot Caribbean wind engulfed the cabin as he pushed it open and activated the stairs. Charlie turned to Amara.

'Do exactly what Christina has instructed you to do. Do not speak to anybody unless she permits you. Do you understand?'

She nodded nervously in reply as she touched the necklace with trepidation.

A tough-looking guy appeared at the bottom of the steps. 'Who is in charge?' he shouted in heavily accented English.

'That would be me,' replied Charlie, standing at the entrance.

He saw about a dozen men grouped around a large, converted Mercedes 600 Pullman. It had been stretched, and the back had a drop-down tailgate installed. Vincent had told him to expect this vehicle, which Mizrahi had specially constructed as Levi's transport when he started using a wheelchair.

'Where is Mr Mizrahi's brother?'

Charlie nodded to the aircraft's rear. 'He is ready and waiting. Is that our transportation?' he asked, indicating the Limo.

'Yes,' he grunted.

'Then you, your men and the driver will, be walking. Our instructions were explicit. If not, we will turn around and fly away.'

The guy turned his back and made a call on his phone. After talking for a couple of seconds, he disconnected and turned back. 'As you wish. Transport is on its way. Now can we unload?' he asked.

Charlie just turned and picked up the intercom to where Sergei was with the capsule. 'Unload, but don't allow anybody to approach.'

'Got it, boss,' he replied as he activated the tail section.

As the rear of the aircraft was opening, a small convoy of pickups arrived to carry Mizrahi's men. As soon as they stopped, Charlie indicated for Chris and Aurora to exit the aircraft and follow him down.

'I am escorting the doctors to the car first. I will need your driver, and anybody in the car, to leave and board the transport,' he instructed.

The henchman turned to shout instructions. The men all moved to the vehicles, and a driver and passanger emerged from the vehicle and followed suit.

'Good. Now you wait here while we inspect the car,' Charlie said, as he and the girls made their way over. He then checked the car for the all-clear. 'Okay, you guys know what to do, sit in the back and hang tight.'

He closed the door and headed back to where Sergei was wheeling the capsule. As he emerged from the bottom of the ramp for one of the pickups, a guy jumped out and made a beeline towards the capsule. Whatever his intentions, it did not end well for him. Before he could even get close, Sergei, with remarkable speed for his size, intersected the poor guy and lifted him bodily off the ground by his head. He then flung him against one of the vehicles, resulting in a satisfying sound of breaking bone, followed by an ear-splitting scream.

When the leader went to move, Charlie put his hand to stop him. 'I wouldn't if I were you. You would not want to see him angry. Just tell everybody to stand back. We will take good care of the merchandise.'

He waved for Sergei to continue, who quickly pushed Mizrahi's brother to the car's rear in plain view of everybody, opened the tailgate and pushed the capsule inside. Moments later, Charlie was seated in the driving seat with Sergei riding shotgun. The doctors had access to monitor Levi. He turned back and then whispered so only Sergei could hear.

'Well, the first bit is over. Wonder how the others are faring?'

# 78

The Eurocopter NH 90 TTH, the latest transport chopper used by France for military and civilian configurations, was used exclusively for missions such as this.

It gently descended into a secluded area close to Mizrahi's hideout. Elliot and his men quickly disembarked and unloaded their equipment. Elliot signalled the pilot to take off as soon as they were finished. The helicopter quickly ascended and moved to a location where the pilots could sit, awaiting the call to exfill the team.

Elliot checked his coordinates, seeing they were only a short distance from their target. The area was sparsely developed as privacy and security were of significant concern for the ultra-rich that inhabited the island.

He sent one of his men ahead to scout the security they would have to contend with. While the men were preparing their equipment, he took the opportunity to reach out to Charlie on the earpiece he had provided.

'Elliot here. If you can't speak, just cough,' he whispered.

Charlie's voice came back loud and clear. 'All clear here. We have arrived and are in the vehicle they provided. We insisted we travel alone. At the moment, we are following his men, presumably to his place. How are you guys going?'

'We are just about to get into position around his hideout. I have sent somebody to ascertain what resistance we have to contend with,' he replied.

'Any word from Sun Yee?' Charlie asked.

It had been agreed that all contact with her would be through Elliot. She had given strict instructions not to contact her unless it was an emergency. It had been decided as soon as she had any word about Aurora, she would alert them both.

Elliot responded. 'Vincent has just been on. She has been in contact. She arrived, and her connection provided her with transport and the requested equipment. When they spoke about an hour ago, she was enroute to where she believes Aurora is being held.'

'Did she say how she was able to locate her?' he asked.

'Sun Yee does not take kindly to being questioned about her methods. Her reply when I enquired was, "Not your concern. Focus on being ready for when I contact you." Then she cut the connection.'

'Sounds just like her. I pity whoever gets in her way. If they do, they better bring lots of body bags,' replied Charlie.

Just then, Elliot's scout returned and filled him in as to what confronted them. After he had reported the intel, he returned to speaking with Charlie.

'It is heavily guarded. Entry will be no problem for my men. But I have to warn you, it will be noisy.'

Charlie gave a big sigh. 'Like most of our plans. They tend to end up that way.'

He signed off just as the convoy slowed down and turned into a private road. They stopped at the gates of a large estate, which opened remotely. They proceeded up the driveway and stopped in front of the entrance to the house. Outside was another bunch of men waiting to escort them inside. Charlie stepped from the car and addressed the guy who seemed to be in charge.

'We don't move or touch anything until we have information about our friend held captive here.'

The guy did not acknowledge him, instead turned to one of the men who disappeared inside. Moments later, a man of short stature appeared. He hurried down the stairs to approach the car.

'Is my brother in there?' he asked as he tried to look inside.

Charlie held up his hand to stop. 'So, at last, we meet in the flesh. Before we continue. I want to speak to my colleague.'

Mizrahi pulled his attention away from trying to glimpse his brother. 'Of course,' he replied, producing his phone and pressing speed dial. Seconds later, he spoke to somebody and handed the phone to Chaz. 'You can ask her if she is okay, but if she tries to disclose where she is held, they will hang up,' he explained nervously, something Charlie took note of.

'Hello, who is there?' Eitan's voice came back. He was speaking to Aurora. 'Tell him that you are okay. Nothing else, understand.'

Charlie could hear Aurora reply softly in agreement and then she addressed him. 'I am okay, but don't trust these pigs,' she screamed as the line was disconnected.

Mizrahi pocketed the phone. 'Well, as you can see, she has been well taken care of. Shall we move inside now?' he suggested, indicating the door.

Charlie nodded, muttering to himself. 'Here we go again!'

# 79

Eitan glanced out the window of the secluded cabin to check that his men were on their toes. He was sure they could not be traced to this location.

He glanced in Aurora's direction. She was sitting in a chair with her wrists and ankles taped. She was still wearing the clothes they had provided. Even though she had been scanned, he had left everything else behind.

'Don't get your hopes up. They still have to deliver Levi, the organs and, most importantly, the crypto. If you think somebody is coming to rescue you. I am sorry, but I am the only one that knows this location.'

'You have no idea what you are dealing with. You moron,' she retorted.

He wandered over and delivered a heavy blow to her solar plexus. Driving the breath out of her lungs. 'I hope your friend's screw up because I have my own surprise waiting for them, regardless of the outcome,' he hissed.

Even with her legs taped, he reflexively stepped back, suddenly remembering how quick she could kick.

'They won't give you the crypto information until they return to the plane,' she taunted, hoping he would reveal his plan.

'Exactly. I would expect nothing less. But you see, my men will attach a little surprise to the fuselage during the night, so as soon as it takes off, *Boom!*' indicating an explosion.

This brought a shudder to Aurora. She knew he had no intention of letting her go.

At that same time, Sun Yee On was making her way on foot along the northeast coastline, intending to approach the location from the inhospitable part of the island. On this side, sheer cliffs descended to an angry sea, and she knew any guards would be posted to the front of wherever they were hiding. She reasoned they had full trust the cliffs would prevent any approach from that direction.

Stopping to check the direction locater, she was glad she had decided to abandon the car. She was making much better time on foot, and she was now only five kilometres from her target.

A voice in her ear caught her attention. It was Charlie. He was speaking to somebody and had activated his earpiece. This indicated he wanted them to hear.

'How long before my friend will arrive here?'

She could not hear the reply, but Charlie replied. 'Okay, we will unload your brother into the house. But remember, nobody except my people will be allowed to touch anything until our business is concluded. Understood?' and then he disconnected.

Sun Yee realised he was stalling as best as he could and was letting them know that arrangements were being made to transfer Aurora to the house. With this news, she increased her pace to arrive before they moved her. Her best chance of success would be here rather than back at the house. Too many moving parts.

*No. Aurora's chances were better left in her hands*, she decided.

# <u>80</u>

Sergei unloaded the capsule and pushed it towards the large entrance, with Charlie clearing a path. Behind them, Christina and Amara emerged from the car.

'Dr Amara, you are here,' Abdiel cried out in shock.

Before he could approach her, Charlie intervened. 'It was only at the insistence of Dr Herrero that she was included. She has been accommodating in ensuring your brother receives the best care. She suggested that we use this method of transport. It ensures a sterile atmosphere. But until we conclude our business, all communication regarding his condition will be through Dr Herrero.'

Abdiel nodded, then blurted out to Dr Amara. 'How is he?' he yelled.

Amara glanced at Christina, who paused momentarily and then nodded to her. As instructed, she said nothing. She just gave the thumbs up and followed the procession inside.

As Abdiel turned to follow, Charlie stopped him. 'Last chance. Do not talk to anybody but me. Attempting to approach your brother will result in disastrous consequences. We expect you to try another double-cross, so precautions have been taken. You have been warned,' he said, as he marched inside.

They were led to the rear of the house to the extension that had been converted into a mini-hospital. No expense had been spared, and it could match any modern facility anywhere in the world. Inside stood a team of medical specialists waiting for their patient.

Charlie put his hand up. 'Before we move inside, the place has to be vacated. Only our people will be allowed near your brother until our business is concluded.' When Abdiel began to protest, Chaz stopped him. 'Before you try whatever you and your pal have cooked up, let me show you something.' Turning to Sergei, he said, 'Show him.'

Bending down, he opened the compartment below the capsule and extracted a medical case used to transport organs. This one had a clear lid, and inside were the heart and lungs supposedly for Levi, kindly donated by some poor soul in the mortuary back in South Africa.

'All he has to do is unclip the lid, and they become useless. So if you hope to help your brother recover, I suggest you follow our instructions.'

Reluctantly, Abdiel took out his phone. Somebody inside the operating room picked up a phone on the wall. It must have been soundproofed because without a sound, they all vacated.

A door opened into the space, and Charlie asked Sergei to move the capsule inside. He then indicated for Christina and Amara to follow. 'Anybody tries to enter; you know what to do.' he instructed menacingly. He then turned to Mizrahi, 'Time to get down to business.'

# 81

Des peeked out from the heavily tinted window of the vehicle that had transported the capsule from the airport. He had squeezed into the compartment below it until Charlie and the rest of them were inside.

The crew had decided not to put all their eggs in one basket. So Des had volunteered to be the backup. This was what he shone at. Being dropped in at the deep end and figure it out as he went.

As they suspected, all the guards' focus was outward. So as soon as they had disappeared inside, he slipped out and darted to the side of the house. Sneaking around to the back, avoiding the windows, he carefully spied around the corner to see what seemed to be a large factory structure attached to the back of the house.

He noticed a side door at the rear, quickly checking to see if the coast was clear. He quickly darted over and tested the handle and, to his surprise, discovered it was unlocked. Peeking inside, he could see it was some form of storage room. It was full of medical equipment and clothing.

He stepped inside and stood silently, listening for any sound. He could hear activity somewhere deeper in the building, but nothing he could distinguish.

He decided action was his best course and joined the medical staff. He stepped out with confidence in his disguise as medical personnel. He was dressed in a white coat, surgical scrubs, a theatre mask and a hair cap. The only giveaway was his blond curls sticking out.

He found himself in a corridor connected to what appeared to be surgical units or perhaps research labs. A couple had people working in them, but they showed little interest as he passed by. When he came to the end, he pulled up abruptly and stepped back out of sight.

Around the corner was a window into an operating room, and inside, he spotted the large frame of Sergei with two women with their backs to him, who had to be Christina and Amara.

Things looked calm enough, so he let Charlie know he was there. Looking around for cover, he realised the unit he had stopped at was unoccupied, so he stepped inside.

It was fitted as a doctor's office with a desk and treatment bed. He sat down behind the desk, taking a folder from a desk beside him. Then while pretending to inspect it, he pressed the activating switch as he'd been instructed and whispered, 'The Eagle has landed,' quoting one of his favourite movies.

# 82

Charlie coughed into his hand to disguise the chuckle when he heard his brother check in with one of his favourite movie quotes. He should never have doubted him when he suggested this plan. Sneaking into places was his speciality.

Charlie realised that Mizrahi was waiting for him to proceed. 'What needs to happen for this to conclude successfully is when our friend arrives, you will accompany us to our aircraft. Bring whatever you need to verify that your money has been released. When we are there, they will provide you with what is necessary to unlock it when you are happy. We will depart, and you won't hear from us again. Try anything, and the first thing that will happen is what I just described. Also, the safety of your brother would be at grave risk. Now where is our colleague?' he demanded.

He noticed Abdiel again becoming uncomfortable and paused before replying. 'He said he had called for a helicopter to transfer them from wherever they were. I am sure it won't be much longer.'

Charlie nodded, then turned and entered the operating theatre, leaving Mizrahi standing outside. As soon as he entered, he stepped behind the casket and bent down to inspect Levi. He pressed the earpiece to contact his friend.

'I know you have been monitoring the conversation. So far, so good. They seem to be playing along,' he whispered.

But it was Vincent who came in loud and clear. 'I am not so sure. His behaviour becomes very guilty whenever you inquire about

Aurora. I don't know if he does not trust his lieutenant, or they have something up their sleeve.'

It was Elliot that spoke next. 'We are ready. All the sentries have been located, and we are ready to go. All we need is the word from you.'

'Okay, guys, just hang tight and hope Sun Yee has some success. Otherwise, we will have to take care of it here when she arrives. Signing off, but keep listening, folks,' Charlie joked as he disconnected.

'Well, what is happening?' Christina asked, concerned by the conversation.

Charlie indicated to Amara, who was listing intently. 'All good. Things are going as you planned it.'

Christina nodded, aware not to blurt anything. While distracted, she failed to notice the cunning look on her friend's face.

# 83

Sun Yee On had heard the conversation but did not respond. She was more focused on the small chalet she could see in the distance. The signal was coming from that location. She could see a small cluster of men standing guard at the entrance in front of a small building, which must have served as their accommodation. Their job was made easy as the approach to the place was by a single path, plus shrubs surrounded the chalet. The sheer cliff protected the rear, and an electrified fence covered the sides at the back.

She edged her way as close as she could without being spotted but was confronted by an open space before she could reach the bushes. Her options were limited as she glanced at her watch. Charlie and the crew had arrived at the exchange point forty minutes ago, and she knew every minute was precious. At any moment, their ruse could be discovered. If that happened, Elliot would have no option but to engage, putting her friends inside in grave danger.

One option was the cliff. Although she believed she could manage the climb, she knew it would take some time and was afraid they might move before she got in position.

Just then, she heard the sound of an approaching chopper. The guards all jumped to attention, ready to receive it. Sensing the opportunity while their attention was focused on the incoming helicopter, she sprang to her feet and ran across the open space, ducking down behind the foliage. Surprisingly, she found a ditch cut around the property to provide drainage.

Dropping in, she was out of sight from their vantage point. She made her way around to position herself in earshot of the guards, who were welcoming the pilot who had just disembarked. They began babbling away in the local dialect, so she had no idea what they were saying. At the same time, the cabin door opened, and a man emerged. She recognised him immediately as Eitan from the photos they had.

He yelled in Spanish, the second language used on the island, '*Voy pronto, estar listo.* Coming soon, be ready.'

Sun Yee settled back into the ditch. *Got you*, she thought, contemplating how she would get by half a dozen guards and the pilot without alerting Eitan.

She shrugged, muttering. 'Okay, now for the hard part.'

# 84

Des was seated behind the desk as he listened to Charlie speaking with Mizrahi. Then, when he entered the privacy of the operating theatre, he updated Vince and Elliot.

He put down the folder and spotted a laptop sitting to one side. Just as he pulled it across, the door opened, and a lanky fellow with unruly hair stepped in and pulled to a stop at the sight of Desmond sitting there.

'Who are you?' he sputtered.

Not perturbed, Des sprang to his feet, extending his hand. 'Brad Pitt here, and who are you, my fine friend?' pumping his hand variously.

While trying to release his hand, the confused chap replied, 'I am Lars Shrider, and can I ask what you are doing in my office?'

'So they did not inform you about my arrival?' Des asked.

The guy shook his head. 'No, which is surprising as I am head of security and was not told.'

Des gave him one of his most disarming smiles. 'That's too bad. I am sorry to have to deliver you this message.'

Lars looked confused for a second just before Des hit him with a solid right cross to his temple, putting his lights out immediately.

By the time he started recovering, Des had his hands and feet bound with some packing tape he had found. Lars shook his head and then began to open his mouth. But Des put a finger to his mouth.

'If you cry out or call for help, I will put you to sleep again,' indicating his fist. Lars nodded quickly, so Des continued. 'We do not wish you or any of your friends harm. Our disagreement is with your boss. So I am going to gag you and put you in this storeroom,' indicating a storage space in the corner.

'If you remain quiet, all this will be over quickly,' he reassured him as he stuffed a rag in his mouth and taped it.

After he was secured. Des returned to the desk sitting for a moment to take stock of what had just happened when he remembered the laptop.

As he opened it, he wondered if he would have to ask the poor fellow in the cupboard for the password, but to his surprise, when he lifted the top, he was greeted by an array of small screens with views from security cameras positioned around the place.

He discovered that hovering the cursor over a particular camera view it would fill the screen. Moving through, he could watch the various activities.

Mizrahi was pacing frantically with his staff trying their best to stay out of sight. In a room behind them was what appeared to be a medical team. They seemed nervous also, muttering together. The place was littered with empty coffee cups. Moving on, he switched to the room where Charlie and the doctors were. He smiled when he saw the familiar face of his brother. His famous scar ran down his eyebrow to his cheek, which was more visible when he was in action. He could see that he was speaking to Christina, probably discussing the next possible move.

Des moved the cursor over some darkened screen when movement alerted him from the corridor surrounding the operating theatre where Charlie was. When he zoomed in, to his shock, he saw it was filled with armed men preparing for an assault.

Vincent was right. This bastard was planning another double-cross!

# 85

Des pressed his earpiece to indicate he was about to speak.

'Charlie, Elliot, it's a trap. They have men positioned in the corridor surrounding you and the girls. What do you want to do?'

Elliot responded first. 'This changes the plan. We were going to silence the guards outside before we made our entrance. But in light of this news, our options have become limited. If they attack you, we will have to come in hard. But you would have to survive for at least fifteen minutes before we could affect a rescue. This puts you and Abdiel in extreme danger,' reminding Charlie of the importance of Mizrahi's survival if they wanted to recover the crypto from his wallet. Without his password, it would be lost forever.

Charlie responded quickly, 'Let's continue for as long as possible. We can use the fact that they don't know we have discovered what they are up to. How could you discover this without being discovered?' he asked.

Des's cheery reply came back. 'I am in the office of the guy that oversees the security. He has kindly allowed me the use of all his surveillance cameras. I am watching everything as we speak. It does not look as though they are preparing to assault at the moment. Abdiel just got off the phone. I suppose he was checking on Aurora's arrival.'

Charlie was not a bit surprised. His brother had an uncanny ability to get into the most unusual places without being discovered.

Elliot responded, 'If they are considering an assault, I think you have to assume they have no intention of exchanging her.'

'Agreed,' Charlie responded. ' Then all we can do is hope that Sun Yee is having some luck.'

He surmised that no response from her was not good news. She had said she would only open communications when she was ready, in case she was distracted. He had to remember she was a trained professional and never wasted time on conversation. Something she had to get used to with the Savage brothers.

'Des, remain where you are and keep us informed. Only tell us if they look like they are about to attack. Otherwise, stay out of sight and wait to hear from Elliot or me, okay?'

With a usual response from him, he replied, 'Am I not always ready?'

Charlie laughed and said, 'Okay, let's hold fire and hope Sun Yee comes through. Stay alert, and keep our fingers crossed.'

He turned to judge Christina's and Sergei's reactions to the news they had just received. He failed to notice Amara's response.

While they were talking, she moved closer to the door they had entered from. She was trying to signal Abdiel surreptitiously of her intention, but he was too engrossed in his phone call.

She had been able to overhear some of Charlie's conversation and realised she would be in the firing line If things went wrong. Regardless of the killer necklace she was wearing, her survival instinct told her the best chance was with her old boss. As far as she could see, he held all the cards.

While Charlie and his friends were distracted, she took the opportunity to wrench the door open and run as fast as her short legs could carry her. She scampered outside, screaming for Abdiel's assistance.

# 86

Sun Yee On had positioned herself close to the shed where the guards and the pilot were.

She had counted five plus the pilot. Her problem was not that she doubted she could handle them, but to do it quietly without alerting whoever was in the house. Plus, there was also the problem that he could appear for his helicopter flight any minute. So she realised she had to act.

The shack door opened, and two guards stepped outside, supposedly to keep a lookout. But in this case, it was to have a smoke. Sensing an opportunity to reduce the odds, she crept closer. She could hear the others inside joking and laughing loudly. Seizing the chance, she stood and, with two perfectly placed silenced shots from her Tactical Ruger Mark V 22, dropped them both with hardly a sound. She quickly approached the shed, but just as she arrived at the door, it opened, and she was greeted by the appearance of the pilot standing at the entrance.

Inside the main building, Eitan approached Aurora with an evil grin on his face. 'Well, much as I would have liked to spend more time together, my presence is required back with that fool and his half-dead brother. It would seem that he is too squeamish to do the dirty work, so I have to get rid of your friends waiting for your return. Sadly, I have to terminate our relationship.'

He went to pick up his gun, which was sitting on a table. She knew she had to try and do anything to stall him, even though she had all but given up hope of being rescued. The longer she kept him occupied, the longer it gave Sun Yee to come through. If anybody could find a way out of this predicament, it would be her.

'What, no kiss goodbye?' she taunted.

He stopped and turned to face her. 'I have to give it to you, I have never met a woman like you. Perhaps in another world, we would have made great partners.'

He stepped closer and bent towards her waiting lips. To his surprise, she responded as he kissed her firmly. Then with all her force, she bit him.

Jumping back and cursing, he felt the blood filling his mouth. He lunged forward and punched her as hard as he could in the midriff, driving the wind out of her lungs. He was about to deliver another blow when he heard a voice from the entrance.

'Why don't you try that on somebody that is not tied up?' Sun Yee On suggested.

## SIX MINUTES EARLIER

The surprise on the face of the pilot at the sight of this slight Asian woman smiling at him was quickly replaced with a grimace when she lifted the gun a shot him in the head.

As he fell back, Sun Yee stepped over him to see that one of the guards was lying on a bed with his eyes closed listening to music with headphones. Moving her gaze around the room, she saw the other two sitting at a table playing poker. By the time they realised they had an intruder, they had already received kill shots, leaving them slumped over the table, blood flowing over cards. By this time, the guy on the bed had opened his eyes to be greeted by Sun Yee pointing the gun at his head.

She put a finger to her lips, indicating silence. 'How many are there in the house?' she asked in a sweet voice.

He pulled the earphones off, so he could hear. Sun Ye repeated herself. He blinked, then, in a quivering voice, replied. 'Only the boss and the girl,' he stuttered.

'Thank you for that,' as she shot him between the eyes.

She stepped to the door to see if there was any reaction from inside the house. When there was no activity, she quickly covered the distance to the side of the house, where she moved silently to a window and peeked in to see Eitan pummelling her girlfriend.

Enraged, she moved to the door and assessed the handle. It was unlocked. Pushing it open, she stepped in and spoke to a shocked Eitan.

For a split second, he did not react, then his training kicked in, and he reached for the gun resting on the table. For all his training, it did not come close to Sun Yee's ability. Before he could get it, she raised her gun and shot. The bullet hit his hand, simultaneously taking his fingers off and shattering the hand.

He let out an ear-piercing scream as he clasped his ruined hand. Instinctively, he tried to save himself by rushing her, but another well-placed bullet entered the other arm at the elbow, passing straight through, taking bone and tissue with it.

He collapsed to the floor. The agony of his wounds paralysing him. She quickly hurried to Aurora's side. 'Are your hurt?' she inquired.

'Much better now that you arrived,' Aurora replied.

As she grimaced in pain, Sun Yee began to untie her. 'Sorry it took so long. But this place is well off the beaten track.'

Aurora stood and immediately went to the stricken Eitan. 'Not so tough now,' she said, and delivered a swift kick.

Sun Yee pulled her away. 'Enough time for that later. We have to get back. Charlie and the others are in trouble. Can you walk?' she asked.

Aurora walked to the table and picked up the gun without saying a word. 'Just watch me,' she replied.

# 87

Christina was the first to spot her escape.

'Amara, stop!' she yelled.

Amara only slowed for a moment, glancing back. When they made eye contact, she just shook her head and continued in search of Mizrahi.

'If she heard our conversation and alerted Mizrahi, he will react. She has to be stopped,' Charlie snarled at Christina.

She ran to the entrance in pursuit. But despite her plump stature, Amara was nimble on her feet. Her shouts had alerted Mizrahi, who stepped out to see what the commotion was about. At that moment, Christina managed to grab her top, but she managed to shake free and continue towards Abdiel.

'Come back,' Christina yelled.

But Amara ignored her, struggling forward to her old boss, who was confused about what was happening.

'Forget her. She had her chance,' Charlie yelled. 'Get back inside.'

Christina stood for a moment as Amara reached her target. Then she looked back at Chaz, then nodded her head.

'I told you there would be consequences,' she muttered as she hurried back.

At the same time, she could see Charlie extend his hand and press a device on the watch Moses's technician had provided. It was the activation device for the necklace that Amara was wearing.

Falling into his arms, Amara began to babble incoherently as she tried to regain her breath. Mizrahi pushed her away. 'Have you gone crazy? Why are you not taking care of my brother?' he screamed.

She managed to croak out, 'They know…' then the necklace began to tighten, cutting off her breath. She clutched frantically at it, trying to pull it free. But the tungsten chain and clasp were too strong. Abdiel watched in shock to see the tips of two of her fingers slice off as the chain bit into her neck. She fell, writhing to the floor as the chain continued to contract inexorably. Biting deeper, it sliced through her oesophagus. The blood spurted out, drenching Mizrahi' trousers as the arteries in her neck ruptured.

By this time, Amara had already expired. The necklace continued its gruesome work until, finally, it cut through her cervical spine, garrotting her. Her head roll grotesquely towards her old boss, who stood riveted to the spot, unable to comprehend what he had just witnessed.

Then he began screaming, bringing his panicked staff, which was equally horrified at the sight of a headless woman.

Christina ran through the door, where Charlie's expression caused her to stop and look at what had happened. She covered her mouth in shock at the sight of Amara lying without her head.

Charlie gripped her as she whispered. 'I had no idea that the device Moses gave me would do that. I thought it was just some deterrent.'

'Well, it sure deterred her. This is not your fault; I had no idea this would happen. Remember, Africa is a violent place, and I guess Moses wanted to ensure she paid for her crimes in the event she decided to change sides.'

Christina ran to the comfort of Sergei's big arms as Charlie stepped outside and yelled, 'This is an example of the precautions we have taken. I don't know what you said to influence her to take this rash decision. You have been warned!'

He stepped back inside and closed the door. 'Well, bad as that was, it probably bought us a little time.'

He looked at his watch. They had been in the lion's den for forty-five minutes already, longer than he would have liked. If Sun Yee didn't come through soon, they may not have much choice but to move to the backup plan.

He shuddered as he realised how much danger that would place them in.

# 88

Mizrahi stood in shock, covered in Amara's blood, unable to comprehend what had just happened. Although he was responsible for so much pain and suffering, he remained insulated from the absolute horror created by his brother and later by Eitan.

To be confronted by the sight of the headless body put him into a blind panic. His first reaction was to reach for the phone to tell Eitan what had just happened. When he received no response, he hurried back to the room where his man was in contact with the guys preparing to breach the operating theatre.

'Are they ready?' he asked.

The guy nodded. 'They are only waiting on the word,' was the reply.

'Are you sure that they understand the importance of protecting my brother?'

The concern in Abdiel's voice was palpable. His reply was succinct. 'As if their lives depend on it.'

'Well, remind them that is what they are risking,' he said, and raised the phone to his ear and reached out to Eitan again.

Charlie pressed his earpiece. 'Des, any sign of movement?'

'Something is happening. One of them is talking on the phone. What's up?'

Charlie explained what had happened with Amara and expected Mizrahi to react.

'Wow, I bet you don't see that every day. I guess she had it coming. Never did trust her.'

Charlie ignored him as he could hear somebody trying to break into the conversation. Only one person could speak at a time. 'Shut up. Somebody else is trying to talk.'

As Des fell silent, Charlie could hear a female voice. It was the call they had been waiting for.

'I have got her; Aurora is safe. Have to go. Hang on, we are on our way,' Sun Yee yelled, then broke the connection.

Back at the house, Abdiel flung the phone down in disgust. 'He is not answering. We have to attack,' he yelled at the startled guy.

'But Eitan said we had to wait for him,' he replied in panic, knowing what Eitan's response would be.

'Well, he is not here, and I am in charge. Do what I tell you,' he roared.

The guy shrugged and pressed the intercom. 'It is a go, breach,' he ordered.

Des was listening to Sun Yee's news when he saw movement from the men in the corridor. They were preparing to attack.

He touched his earpiece. 'Bad news, they are preparing to break in. They are assembling at the rear entrance.'

At the same time, Charlie was speaking to Elliot, and they both heard Des's warning. 'It seems we have no choice but to go to our fallback plan. Are you ready?' Charlie asked.

Elliot replied. 'On your mark. But it could take us fifteen or so minutes to gain entrance. Can you hold out?

'We will find out soon enough. So let's go for it!' he yelled. Then to Des again, 'As soon as they attack, try to make your escape. Good luck, brother.'

Then he turned to the others and explained what was about to happen. 'Sergei, you know what to do. Christina, take cover where I told you,' indicating a steel cabinet alongside the wall.

Then he and Sergei pushed the capsule up tight against the door from which the attack was coming. They ran back to join the ladies, crouched behind the cabinet, and waited for the action to begin.

## 89

Sun Yee dragged Eitan to his feet. 'Move, or I will put another hole in you,' she warned as she hurried Aurora out the door.

She knew that the team back at the hideout was in big trouble, having heard the interaction over the earpiece. Pushing Eitan in front, she began to search frantically for some vehicle when they got to the shed with the two dead guards in front.

'You?' Aurora asked, pointing at the dead guards.

Sun Yee nodded and continued searching for where they might have parked their transport. 'What about the chopper?' as Aurora pointed in its direction.

'The pilot is indisposed,' was her curt reply.

She realised that even in a four-wheel drive, it would take hours to get back to help the others. Then she saw Aurora striding toward the helicopter.

'Where are you doing?' she yelled.

Aurora turned. 'I am going to get transport ready, are you coming?'

She hopped into the pilot's seat and began working with switches and instruments. A few moments, Sun Yee arrives, dragging a moaning, delirious Eitan. Peering in at the busy Aurora, she asked, 'You can fly this thing?'

Shouting over the rotors starting to spool up, 'I was the traffic and rescue helicopter pilot for the NSW Special Squad. Get in. We can talk in the air.'

After Eitan was secured in the back. They had put tourniquets on both his shattered arms, causing him to pass out. As soon as Sun Yee was in the co-pilot seat, she placed headphones on so they could speak. Aurora yelled instructions to get her some headings.

Sun Yee used her phone the get coordinates to the hideout. As soon she input them into the satellite navigation, Aurora engaged the cyclic, increasing the power as they took off. She put the aircraft on its headings, then relaxed as the old skills came into play.

Glancing at her friend, she asked, 'Okay, how did you do it?'

A smile crossed Sun Yee's lips. 'I have no idea what you are talking about.'

Aurora snapped back. 'Stop kidding around, how did you find me? I know for sure it was not a tracking device. I have been in my underwear since they captured me, and my clothes and whole body have been scanned, and they found nothing.'

'Girlfriend, I know you pretty well by now, and I am well aware that sometimes you act on impulse.'

Aurora began to protest, but Sun Yee put her hand up. 'Allow me to continue. I thought it only fair, for my peace of mind, that I devise something. Remember when you asked if I knew a good dentist, and I sent you to an old friend when we were in Poland?'

Aurora gasped, 'You had her put something in my tooth!'

'Not exactly. She put a small screw in your jaw, which dentists use frequently and would not attract attention. Except for this screw was special, it had a tracking device, smaller than a pin head inserted,' she explained.

Confused, Aurora asked, 'But that does not explain how it wasn't detected?'

'Some very clever East European scientist created this device when the homing device is not tracking it. It becomes dormant, therefore, undetectable. I hope you will not be angry. It was only out of concern.'

Aurora could not contain herself and started to cry, 'How could I possibly be angry? You have just saved my life, and more importantly, it makes me feel very special.' Then she asked, 'How long to the destination?'

Sun Yee checked the sat nav. 'Fifteen minutes. A lot can happen in that time,' she replied.

They stared out of the cockpit to the ground below, wondering how their friends were faring.

## 90

Charlie pressed his earpiece to speak to Des. 'Brother, we just heard Elliot is on his way. We have no option but to go for the drastic plan. So things are going to get loud. If you can hang fast, let me know when his crew is about to breach. Then get the hell out of there. I will see you when this is over, and we will have a drink.'

'No problem, bro, I will hold you to that,' he replied as they disconnected.

Charlie turned to his companions. 'It's going to get very noisy at any moment. You know what to do.'

They nodded and covered their ears. At the same time, Des's voice burst in his ear, 'Here they come!' he yelled.

Charlie pressed the remote on his watch again, and the explosive device Moses had hidden in the case carrying the donated organs detonated. The result was devastating.

They had placed it closest to the end against the door, directing most of the energy against where they were about to enter. The force shattered the door, and most of the back wall separating the operating theatre from the corridor where the men ready to assault were crowded. Most of them were blasted by the explosion, while the rest were showered with fragments of the capsule and numerous parts of Mizrahi's long-dead brother. It was like a giant grenade, but thanks to most of the force being directed outward, Charlie and the rest of them inside the operating theatre came out relatively unscathed.

They were showered with debris, and the noise of the explosion had left their ears ringing, but they had avoided the brunt of its damage. Christina was the first to react and gave a thumbs-up. Sergei responded with the same. At the same time, Charlie was trying to recover his breath from the stunning blow he had received to his side. Reaching down to feel what was wrong, at the same time, he began to stumble, raising his hand. It was covered in blood.

'You are bleeding,' Christina cried as she leapt to his assistance.

He slumped down. 'First time I have ever been shot...' he muttered, a confused expression on his face.

She moved his hand aside to expose a deep groove carved into his side. 'You are lucky; it missed any arteries. Keep pressure on it until I find something to staunch the bleeding.'

While she was doing this, Sergei had begun to explore the room's shattered remains. The walls and ceiling were peppered with holes of all sizes, splattered with the remains of Levi and his cubical. Stepping carefully to the gaping hole in the back wall, he looked in to see what they had to contend with. When he saw the blast result, the corridor was littered with dead and maimed attackers.

He shrugged and hurried back to where Chris had just finished patching Charlie. 'We are clear to retreat out the back,' he informed them.

'And we are ready to go,' Christina announced, satisfied with her work.

Sergei stepped in and quickly picked up Charlie's 110-kilogram frame like a baby. 'Best thing I have heard today, follow me,' he instructed.

Sergei returned to where he had been before, to the point of entry into the passageway. The damage was extensive. Christina gasped, putting her hand to her mouth in horror.

'I would have thought you would have been used to the sight of blood?' Sergei muttered as he searched around for an avenue of escape.

He had no idea whether there were reinforcements on the way. She tugged on his sleeve, pointing towards what remained of the door and capsule.

All around were the dead and injured. Then he glimpsed what she was pointing to.

'Levi,' she gasped.

The pieces of what she assumed were Levi's remains were confirmed when they spotted his heavily made-up head, sitting propped against the wall, with a grotesque grin on his face.

They stared momentarily, then just stepped around the pieces of flesh littering the floor. They ignored any of the remaining guards who were still alive, as they were long past offering any resistance.

Christina moved in front of Sergei at his behest. This way, he could watch behind and in front. He shifted Charlie in his arms to reposition him.

'You can put me down now, big guy. I think I can walk.'

Sergei shrugged and placed him down. Charlie stood for a moment the test his balance. The wound on his side hurt, but he could manage once he kept the pressure on it.

'Let's go, lead on,' he said, stepping between the others.

Groping in the dark, they tried to orientate themselves. Some lights were functioning, so Christina began to check those first. They had yet to find an exit, all passageways leading to dead ends.

After retreating to the central passage where they had started, they moved into the darkness of what appeared to be a service passageway. This time Sergei took the lead with Charlie at the rear. Christina now used her mobile to shine a pencil light around to give them some idea of where they were going. As she shone the light on what appeared to be an intersection, the beam caught one of the guards who had survived launching himself at Sergei. Thanks to the light, Sergei grabbed him and the hand that held the machete, just in time. Spinning him, Sergei slammed him into the wall, twisting his arm as if it was a piece of string. Using the attacker's hand, he turned it in a circle cutting the guy's throat with his own weapon.

As the dead guard dropped to the floor, Sergei shrugged at the horrified expression on Christina's face. 'Him or me. Let's keep moving,' he said.

They decided to take the direction that the guy had appeared from. In the distance, they could see a door to the outside ajar.

'There is a door,' she indicated.

Sergei led the way. At the door, he pushed it fully open with his foot, and they stepped out into the bright sunlight to be greeted by the sight of two gunmen fumbling to bring their Uzi's up to fire.

# 91

Elliot and his men had already begun silently disposing of the guards blocking their entry point. His well-trained men made easy work of them.

But that all changed as soon as Charlie detonated the bomb. They had been expecting this, so their tactics adjusted at once. They went from stealth to complete action in a heartbeat. Although they were outnumbered three to one, they disposed of their targets without suffering a scratch, except for one of them receiving a couple of hits from a lucky burst of machine gun fire to his bulletproof vest. Regrouping at the front entrance, Elliot spoke to the men, instructing them what he wanted.

He sent the bulk of his force to the front; their job was to secure Mizrahi and subdue any resistance. He reminded them of the importance of their target being able to speak. He knew they would have no problem identifying him as they had studied many photos of him.

As his men entered the front, Le Blu and Le Rouge went for the side of the house as the schematics showed a large factory-like structure built on the back. Elliot planned to approach the skirmish from the rear and assist the others as he searched for an entrance.

He became concerned when his earpieces fell silent. He hoped it was some equipment failure and not that his friends had suffered any harm.

## EIGHT MINUTES BEFORE

Abdiel Mizrahi stood rooted in the horror of what he had just witnessed.

He had just advised his men about where they had pushed his brother's casket when the whole thing exploded!

In front of his eyes, he saw his brother's capsule disintegrate as pieces of it and its contents blew everywhere. The force of the blast blew out the window that separated the theatre from the house, showering him with debris. Inundated by the screams of the wounded guards coming through the broken window, he put his hand up to wipe his face. As he took it away, a guttural wail came from his mouth. His hand was covered with tiny particles of his brother's brains.

Suddenly, he was grasped from behind and spun around. One of the medical staff was shaking him. 'Come with me; we must get you to safety,' the medic urged, shaking the horrified Mizrahi.

Hesitating momentarily, he nodded blankly and followed. The medic led him away from the horror he has just witnessed.

As he stumbled along behind, he asked, shakenly, 'Where are you taking me?'

The medic replied with a sense of urgency, 'To the safest room in the house. You can remain there until the authorities arrive. They must be on their way by now.'

They hurried to part of the house reserved for the staff. Passing one of the rooms, he could see many of the medical personnel huddled in fear of the gunfire. The medic waved and got some weak responses from his colleagues.

Just beyond there, they arrived at a steel door. 'Inside,' the medic indicated. ' I will seal the door. Don't open it for anybody unless it is the police; good luck.'

And with that, he pushed the heavy door closed.

# 92

M. Rouge waved his boss forward. They were at the side that led to the rear of the house and had encountered little resistance, except a sentry trying to flee. But a well-placed shot dropped him in his tracks. They moved along the path leading to the rear, and as they stepped around to the back, they stopped abruptly.

The sight of the giant Russian, Sergei, and Christina greeted them. She was supporting Charlie. To their horror, they could see that two guards facing them were about to shoot!

M. Rouge reacted first, crossing the distance to the gunmen in a couple of silent strides. He drove his C.A.C. folding short-blade killing knife into the first one's spinal cord, severing all connection to the nervous system. His lifeless body dropped, and as the other gunman was just reacting, he was gripped by the collar and violently wrenched back. He fell backwards, dropping his rifle, trying to recover his balance. He looked up as he was falling, and the last thing he saw was the masked face of Elliot placing a bullet between his eyes.

This had all taken place in what seemed to be a blink of an eye to the startled stare of Sergei, who had moved to shield Christina and Charlie behind his colossal frame before the guards could shoot.

Like phantoms, two masked men clad entirely in green disposed of them. He had never seen men move so fast and efficiently, even during his time in the GRU forces.

'It has to be Elliot,' he could hear Charlie say as he leaned on him for support.

Sure enough, as they approached, removing their masks to reveal the smiling face of Elliot and one of his men. Sergei embraced them, almost crushing their ribs.

'You are hurt,' Elliot exclaimed as he spotted Charlie being helped by Christina.

'My first bullet wound,' he declared, brought on by the Savage brother's flair for the dramatic.

The sound of sporadic gunfire changed the subject.

'Let's get you all to cover,' Elliot ordered, then began to enter the door they had just emerged from.

'Not a good idea. It's a bit of a mess that way. I believe the front would be a better option,' Sergei suggested.

Taking his advice, they returned to the front of the building where they were greeted by the one who was assigned the colour green, M. Vert.

'Just clearing up some stragglers, let me check,' as he spoke to somebody through his intercom. 'All clear, this way,' as he indicated for them to follow.

'Any sign of Mizrahi?' Elliot asked.

'Not yet. We are clearing the place room by room. The only people we have located so far are the general staff. We have placed them in a separate room from the medical staff until we discover their involvement.'

Elliot nodded. 'Take me to the medical people first.'

As they entered a large reception area with doors leading to different locations, one of the men called, 'Over here!'

When they got to the door, they could see what seemed to be a recreation area. It was crowded with medical staff hiding from the battle that had raged outside.

Elliot stepped forward. 'Is there anybody here that can help locate Mr Mizrahi?' he asked the crowd huddled inside.

One of them in a white coat and haircap stood. 'That would be me,' he announced.

Elliot looked at the man for a moment, then replied, 'Of course, it would be you, Desmond!'

They both burst out in laughter.

## 93

After they got over the additional shock of finding Des disguised as a medic, he began to explain how he had located Abdiel. While he talked, Christina put Charlie on a comfortable couch where she had plenty of willing helpers to attend to his wounds. Des continued to relate what happened from when Charlie had told him to find his own way out. As soon as he had said go, he had dashed from the office into the corridor. He had only just passed the entrance when the blast from the explosion flung him to the ground, where he picked himself up and continued running, coughing and spluttering until he came into the clear.

He had now found himself in the reception room. A door then opened as he was trying to figure out where he was, and a nurse appeared. She gestured for him to take cover. Before he could respond, an ear-splitting shriek caused the nurse to retreat and slam the door.

'I decided to follow the noise. That's when I discovered Mizrahi was the source. He was standing there, brandishing a gun. He was covered in the remains of his brother. As you can imagine, he was a bit upset.'

He continued with the story, dragging the most out of it.

'So I decided to kill two birds with one stone. Help him out and secure him at the same time. I grabbed him and told him I was there to help him. I took him somewhere he would be secure, put him inside, and told him not to open the door to anybody but me or the authorities.'

It was Charlie from the couch that had enough of the story. 'So, enough already. Where is he?' he yelled, causing him to grimace in pain.

'All right, no need to be rude. Follow me,' indicating Elliot and some of his men to follow.

They turned and crossed the hall to one of the doors opposite. Entering, they could see a storage area filled with medical supplies. Every possible medical emergency was provided for at the insistence of Mizrahi. All for his brother. Des led them to a corner where the solid door to a cold room faced them. He banged on the door.

'Mr Mizrahi, it is me. I have brought help.'

When he got no reply, he released the catch and opened the door. They could see Mizrahi sitting on some boxes, shivering so violently that he probably would have bitten his tongue off if he had tried to talk. Desmond glanced back when he saw their expressions.

He shrugged and said, 'I never said he was comfortable!'

## 94

They managed to get Abdiel thawed out enough to transfer him to the room where most activities occurred. His desk and computers were facing a wall where one of Elliot's men had already discovered his safe. It was disguised as a cabinet and firmly cemented into the floor, so it would have to be opened if they wanted the contents.

Elliot's men had continued mopping up operations and had transferred those survivors that could walk to the room where they were guarding Abdiel. The domestic staff had also assembled there, where one of his men that could speak Spanish had explained that they were in no danger, and that their argument was with their boss. They were delighted to assist when they were released, hurriedly preparing refreshments while the medical staff tried to help the badly wounded.

While this was going on, Christina had Charlie transferred into the same room. He was seated comfortably while Christina gave the other doctors a hand. When they secured the area, they reached out to Vincent and everybody back home on a secure video link Axel had set up. They told them they had succeeded and, most importantly, that Aurora had been rescued by Sun Yee. She was safe and sound, and were on their way to meet up.

'Great news on that front,' Vincent congratulated them. 'I had just been on to the police in Aruba when I heard you would set off the explosions. I contacted them, representing myself as Mizrahi's lawyer, to explain that they were practising for an upcoming party with fireworks and numerous other noisy activities. They thanked me and offered their assistance, which I declined but said to keep their eyes out for a surprise.'

This brought a relieving laugh from the surrounding crew.

'It won't be the one they are expecting,' Des chimed in.

Axel intervened. 'Have you had any luck with the wallet and his laptops?' she asked.

This time, it was Elliot that took charge. 'My men are loading up every piece of computer hardware. It would appear that he did all his operations from here.'

'When you discover where he has the wallet, you will almost certainly find some hard drives. This is where he will have his most closely guarded secrets,' she informed them.

Elliot glanced in the direction of Mizrahi, whom M. Vert was watching. They had put a blindfold on him and headphones, which served two purposes. They could talk freely, and it was scaring the shit out of him!

'I am just letting him stew while we prepare to evacuate all of the Umbrella crew,' he replied with a chuckle.

At that moment, the sound of an approaching helicopter brought an immediate response. M. Rouge leapt into action, directing two more of his men to the outside in case this was reinforcement for Mizrahi.

Despite the headphones, Abdiel could hear the sound of a chopper, and his hopes soared. *This might be Eitan arriving after taking care of the girl. He will know how to handle this situation.*

His brother was now forgotten as his survival had become paramount. He swivelled his head from side to side to try and pick up anything that would tell him what was happening.

'Somebody has come to visit you,' he heard as the headphones and blindfold were removed.

He could hear the helicopter spooling down and voices approaching from the front entrance. His heart dropped when Aurora marched in, dragging a sorry-looking creature behind her. He could see that the guy was missing part of his right hand, and his left arm hung uselessly at his side, dripping blood, despite the tourniquet wrapped tightly around it. To his horror, he realised it was Eitan Zoabi, or what was left of him. At that moment, he knew he was totally screwed.

Aurora was followed by an attractive Asian woman who, when she spotted him, her glare almost gave him a heart attack. While their friends greeted them with great excitement, Eitan, having reached the limits of his endurance, collapsed to the floor.

M. Rouge dragged him to his feet. 'What do you want me to do with this crap?' he asked.

Elliot responded. 'Take him to our chopper. We will deal with him later.'

This brought a gasp of horror from Abdiel. Elliot acknowledged his existence for the first time since he had been released from the freezer.

'Don't be concerned. We are not going to kill him. We have so much to discuss. Sadly his condition does not give me much time,' he explained to the stricken Mizrahi.

Des sprang to his feet and looked at his brother imploringly. 'Can I make the introductions,' he pleaded.

Charlie nodded. 'But of course, after all, he is your friend.'

Grinning from ear to ear, he turned his attention to Abdiel. 'Allow me to introduce you to Colonel Elliot Blanchet of the French Secret Service. He is retired but has returned for this special assignment. You see, he is the father of Estelle Blanchet. If you don't recognise the name, she is the girl you and the bleeding creature standing there kidnapped and removed her kidney for your worthless brother. He is very keen to chat with you.'

Abdiel whimpered and passed out cold!

# 95

Abdiel was revived by a jug of water being flung over his face, and he nearly passed out again at the sight of this Frenchman standing over him.

Elliot began to speak to him in a soft voice that carried so much menace. 'Let me explain what is going to happen. Shortly you and your friend will be transported to another location where you will be asked to provide some information. You almost certainly will refuse. But I can assure you, you will provide the answers we require. But before we leave, we can put that to the test. You see, we need some of the contents of your safe, so we require the combination. Now I see by your expression some reluctance to provide that. So if anybody is squeamish, I suggest you step outside while we discuss your reluctance.'

Nobody moved. To Charlie, it appeared no love was lost with his employees, and considering the horrors he was responsible for, none of his captors had any ideas of moving either. This didn't really come as a surprise.

Elliot took out a cigar and removed a device for clipping it. He placed the opening over the tip and depressed the trigger, taking the end off. He then began to light it slowly, savouring the aroma. He moved closer to the terrified Abdiel, who was starting to hyperventilate.

'Are you right or left-handed? I need to know in the event we need you to write something,' he asked pleasantly, dripping with venom. When he did not reply, Elliot shrugged. 'Well, left hand it is. Most are right-handed, so here we go.'

Placing the device over his ring finger and swiftly snipped the top off. The screams reverberated around the room. Most turned their heads. But all the Umbrella crew kept focused, remembering what he was responsible for. Elliot asked one of his men to give him something to staunch the bleeding. Then he placed the clipper on the next finger.

'It usually takes two, sometimes three with the stubborn ones, before they talk. With you, I am guessing one.'

Mizrahi began to blubber 'Stop. I will tell you.'

As he recited a number, Elliot indicated for M. Rouge to try unlocking the safe, and seconds later, the contents were spread on the ground.

The hard wallet was located along with a second hard drive. They were added to the computers they had collected, along with a pile of documents.

Elliot ordered them to be loaded on their helicopter along with their captives. M. Rouge called out, 'What should we do with this?' pointing at a large box he had pulled from the bottom of the safe.

The lid was open, exposing the contents. On top was a small sack crammed with diamonds and precious stones. Underneath was stuffed with US dollars, a small fortune. Elliot approached Des and Charlie.

'This decision is up to you. My men nor I want any part of it. We have our compensation,' glancing at Abdiel.

Charlie quickly decided for them. 'Give the money to the staff,' he replied, then flicked the bag with the stones to his brother. 'Here you take care of these, seeing as you have some experience with them,' referring to the diamonds Des had "procured" in a previous adventure.

Elliot announced to the staff that they would leave the money for them to distribute amongst themselves. He suggested that deciding who in the medical personnel deserved a portion would be up to them. He then moved to where the others were waiting.

'We are ready to depart and will link up with you back in Bogota. I would expect to have the password for the wallet before you depart for home.' He then turned and instructed his assembled crew. 'We will wait here until my men transport you back to your plane.'

'No need for that,' Aurora announced, 'I have just been on to the pilots to prepare for take-off, and we will be arriving by helicopter. I will fly our crew in on the one Eitan gifted me.'

Minutes later, the military chopper lifted off and disappeared into the distance. Aurora had waited in their much smaller aircraft until the wash of the larger one had passed. Inside they squeezed Sergei's large body in the back alongside Des. Charlie had Christina alongside in the second row with Sun Yee as co-pilot.

'Hold on, here we go', Aurora yelled over the rotor as they climbed and turned toward the airport.

# 96

The chopper descended into the airfield and landed alongside their aircraft less than ten minutes after their departure, greeted by the pilots standing by to help transfer the injured Charlie, whom Sergei had carried to the plane.

After he was seated, Aurora checked the precious wallet, and the hard drive was secured beside him. When everybody was on board, one of the pilots pointed to the helicopter.

'What do you want to do about that?' he asked Aurora.

She glanced at the Sun Yee, who shrugged. So she replied, 'It is yours. I am sure an enterprising chap like you can figure out what to do with it.'

'Won't the owner be looking for it?' he asked.

'Not a chance. He has a much bigger problem than that,' she said.

They had taxied to the start of the runway, where Aurora could hear the pilots finalising their take-off check list. Something nagged in her mind that she felt she had forgotten something.

The last few days' events kept flashing into her thoughts, and then something Eitan had said sprang into her mind, causing her to unbuckle her seat belt and leap up, running into the pilot's cabin, screaming at the top of her voice.

'Stop!'

The urgency in her voice caused the pilot in charge of the take-off to abort. 'What's wrong?' he demanded.

She turned to her startled teammates. 'Sorry, I forgot there is a bomb attached to the plane,' she mumbled, burying her face in her hands with embarrassment.

She explained that while Eitan had been delivering one of his beatings, he had let slip that his men had placed a bomb under the aircraft that would detonate when they reached cruising altitude.

Thirty minutes later, they were all back inside the aircraft after Sergei had discovered the bomb in the undercarriage well and was safely disarmed.

'Are you sure that thing is safe?' Des asked Sergei as he brought it back on board.

He gave a big laugh. 'Irishman, I thought you people know all about bombs,' as he tossed it to him.

Des caught it as if it was a hot potato. 'Are you crazy! Just like all Russians are not in the mafia, all Irish are not part-time bomb makers,' he yelled, handing the bomb carefully back.

'It is harmless without the pressure switch. It is just a doorstop. By the way, all the Russians I know would love to be in the mafia!' Sergei roared, laughing again.

Forty minutes later, they were taxiing to a stop in the airfields where Elliot was operating from. As soon as they arrived, they began preparations by transferring to Christina's dad's jet for the return trip home. While that happened, Aurora and Sun Yee caught up with Elliot to see how he was progressing with the Wallet password.

'He is being surprisingly stubborn. He asked to speak to Eitan, who had been stabilised but will not be playing the piano anytime soon,' he quipped. 'Whatever they discussed seemed to firm Abdiel up. I am just about to continue questioning him.'

'Before you do, has he made any requests?' Sun Yee asked.

'No, nothing of note, except he kept asking where his wallet was. I told him it was safe and flying back with you. He seemed relieved.'

Sun Yee explained about the bomb.

'This must be what they are holding out for if the wallet and hard drive were destroyed. Our only hope of retrieving anything is if they are alive. I think it is time for them to have a visitor.'

Abdiel was surprised when Eitan was wheeled into the room where they held them. Since he had told him about the bomb, he had kept his mouth shut. Hoping word of the downed aircraft would reach them before the French father of the girl took more of his fingers off. Looking at the dejected figure of Eitan, with his useless arms strapped to the chair, they exchanged nods as Elliot strode into the room.

'Before we begin, you have some visitors.'

He stood to one side, allowing Aurora and Sun Yee to walk in. The shock on their faces at the sight of Aurora and her friend was something to behold, as all hope disappeared.

'Surprised to see us. You forgot that while amusing yourself by hitting me, you talked a lot. You forgot that you boasted to me about this,' as she flung the detonation device onto his lap.

They sat in stunned silence. Then Mizrahi lost it.

'You idiot! Your desire to settle the score with this woman has ruined everything.' Turning to Aurora, he pleaded, 'This was all his idea. You have to believe me.'

'It is not me you have to convince. If I were you, I would be more concerned with the father of the girl you intended to sacrifice for that worthless brother of yours. I suspect this is the last time we will meet. No point in wishing you well. I think that would be a waste of time.'

Turning to Elliot, she then said, 'I will leave you to continue your conversation,' and marched out.

They were halfway through their journey back to South Africa when Elliot called on the radio. 'I have that information you wanted,' and recited the password.

# 97

They had been back at Christina's clinic for two days. Elliot and his men had arrived the previous day, and his men had already departed for their respective homes with little fuss.

They had tried to convince them to stay and enjoy their success with the rest of the crew. But as Elliot explained, that this was just another day at the office for them and interaction with those involved was something they avoided. So after Aurora and all concerned had thanked them, they boarded their transport plane and disappeared into the sky.

Elliot remained to be reunited with his wife and daughter and agreed to stay on while Axel went to work on the wallet and the hard drive.

Charlie was revelling in the attention he was receiving due to his "bullet wound". As far as he was concerned, he was the first of the Savage brothers to get shot. Chris had not got the heart to burst his bubble by telling him the "bullet" was a piece of Levi's capsule.

Commander Moses was delighted to see them return safely. When he had greeted everybody, congratulating them on their success, he then turned to Elliot, asking as to the fate of Mizrahi and Eitan.

A blank expression crossed his face as he replied, 'They both decided to become organ donors. Already their donation has saved the lives of over a dozen people.'

Desmond, as usual, interrupted. 'I thought you had to be dead to give your organs?'

He just smiled and replied. 'As usual, you are right, Desmond.'

When Des saw the expressions on the faces of his pals, the penny dropped! 'Of course, I knew that', he blustered, his face bright red.

Charlie stepped in to save him from embarrassment. 'Speaking of deaths. The necklace you gave us to control Dr Amara did its job. It had no half-measures. Did you know it would take her head off?' he asked Moses.

'Well, my friend, I knew the type of person she was, and that she could not be trusted. She had the opportunity to do the right thing. But she chose wrong. I knew you wouldn't activate the device if you knew the outcome. So I made that decision. Nobody is responsible for her demise except herself.'

Elliot stepped in. 'Regardless of our decisions, I have no regrets for any actions I have taken in this regard. Let's not forget the pain and suffering these people have caused. Not only physically but also shame and financial ruin to so many. Nothing we have done could compare to what they deserve. I, for one, will offer whatever assistance the Umbrella Crew should need in the future.'

Moses stuck his hand out. 'You can count me in on that also, Le Blu,' he added as they exchanged handshakes.

# 98

Axel had woken them at 05:30 in the morning, yelling for them to follow her.

Back in the computer room where they were gathering, wiping the sleep out of their eyes, Vincent, being the last to arrive, was not at all happy at being awakened.

He growled, 'What the hell is happening?'

'We have the crypto. The wallet is open, and I have removed the currency and begun to distribute it back to his defrauded clients,' she bubbled with excitement.

'How much is there?' was the first thing Charlie asked.

'Hold your breath,' she said. 'There is over 2.4 billion in Bitcoin and another few million in assorted cryptocurrencies,' she announced, which brought a gasp from the crew.

His next question was, 'How much is due to the people he defrauded?'

'I can't be exact, but from his records on that second drive. He kept a list of all the people he defrauded. So they are about to get a big surprise when their crypto is miraculously returned. Also, because they don't have to liquidate to cover their losses, it will help to support the price of the Bitcoin, allowing the balance to be transferred to Christina's trust fund to provide for the victims of his crazy scheme.'

Desmond was next to jump in, 'But how much is that?'

She paused, then replied in a hushed voice. 'In excess of one and a half billion US dollars. More than enough to provide for all of his victims. Not only their rehabilitation but to provide for their future education and to aid in locating relatives where possible.'

Christina could not contain herself, bursting out in tears. 'This is a miracle. We can also expand our assistance to many others with these funds.'

While the discussion was going on about this fantastic windfall and how to distribute it best, Charlie noticed Axel was silent, as if waiting for a chance to continue.

'Everybody, I think Axel has some more news for us. Is that correct?' he asked her.

She nodded furiously, hardly able to contain herself. 'I found the stolen computers,' she cried, referring to the Bitcoin computers stolen from her home country, Iceland.

'Where are they?' Vincent asked.

'You won't believe it when I tell you,' she said, and began to relate her discovery.

# 99

## REYKJAVIK, ICELAND

Jon Sigurdsson held the door of the old warehouse, one of many abandoned by the US military, for his girlfriend Kristin Jonsdotter to enter. This had been the daily task since 2014 when the mysterious MR X, as the press had nicknamed him, had approached them.

They were in their IT services shop when a guy came in, who, from time to time, brought them Items to sell. They never questioned the origin. But they suspected he dealt in dubious activities. Still, as crime in Iceland was almost non-existent, they gave him the benefit of the doubt.

Then everything changed.

He came in one day very excited. 'I have a wonderful opportunity for you. A business associate of mine is looking for somebody to service and maintain a computer hub here in Reykjavik. It would suit you guys down to the ground,' he exclaimed.

But when they questioned him for details, he told them it was all very hush-hush, and they would have to be bound to secrecy if they were interested. The temptation was too much for them, so they agreed, and the following evening they got a call to meet them at one of the old warehouses that dotted the landscape. When they arrived, the guy they knew as Rolf, introduced them to a stocky man who looked like a banker.

'This is Mr X. (Alex explained this was Mizrahi). He will explain what is expected of you,' handing the conversation over.

'This will be the only time we will meet face-to-face. I operate my business on the internet. From now on, we will establish an untraceable link to communicate. I operate a Cryptocurrency Exchange. I presume you are familiar with what we do?' he asked.

Kristin replied excitedly, 'Yes, we have upgraded some computers for our friends so they can trade.'

He nodded. 'Good, so then you are familiar with Bitcoin. Shortly some special computers constructed to mine for Bitcoin will arrive here. You will monitor and service them as they produce new currency. For this service, you will be paid a percentage of every Bitcoin mined,' he explained. 'Before you decide to undertake this task, there is somebody I would like you to meet. This is my brother, Levi,' indicating a guy that stepped from the shadows.

He was the exact opposite of his brother in appearance. The cold look on his face sent a shiver through them. 'As you can imagine, this will produce a large amount of wealth, and with that comes risk. Any mention of this will bring repercussions. Do we understand each other?'

Jon turned to his girlfriend to discuss it, but greed took over before he could utter a word, and Kristin responded. 'We are in.'

Later that evening, a truck pulled up at the warehouse and started to unload the computers. They were about the size of a carton of cigarettes. But what shocked them was the amount. There were over 900 of them!

The following day after a restless night, they awoke to the news of the brazen theft of Bitcoin computers from a government-sponsored crypto mining centre. When Jon started to panic, Kristin slapped him.

'Enough. I have had enough of scraping by. This is our chance, and we are not backing out,' she informed him.

So they moved their business to the warehouse, providing a perfect front for them after the initial excitement of such a giant robbery and the subsequent capture of the people that carried out the theft. But no trace could be found of the mysterious MR X. Over time, they settled into their new career, enjoying their newfound wealth. Their only contact with the mysterious Mr X was through a secure line, where they would be contacted from time to time with instructions.

A few weeks back, someone contacted them to provide new contact details. At the same time, he asked them to step up production. Since then, they had not heard from him, which was normal, as often weeks passed without hearing from him.

They entered the area this night where the computers were housed and were about to commence work when, on their security cameras, they saw some cars pull up, and some people in uniform step out.

'It's the police,' Jon gasped.

'Calm down. It is probably a security check,' Kristin snapped.

A loud rapping on the door made them jump. 'Go and see what they want,' Jon urged.

She rolled her eyes and groaned as she headed to the door. 'We are closed; who is it?' she asked.

The banging continued. Then, with a crash, the door burst in.

Kristin was flung onto her back to be surrounded by armed police. 'Kristin Jonsdotter, you are under arrest for government property theft and misuse. Where is Jon Sigurdsson?' the policeman demanded.

Within minutes they were handcuffed and advised of their rights. As they were being led out to the police car, a reporter stepped forward accompanied by a camera crew, shining bright lights into the forlorn faces of the pair.

'Have you any comment for the people that have been affected by this theft?' Pulitzer nominee and intrepid reporter Sharlene Nolovu asked in English as she thrust the microphone in front of them.

# 100

**TWO WEEKS LATER**

The world press had descended on Reykjavik when news broke of the recovery of the Bitcoin computers, thanks to Axel releasing all the documents to the internet and also to the international authorities.

One week later, Sharlene Nolovu went on prime-time television with an expose of the false accusations brought against Gunnar Sigurdsson, the guard that had been put under suspicion of the theft, resulting in his untimely death.

Immediately after the pressure from the public for a full investigation, an inquiry was launched. With the irrefutable evidence provided by his daughter, Gunnar Sigurdsson was quickly exonerated and was posthumously awarded the country's highest honour, the Medal of Valour, for his services.

Axel had travelled back to her home country as soon as Commander Moses Khumalo contacted the police in Reykjavik. He had assured them she had been cleared of an investigation in South Africa. He also used his connections in Interpol to convince them that her efforts were the reason they had brought down the organ harvesting scheme, resulting in her name being taken off the watch list.

Vincent Savage worked diligently with Christina to ensure the true story came out. When the Icelandic government tried to play the whole affair down, he quickly stepped in and informed them that unless they wanted another banking crisis, he would have no option but bring to light how no proper investigation was ever carried out. Added to this, Sharlene's TV special quickly prompted the subsequent action.

Helga Sigridsson embraced her daughter, delighted that she could return home. She had brought Sharlene with her. When Vincent had outlined their plan of attack regarding the story's release, he insisted that she remain anonymous. The information was attributed to an inside source who had contacted Sharlene. When she explained to her mother who she was and how she had helped clear her husband's name, she hugged her, crying joyfully.

'How can we ever thank you? Gunner would be so happy that the truth has come out,' she sobbed.

Later, when they had given her mother a sanitised version of what had happened, they opened a bottle of schnapps to celebrate.

During the evening, neighbours and friends began to call. First, to apologise for doubting her husband and secondly to congratulate her on the truth coming out.

Helga could not have been happier, just glad to have their family's honour restored.

Later that evening, when everybody had left, Sharlene excused herself, explaining that she had an interview with the President. Since her success with the organ transplant story and now this fantastic follow-up expose, she had become the darling of many world leaders and was lauded as the most prominent reporter of colour, which had opened the door for her to be flooded with offers from TV networks around the world.

After she had departed, mother and daughter sat together, enjoying this particular time, when Helga sprang up.

'I almost forgot!' she cried, hurrying to a table to fetch something. 'Look at this,' thrusting something into Leslie's hand.

It was a cheque for 800,000 Krona, equivalent to about 600,000 US dollars.

'This arrived yesterday. Somehow, the authorities discovered a glitch in their computer system, which had just been brought to their attention. Disclosing that they had failed to maintain Gunner's pension payment current. Resulting in them sending me this. It even includes interest!' she gushed with excitement.

Axel answered. 'I wonder how that happened?' hugging her mother, as a big grin crossed her face.

# 101

Something that had become a custom was a party-come-reunion after their adventures.

The entire crew were gathered at Christina's place. They were expecting her parents, Felipe and Rosa Herrero, who were flying in on their private jet, accompanied by Desmond's girlfriend, Maria Heart, Bill's daughter. She had brought along their family 'home manager' Dawi Wayan.

Dawi was Balinese and had unofficially taken charge of the day-to-day running of the Heart house. She had been 'adopted' by her family in mysterious circumstances and had become part of the family. Vincent Savage had struck up a relationship with her when helping his brothers out of a spot of bother in her home of Mallorca.

Vincent had jumped at the opportunity to spend some time together. It was an afternoon affair. The staff had prepared a typical South African barbecue, a *braai*. The meat was cooked in a pit on hot coals and then buried to cook slowly in their juices.

The Savage brothers were trying to outdo each other with their stories, much to the delight of the assembled crew. Aurora and Sun Yee were the happiest they had been since they had begun this adventure, which seemed a lifetime ago.

'You never told us how you located Aurora on Aruba?' Charlie suddenly decided to ask them.

He had become tired of the competition with his brothers, especially as they were questioning him for information about the story behind the scar that ran down the right side of his face. Something he wanted to avoid.

Sun Yee looked at her companion, then with a grin, replied, 'We girls have our secrets. If I told you, I would have to kill you.'

This brought some nervous laughter, considering her previous role as an assassin. Then they both burst into laughter.

'Got you!' they cried in delight.

Elliot and his family had joined them, accompanied by Sergei, who had taken to following Estelle around like a puppy dog. This giant of a man had become her chaperone, and much to the delight of her parents, she seemed to embrace his attention. She had recovered wonderfully from her ordeal and was enjoying the company of her rescuers and new-found friends. Especially the antics of the brothers and their Irish humour, which was rubbing off on everyone.

Axel and her mother had arrived from Iceland earlier, along with Sharlene, who had finished her interviews with the authorities, who were anxious to discover the source of her breaking story. Something she bluntly refused to reveal.

The evening continued with plenty of drinks being served as they waited for the arrival of Christina's parents, who had just landed and were on their way to the house, which led to more stories that only seemed to grow the more that drink was consumed. Des was in fine form, describing how he had fooled Mizrahi into believing he was saving him.

'I nearly froze the bugger to death. When we opened the door to the cold room, he looked like a snowman,' he declared, bringing roars of laughter from the room.

The sound of someone arriving brought a cry from Christina. 'My parents are here.'

At the same time, her dad and mum were ushered in by the servants, accompanied by Maria and Dawi, all rushing to embrace their loved ones.

While this was going on, a loud voice from the entrance sent a cold shiver down the backs of the Savage brothers. They stood in shock at the sight of their father, Charlie Savage Sr, standing in the doorway with a wild look on his face.

'Where the hell is my money I sent you to find?' he roared.

# 102

The brothers stood in shock, unable to believe their father was here in South Africa. This was a man that liked to be close to his local and only travelled when there was a promise of free drink.

Vincent was the first to react. 'What the hell are you doing here?' he asked.

At that moment, Charlie remembered the reason Desmond had come here in the first place. 'He is here about his money,' he sputtered.

Charlie Snr strode across the room and started prodding Desmond in the chest. 'You completely forgot about me. It is always the same. As soon as the three of you and your Umbrella mates get together on one of your quests, anything your poor father needs is forgotten.'

Poor Des was lost for words, which seldom happened. Ever since the brothers had discovered a small fortune on their first adventure, their father had quickly adjusted to going from being dirt poor to having more money than he could earn in two lifetimes. This did not stop him from thinking they were still his little boys and at his beck and call.

Charlie stepped in to save the day. 'You have got it all wrong, Dad. If Des had not been looking for a top hacker to recover your money, we would never have caught the people responsible for those terrible crimes.'

When he saw the confusion on his father's face, he gave him a condensed story of the events that had led to Axel's involvement and the journey it had taken them through.

It was Vincent's turn to interrupt. 'Do you mean to tell us that Desmond came over on some wild goose chase to try and recover the money Dad was duped out of?' he asked incredulously.

'I was not duped!' his father roared. 'It was the bank's fault. They were letting these crooks use their website.'

Charlie gave Vince a glance to try and get him to leave it alone. Thankfully, Axel stepped in and saved the day.

'Hi, I am Axel. Des helped to get me out of jail. He told me about your problem, but unfortunately, the rescue of those poor people distracted us.'

Charlie Snr's attitude changed at once at the arrival of this gorgeous blonde woman. A big smile broke across his face. 'Don't tell me somebody as pretty as you are involved with these crazy sons of mine,' he said, ignoring all convention and embracing her in a big hug.

Before she could respond, a voice yelled from the doorway, causing Charlie Snr and his sons to jump. 'I leave you for five minutes and here you are embarrassing that poor girl.'

Helen Savage was standing there. Their mother had come also!

After everybody calmed down and introductions were made all around, and as was customary, whenever the Savages were together, drinking was involved.

The rest of the evening was spent discussing all that had happened, with Charlie Snr continually returning to the subject of his problem.

Vincent had enough. 'You are never happy when we had nothing. You were always complaining. Now you have more money than you could drink in a lifetime, and you are still not satisfied.'

Not to be outdone, Charlie Snr came back with his own response. 'It is not the money, but somebody has to teach those people that you can't take advantage of innocent people,' he retorted.

This brought roars of laughter from his sons and wife.

'This, coming from somebody that would steal your shoes if you were not standing in them!' Helen taunted.

The laughter drowned out his protests. As the night wore on and everybody was well-oiled and merry, Axel assured him she would try to fix his problem. This prompted him to insist they toast with another round of drinks. This went on late into the night as everybody discovered how the Irish celebrate a victory.

By getting blind drunk.

# 103

The following day at breakfast, as they sat nursing sore heads, Charlie Snr arrived without a bother on him. His years of going to the pub every day had hardened him. He sat down, tipped some whiskey into his tea, and gulped it down in one go.

'Nothing like the hair of the dog to get the heart started,' he gasped as the fiery liquid coursed down his throat.

'You lot look the worst of wear. I hope you will not use this as an excuse to put my job on the long finger,' he said, giving his sons a warning stare, which brought groans from them.

Axel stepped in again, seeing the frustration on the lad's faces. 'Okay, so explain to me how they tricked you out of your money?' she asked.

This made him flush with anger. 'I don't know what that son of mine told you. But anybody would have believed them. I was sure it was my bank,' he snapped.

'I was not suggesting that you could be easily fooled. These people are well organised. That is why they are so successful,' she quickly replied, trying to nurse his damaged ego.

After he calmed down, he explained how they had got his bank details and removed his money, avoiding that if Vincent had not spotted they were trying to access the family trust, things could have been much worse.

'Have you got the phone that you used with you?' she asked.

He produced the phone and handed it to her. She quickly scrolled through it until she pointed to a number that appeared. 'Is this the number they called you from?'

He nodded. 'How did you know?' he asked.

She laughed and started clicking away at her keyboard, her gaze fixed across the screen as lines of code scrolled across. After a few minutes, she sat back. 'Now we wait,' she said to a very confused Charlie Snr.

'Whatever you say, young lady, The language of young computer people today is from another world. What chance has a dumb Irishman got against the likes of you?' he spluttered in awe.

'You were smart enough to send me to find a genius like this young lady you are so in awe of!' Des snapped, bringing a titter of laughter from his dad.

A couple of hours had passed before Axel yelled out, 'Got you!' bringing Des and his dad running!

'You found him already?' Des asked.

She put her hand up. 'Not so fast, cowboy. It's not that easy. These people cover their tracks very well. I have traced the number to a cluster located in Ireland. It leads me on a chase around the globe. They covered their tracks very well, but I found the source of the call. It is an operation here in South Africa. That is unsurprising. The corruption here makes catching them very hard.'

'So what happens now?' Chaz Snr asked.

'We are waiting for them to call you. When it traced the connection to here, I planted your number in their lists of numbers to call. When that happens, then the fun begins,' she replied.

'What if they recognise it?'

She laughed. 'Have you any idea how big this business is? Computer scams generate billions of dollars in revenue annually, and few are ever caught. This is a numbers game. The calls are on an automatic dial. The scammer only responds when he gets a bite. So, no, no chance of you being recognised. In any case, we will let one of your sons do the talking, and before you say it, I will tell them what to say. So, go and amuse yourselves. I have some people to talk to.'

# 104

It was the morning of the second day before they took the bait.

It had been agreed that Vincent would take the call and play the victim. His task at first was to stall until Axel could initiate a trace. Then as soon as they disclosed their scam, he had a prepared list of responses, depending on what they asked.

Letting it ring briefly, with a nod from Axel, he answered. 'Hello, Terrance McQueen speaking,' following his brother Des' love of the cinema and using his favourite actor's real name, Steve McQueen.

'My name is Lethabo Nkosi. I represent the Law firm Cliffe, Dekker, & Hofmayr.'

Vince knew they were using the name of a legitimate business, which was common practice, as most people never checked.

'We have been trying to contact you regarding a large inheritance bequeathed to you by a distant relative. We know this because of the extensive investigation we had to do to trace you.'

Axel gave the thumbs up for Vincent to proceed. Every instinct in his body wanted to resist doing what he had been asked, which was 'act the idiot.' This scam usually started by requesting small amounts of money until they had the hook in deep. Axel had set up a plan for this, and it was going to be the scammer's downfall.

Taking a deep breath, he began to act out the script. 'My goodness, I can't believe it. This must be my wife's side of the family. I believe they were from Africa. The Lindenbergs, I believe.'

Not wanting to overplay his hand, the scammer replied, 'I don't have the details in front of me, but that sounds like what was described to me. What we need to do now is set up an international account to enable us to transfer the funds. There will be a small charge for this.'

He paused for the reaction, and Vincent continued with his act. 'Of course. Can I ask how much I will get?' he said, not wanting to sound too gullible.

The scammer cursed to himself; he was so happy to have found this guy that he had forgotten to dangle the bait. 'My apologies. I was so happy to find you. I forgot. The bequest is in the order of $1.6 million.'

Vincent gave a fake gasp, again following the instructions. 'I am not very good with computers. If I give you my e-mail, can you help me set up this account?' he asked.

By this time, the guy was surrounded by his mates to watch the perfect scam. Within minutes, he was in control of Vincent's computer. At the same time, within seconds, Axel had piggybacked in and turned on all the cameras on their computers, giving her visuals of all the participants but also allowing her to plant bugs on all their equipment. From that moment on, they were in her hands. After the guy had extracted a couple of hundred dollars from Vincent, he told him he would receive a receipt and further instructions shortly.

Hanging up, Vincent could barely contain himself. 'How does anybody fall for this crap?'

At once realising his father was standing there, he quickly tried to cover his tracks. 'We need more people like you, Dad, doing something about it. So what happens next?' he asked, changing the subject.

'They will try to bleed as much as they can from you. That's not going to happen. Their world is about to change in a big way. We are going to take these guys apart. What do you think, Charlie Snr?'

'That's just what the doctor ordered,' he replied.

When Vincent saw the confused expression on her face at the reply, he intervened. 'He is just using one of his old Irish expressions. It means "Great".'

## 105

'I want you to meet Mr Lethabo Nkosi, AKA Lubanzi Diamini, a well-known scam artist,' Axel informed an increasingly frustrated Charlie Snr.

Over the last few days, the scammers had extracted money from Vincent, each time the amount increasing until they had received over fifteen hundred dollars. She continued to explain.

'I, or we, Commander Moses, did the hard work and from the face scans we provided from our cameras, he identified all the staff. All have a record of some extortion and are believed to be part of a highly organised gang operating here in Johannesburg.'

'So, when do we start getting money and stop giving it?' Charlie Snr croaked.

Vincent was about to explode at him, but Axel defused the situation by replying, 'The next time they call is when we give them the shock of their miserable lives. Oh, and at the same time, we will get you your money. How much did you say they cheated you out of?' she inquired cheekily.

'Robbed, not cheated!' he replied, in horror that this lovely person would think he was an idiot easily duped out of his cash.

'Of course, that is what I meant,' she replied with a grin. She had become quite adept at handling this weird Irish family she had become part of.

'85,000 Euro, which Vincent tells me is about $120,000,' he replied sheepishly.

While they were carrying on this banter, the phone they were using for this sting began to ring. 'Looks like we are in business. Are you ready, Vincent?' Axel said.

'More ready than I have ever been in my life. Are you sure you can let this prick see my face before we finish?' She nodded. 'Then let the games begin,' was his reply, picking up the phone.

Lubanzi waited with excitement for the phone to be answered. He had been so successful with his gullible mark that he was ready to go for the kill and convince him to give him access to his bank account. His cronies surrounded him as the call was answered. He signaled for silence as Vincent spoke.

'Hello, this is Mr McQueen. Who is speaking?'

'It is me, Mr Nkosi. I have great news for you. Your money is ready to be deposited in your account. We can begin the transfer as soon as you give me the details.'

'Of course,' he said and handed control of the computer over and provided the account number and password. 'While you are doing that, could I speak to the person handling this claim? You have only referred to him by his name, Mr Ndlovu. And I would like to thank him personally.'

Lubanzi grinned at his friends. 'Of Course, I will transfer you to his office,' transferring the call to his brother, sitting beside him.

'This is Omphile Ndlovu. How may I assist you?

By now, Charlie Snr and all the others were gathered around the screen watching the antics. While all this was happening, Axel rapidly typed away on her keyboard. When Vincent glanced at her, she held up five fingers, indicating she needed five minutes more, so he continued the charade.

'Thank you for taking my call. I just wanted to thank you for the opportunity to do something for my family, especially my father, who is here with me to celebrate this great occasion.'

Omphile could hardly contain himself so much that he failed to see the confusion on his brother's face as he typed furiously.

'He would like to say something to you. His name is Charles,' as he handed it over to his dad.

As this was happening, Axel sat back, giving the thumbs up. It was time to have some fun.

Charlie Snr was in his element. Like many Irish, he was born with the gift of the gab.

'Hello, you have no idea how long I have been waiting to speak to you. It has been such a long time coming. We have a very tight family. I see you kept it in the family also. How do you like working with your brother?' he asked.

He had asked so naturally that the guy was surprised at first but glanced at his brother and the sight of his face, which was locked in horror. As he gestured to the computer screen, he realised something was wrong.

'What up, Lwandle. you look worried?' Charlie Snr asked, using his real name, which Moses had provided.

'Noth…' he began to reply until he realised he had used his real name. 'How do you know this name?' he screamed, forgetting his cultured accent.

'Calm down, you will have a heart attack. Your brother is upset enough.'

Completely losing it, as his reality dissolved around him, he yelled,

'Who are you? How you know all this?' he spluttered in broken English.

'I will hand you back to Vincent. He will tell you how we screwed you,' unable to help himself using the Irish favorite swear word.

Vincent took over. 'It's me again. By now, even somebody as stupid as you will have figured out things are not going as planned. I think you should speak to your brother before he collapses.'

'How you know I have a brother?' he ranted, while at the same time, his brother was trying frantically to show him something on the monitor.

'Smile, you are on camera. Wave to the crowd, and in answer your question, your brother is standing beside you, doing his best to show you that all your bank accounts are empty and being redistributed to all of your victims whose details you kindly provided from your files.'

By this stage, the place had disintegrated into chaos as what had happened began to dawn on them. Lethabo, real name Lubanzi, completely lost it.

'We will find you. You have no idea where we are. We will hunt you down and slice you into little bits, you and all your family. There is nowhere you can hide,' he threatened the cameras.

'Hold on, no time like the present. Let me introduce you to the people that ruined your lives. It started when somebody from your crew mistakenly targeted this gent.'

At that moment, Axel opened a video connection to all the computers in the office. Charlie Snr's face flashed up.

'Hello, how does it feel to be on the receiving end? I don't know which one of you took my money, but I am sure you will have plenty of time in prison to figure it out. Don't drop the soap,' he giggled as Vincent took his place.

'I would love to introduce you to everyone, but we will have plenty of time for that when we meet face-to-face.'

Lubanzi thrust his contorted face into the camera. 'You will never find us. We will be up and running again by tomorrow,' he boasted.

'The man just about to knock very hard on your door might have something to say about that,' Vincent said.

With a thunderous crash, the door behind Lubanzi burst open, and Commander Moses and a team of soldiers flooded the site. They watched the screen as everybody was rounded up and handcuffed.

Moses spoke to them from the other side of the screen. 'Our plan went like a dream, Axel. Your location was spot on. I will collect all the hard drives for you to inspect. We have surely put a big dent in their operations. See you back at base.'

'I told you I had a plan for that!' exclaimed Alex with delight as she received hugs from all around.

Charlie Snr could not contain himself. 'Did you get my money back?' he asked her as soon as they stopped hugging.

'You were first on the list. It is in your account as we speak.'

He was momentarily speechless as he looked around at this eclectic bunch of people gathered around his three equally different sons. Finally, he got his voice and yelled with a big roar, 'This is the best fun I have had since my wedding night! From now on, you can count me in on your adventures!'

Which brought a collective groan from his sons.

$$?$$

## EPILOGUE

## SOMEWHERE OVER MADRID, SPAIN

The Savage family were on the final leg of their trip home to Ireland. They had hitched a ride on the Herrero family jet, a Boeing 737.

They dropped the Heart family back on their home island of Mallorca, continuing to Dublin. Charlie Snr was asleep alongside Vincent, who was deep in thought. His attention drifted to his brothers, who were having one of their discussions as to which was the best movie they had seen. Growing up, he had always been the odd one; his two brothers always had a special bond. They had a loyalty to each other that was unbreakable.

Despite his great success as the leading defence lawyer in the EU, his older brother Charlie remained the bedrock of their family. He had an iron will and an uncanny way of dealing with whatever problems the family had faced in more challenging times before their fortunes had changed. He glanced at the scar that ran down his brother's face, the origin which remained a mystery and a taboo subject.

He shifted his gaze to Desmond, whose superpower was that he could sell ice cream to the Eskimos! Bringing a smile to his face as he recalled all the scrapes he had been responsible for, yet came out smelling like a rose!

Seated behind them was Aurora. The latest member of the family and her friend Sun Yee On. They were chatting and laughing, obviously happy together. Behind them was the not-so-gentle giant Sergei, sleeping soundly, who had decided to spend some time with them in Ireland.

'To learn what makes you guys as crazy as us Russians, ' he had explained when asked.

Vincent recognised that this strange group of entirely different characters somehow gelled together to create a formidable team, recalling his conversation with Axel, who had returned to Iceland. Her sharp mind knew what he was asking when he asked her plans for the future.

'Always wanted to spend some time in London. I am sure you guys will find something for me to do.' So with that, she joined the 'Umbrella Crew'.

He began to plan how he would formalise the organisation and incorporate it into the broader business that he and Bill Heart operated. As the attractive flight attendant hovered over him, asking him if there was anything more she could do for him, the offer was thinly veiled to include something more.

'Not at the moment, perhaps later,' he replied, with a smile, bringing an expectant colour to her face.

As she moved off, he heard a voice. 'You are away there,' mumbled his father with a wry chuckle.

Umbrella Inc. was the name Vincent decided was what he would call the new organisation. He began to plan how to structure it to utilise the available talents, whether it was Charlie's fantastic ability to find a way to prevail in the worst situations. Or Desmond's ability to find a way to make a profit, recalling the bag of precious stones the had 'recovered' from Mizrahi.

Pondering the unique team Aurora and Sun Yee On made, he began to wonder where their next 'assignment' would be.

Only later would he think back to this moment on the plane and realise how little he knew this 'next assignment' would threaten the very future of the whole Umbrella Crew!

www.ingramcontent.com/pod-product-compliance
Lightning Source LLC
Chambersburg PA
CBHW051238260626
47162CB00002B/503